Dear Reader,

In life we don't often take time to acknowledge the people who make a difference in our journey, so I want to take these few minutes, the time between flipping from the cover to the beginning of this story, to say *thank you* for being a part of my journey. If you are anything like me, the TBR pile is overflowing with great stories, and there's never enough time to read them all, but you've picked up this book, and I am so very grateful. Thank you.

If you enjoy the story, I hope you'll spread the word and recommend it to friends, and then start a discussion about your favorite characters using the hashtag #ENtheBook. Again, thank you & enjoy, and watch for book two coming in 2019.

Your friend & lover of books,

Michelle

EN

Book 1
The Girl, the Pendant & the Portal series

Michelle Reynoso

Available through Ingram Book Company and Ingram's global distribution partners, or order directly through the author's website at www.MichelleReynoso.com.

General inquiries: mtr@michellereynoso.com
Direct order inquiries: order@michellereynoso.com
Press & media: press@MichelleReynoso.com

Publisher's Note: This is a work of fiction. Names, characters, places, and incidents are a product of the author's imagination. Locales and public names are sometimes used for atmospheric purposes. Any resemblance to actual people, living or dead, or to businesses, companies, events, institutions, or locales is completely coincidental.

Book Layout © 2019 BookDesignTemplates.com
Title page graphics by George Ingram
Front Cover design by GermanCreative
Author photo by Jane Button Photography

En/ Michelle Reynoso. -- 1st ed.
Hardcover edition ISBN: 978-0-9997189-5-7
E-book edition ISBN: 978-0-9997189-1-9

For Dad—I hope you are looking down from heaven and smiling. See, I did it 'my way'. Hope you are proud. Love you.

I am invisible. Not the literal kind of invisible but something worse, something a step lower than feeling 'less than.' I am a zero.

No one wants to be associated with a zero, I remind myself shoving forward through a teen mob of fitted jeans, team shirts, cellphones and earbuds, trudging the halls with my head bent and my eyes up just enough to see the way through the post bell crowds of Madison High School. I am a ghost in daylight. That's how I feel anyway. I push forward into the science wing where the crowds thin, and I make a sharp right turn to the bathroom at the furthest end of school, pushing at the door and stepping into the stench of mildew and sweat. It's empty as usual, and I head to the last stall. And then I see it...good god there's pee on the toilet seat.

Seriously people?

'If you sprinkle when you tinkle, please be neat and clean the seat.'

Have these Neanderthals not heard this before? I want to scribble it on the wall in permanent marker, but I don't. Instead I clean the toilet seat. Twice. And settle in.

I've been at this dump-of-a-school for three months and the only thing I've learned is to lay low; that, and master the stall perch with my ass on the back of the toilet seat, feet stretching up to the toilet paper holder and back resting against my bunched up sweatshirt. Comfortable—I try to convince myself—but it's not really, and today is not a good day for me to be so isolated, I know that, but it doesn't change anything. Tomorrow will still come, and with it comes the three-month anniversary of my mother's death. I can't be with people right now. Not *these* people – strangers who look at me with pity, who see me as someone who *needs* them. I don't need them. What I need are my real friends from back home. I need my glue, my Kiara, my modelish African queen bestie, because without her I'm falling apart. All the technology in the world doesn't bring me Kiara in the flesh—her Colgate-smile, stellar hugs, and super sappy 'therapy-voice'. I call it her phone sex voice. We joke about it all the time. She calls me crazy because I call her KiKi sometimes, which sounds like a phone sex name to me.

Kiara—Kiki, I don't care. What's in a name anyway? Except when you've got my name that is – Faith; hard to justify a name like that when you've got no faith at all. Which is exactly why I need to talk to Kiara. She keeps me sane on these days when mom is heavy on my mind, and my brother Eddie (aka Six-Foot-Gestapo-of-the-House) is being a pain-in-the-ass, which he was this morning when he snagged my phone for 'wise-assing', which is why I can't call or text Kiara. Honestly, I think Eddie just wants an excuse to keep tabs on me, but whatever, phone or not, I'll find a way to talk to Kiara, because if I don't I might just barricade myself in this bathroom all day long. I do have a plan though, I do, and like a spider-in-wait for prey, I wait in my stall for the next girl to walk in.

The bell rings, and after a few minutes the bathroom door opens and a group of girls enter in the middle of a rapid fire discussion. Their individual voices are hard to distinguish over the sound of shuffling feet and the mixed conversations of late students rushing to class in the outside hall, but once the door closes, the girls' voices echo around the small space. There are three of them, none of which I recognize by their voice, but then again, I barely know anyone. Purses open & close and makeup compacts click. I imagine them preening in front of the mirror, grooming themselves for one of the guys on the football team.

"Give me one," screeches one of the girls. Then the sound of a lighter's spark wheel ignites with a thumb flick. I can hear the exaggerated sucking of air and the exhaling of smoke.

I wonder if I should wait for someone else. Chances are slim anyone else will walk into this bathroom now that classes have started, and besides, Kiara will be heading to her Bio class in about ten minutes. The clock is ticking.

I flush the toilet to alert the girls they aren't alone, and slide my feet off the toilet paper holder to the floor.

"Put it out, put it out!" one of the girls squeals, rushed and desperate. I can hear her moving her arms in the air to disperse the smoke. Then the smell hits me – strong and skunky – and I know that cigarettes aren't the only thing they're smoking.

Shit.

One of the girls turns from the mirror—I hear her feet scuff on the floor, and then the thwack of flip flops knocking the tile as she walks the narrow space in front of the stalls. I can't back out now, it's now or I don't get to talk to Kiara.

"Hey, can I ask a favor," I say in a small voice through the door, trying to sound casual and nonchalant.

The girl's footsteps stop in front of my stall, but she doesn't answer.

"I know you're out there, I can see your flip flops," I say.

"What are my flip flops to you?" the girl finally answers in a high, flippant voice.

"I just need to borrow a phone," I say.

"You got twenty bucks?" The girl asks quickly.

"Twenty bucks, are you crazy?" I reply.

"It's twenty, or nothing; the price goes up in 10 seconds," she says. Her friends giggle.

"Fine," I say through my teeth. I stand up, pull out the last bill I have in my pocket—from my brother for lunch—and pass it to the girl over the top of the stall.

"Here," I say. She pulls it from my hand with a quick sweep and places a pink jeweled phone where the bill had been.

"You've got one minute," she says, "After that it will be another twenty."

I feel my cheeks flush. I want to punch this girl in the mouth.

"And if you drop it, you're dead," the girl says.

I move to the corner of the stall that faces the back wall, mimicking the girl silently. I hold the girl's phone in my hand, and for a minute I contemplate dropping it in the toilet, but it's just a momentary thought before I slide my fingers over the touch screen, dialing Kiara's memorized number. She picks up after the first ring.

"'ello?" She answers, obviously not recognizing the number.

"KiKi, it's me," I whisper into the phone.

"Faith? Hey girl, where've you been? New cell?" Kiara asks with sunshine in her voice.

"No, borrowed it," I say lowering my voice.

"I can barely hear you. Why do you sound so far away?"

"I've got company," I say raising my voice slightly at the end so she can hear me, "Eddie swiped my phone this morning."

"Damn. What did you do?" Kiara asks.

"Why did *I* have to do something?"

"He took your phone, dumbass," Kiara says.

"Screw you," I say.

"I'm just kidding," Kiara says.

"I need 'kidding' like a hole in my head," I say.

"Hey. Don't joke about that," Kiara says, her voice turning serious.

"You're supposed to be making me feel better, not worse. You know what tomorrow is, right?" I ask.

"I know. Talking about that, I was thinking I'd come up to see you tomorrow night. We can spend the anniversary together," Kiara says.

The girl outside the stall shuffles her feet. "Are you done talking to your girlfriend? Your minute is up. Phone or twenty," she says, her hand out-stretched & extended over the stall.

"Were you listening to my conversation?" I say through the stall door.

"So? Think of it as terms of our contract, which is now up. Give me back my phone," the girl snaps.

"Is someone charging you to borrow their phone?" Kiara asks.

"Bingo," I say.

"Kick her ass," Kiara says and then laughs, her laughter so loud it echoes inside the stall. I can't help but chuckle. See, she makes me feel better.

The girl outside the stall rattles the door, "Phone or twenty bucks," she demands.

"That's my cue," I say to Kiara.

"I'll call you later at home, we'll plan for to-morrow. K?" Kiara says.

"No softball?" I ask. Kiara feigns a pained voice, "*Mom my stomach reeeeeeally hurts. I think it's cramps.*"

"Oscar worthy," I say.

"Yeah, one practice isn't going to kill any-body. Besides, It's not like I play all that much, I'm nothing more than a glorified bench-warmer."

I chuckle again.

"Talk to you later," I say.

"Later," Kiara says. I click off the call, take a breath, and open the door to find the girl stationed in front of the stall, hands on hips as her mouth snaps gum through her teeth. I recognize her immediately, Olivia Johnson—soccer captain and Class President. She's wearing a tight fitting white tee, black polyester training pants that hug her hips, and flip flops with white socks that push into the thong. She's flanked by two Miss Teen Beauty Pageant contestants in cheerleading uniforms, one with short black hair and the other with a red cropped cut.

"Freaky new girl, give me my phone," she says.

"Here," I say, shoving the phone toward her.

"Eww, it's freak germs," she says, taking the phone with the tips of her fingers and wiping the screen on her pants.

"Shut up," I say. It's the only reply that comes to me.

"Why, you going to make me?" She asks. Kiara is right, I should just kick her ass, but she's not worth my energy.

"Just move. *Please*," I say.

"You hear that girls, freaky girl's got manners," she says.

Olivia steps up close, invading the barriers of my personal space, the smell of high end perfume and marijuana soaks her clothes. I push at her chest, hard enough to force her back two steps, her black hobo handbag whipping backwards. Without hesitation, Oliva glides over the floor with the grace of a ballerina and the hardened face of a hockey player. She shoves at me, her hands square to my shoulders, barreling me back into the hard metal frame. The stall rattles behind me. Olivia lunges again pinning my hands to the wall, and shoves her knee into my crotch. I try to wriggle free, but I can't move. She leans in—eyes red and irritated—her hot breath on my cheeks, turning the air between us thick and stifling.

"If you ever touch me again, I'll kill you," Olivia says, ending the sentence by weirdly sniffing the air like an animal searching for the scent of fear. Then she turns away from me and walks to the mirror.

I get the message. I'm not a threat.

Standing at the mirror continuing to ignore me, Olivia pulls out a small Visine-type bottle from her purse and like an automaton snaps her head back—her eyes rolling up to the ceiling—and releases a thick, marigold liquid into her eyes, and then drops the empty bottle into the trash. She blinks several times. And then she turns toward me and starts to talk, in a voice not her own, in a tone an octave deeper—a male voice, in breathy and broken speech like a patient relearning to speak again—"Your mother *tried* to hide you," Olivia says.

"Are you making fun of my mother?" I ask from my spot against the stall door, my insides churning between anger and tears.

Olivia continues with the altered voice, "She can't hide you anymore. I have found my way to you."

"Are you on drugs, seriously?" I blurt out before remembering what the girls were smoking.

"Very soon Faith, we will see each other very soon. We have much to discuss," Olivia says, and as she utters the last word a puff of marigold dust bursts from her eyes, instantly disappearing into the air, and her pupils' return to their normal green.

The red cropped-cut sidekick steps up to Olivia and pats her on the back—'That was awesome! So creepy," she exclaims.

"Those acting classes are really paying off," the other sidekick chimes in.

"You're all nuts," I say and move away from the stall and toward the door.

"We're not done," Olivia says in her back to normal flippant voice, as she adjusts her tee shirt over her sweats.

"What are you playing at?" I ask through gritted teeth.

"You don't make the rules here missy. I do. And you go when I say you go," Olivia says.

"You're such a bitch," I say.

She doesn't hesitate, she drops her purse on the counter and lunges forward toward me, ramming the heel of one hand into my ribs and the other into my chest, punching the air out of my lungs. A voice screams inside my head—*block! block!*—but I can't for some reason. I stand there, frozen—like in my dreams when I want to scream but I can't—even as I hear the remaining air leaving my lungs, traveling up through my mouth in a forced exhale. There is no air left. I gasp, clutching for a breath, but I can't get more than a hiccup of air. My chest is heavy and my head dizzy. A kaleidoscope of white stars fills my eyes. I double over, and crumble to the floor. Olivia lets me fall.

"We *are* done now," she says, twirling on her heels, fetching her pocket book, and walking toward the door, "And word of advice, ditch the sweatpants and UGGS, they're so passé." She exits the bathroom with her sidekicks in tow, laughing and chirping like chickens as they leave. I stay on the floor, even after the door closes behind them.

I know I can't stay here, even though this floor with its cool tiles on my burning chest and aching ribs feels like my only friend, this is the worst place for me to be. The bathroom still reeks of lingering smoke and marijuana. I need to get up and out of here before someone walks in.

I force my eyes to focus, noticing a wad of toilet paper by my cheek, and then another further to the left by the trash, and another stained yellow with god knows what. There are wads of pink gum turned black that dot the tiles, and hair on the floor by the mirror. And then I think, how many feet have walked across this floor with shoes streaking the tile with piss and dirt, and cigarette ashes, and—*good god*—period blood? I dry heave sending another sharp pain across my ribs, but I ignore it and force myself up, dragging myself to the garbage. Olivia's transformation and that marigold liquid are important, familiar, but like a word at the tip of my tongue I can't pinpoint why. I grab the discarded bottle, tilting it so the remaining drops of liquid pool together at the bottom corner.

It's important, I know it.

I stuff the bottle in my backpack, and wait for the next bell.

❦

CHAPTER TWO

MISTAKE NUMERO DOS

W hen the bell rings I'm ready, quickly threading my right arm through my backpack straps, holding my left hand against my ribs as buffer, and exiting the bathroom. I keep my eyes trained for Olivia and her Pom-Pom sisters.

I just have to make it to the door. Then to the bus. And home.

Two boys wrestle each other beside me, one in a Yankees baseball hat and a significantly shorter one in a solid black tee shirt. Yankees-baseball-hat-boy shoves the shorter one who ducks behind me. I keep my focus on the door, trying to ignore them, until black-tee shirt-boy grabs my backpack using it like a shield; his weight and the backpack smash down on my ribs and a wave of pain rips through my torso.

"Get off me punk ass!" I yell, shaking the boy off. His friend shoots me the middle finger as they both dart ahead, pushing through the crowd. I breathe through the pain like an expectant mother, and exit through the main doors.

Much of the bus ride home is a blur—potholes and sharp turns, and a countdown of stops. The pain spikes a few times. I swear at the boys under my breath, and Olivia, and MHS. Once I'm home, I toss the backpack to the floor, and make a beeline to Eddie's medicine cabinet. I find his Ambien at the front. I take a couple. I just want to sleep. And forget. I strip off my bra and sweatshirt, and slip one of my sleep shirts over my jeans. My ribs ache. I still need something for the pain. I head back to the medicine cabinet, foraging through bottles of cough & cold medicine, antacids, vitamins, and then I find it, tucked behind a row of hair products, is Eddie's old prescription for Vicodin. I take two, and drop on the couch, and wait for the medicine to work.

"Faith," my brother Eddie says in a whisper as if his voice is distant and far away. Then he says my name again, but this time his tone is sharp and angry and in my face.

"Why do you have my prescription in your hand?"

I open my eyes to find Eddie standing over me, his tall, husky frame hunched by the weight of the work bag hanging from his shoulder, and the stress of mom's death evidenced in the extra pounds he's gained.

"What?" I answer, groggy, half asleep, and slouched on the couch.

"I said, why do you have my prescription?" I look at my hand. The Vicodin bottle is there, I never put it back in the medicine cabinet.

Idiot.

"I needed it," I say, straightening myself on the couch, hoping my matter of fact response will ease him off the subject.

"No, you don't NEED to take Vicodin, or any of my prescriptions. They are MY prescriptions Faith. Is this something you've been doing regularly?"

"Just today," I say sitting up. He opens the prescription bottle and counts the pills.

"You don't believe me?" I ask him.

"Off limits. Understand?" He says.

"I just took two, that's it," I say.

"Two today, two tomorrow, it's not even your medicine, why would you need it?" Eddie asks. He's got that look in his eyes, probably the same look given to accused witches at the Salem Witch Trials. I'm not telling him what happened. He won't listen anyway. He never listens to me anymore.

"No reason," I say.

"What's going on with you?" Eddie asks.

"Nothing," I say quickly.

"'Sis I love you, but you keep pushing me away," Eddie says moving his bag from his shoulder to the floor.

"Likewise," I say. Eddie's mouth moves to respond but he stops himself and takes a breath. He motions for me to make room for him on the couch. "I'm new at this, and it's not easy. I'm still trying to figure it all out," he says sitting next to me.

So am I," I say.

"That's the thing. I don't see you figuring anything out. I see you giving up," Eddie says.

"Can't you just trust me?" I ask.

"How can I trust you when you pull things like this?" Eddie says holding up the prescription bottle.

"It's not what it looks like," I say.

"Your grades are in the toilet, you get in trouble at school..."

I interrupt, "That wasn't me, it was the kids pranking me..."

"So why was it *you* got in trouble Faith? Step up and take responsibility. It's time to move on. Drugs are not the answer, you know that right?" Eddie preaches as if he's my father.

"I KNOW!" I yell.

"THEN WHY?" He yells back.

"You're not listening to me!" I yell.

"And you're not talking! One and two word answers tell me nothing. Mom is dead, Faith. Dead. She's not coming back. It's time to move on," Eddie yells.

"How can I move on when my mother is dead? How can I move on Eddie? How would you suggest I do that?" I yell.

"You just do," Eddie says.

"You do. I can't!" I yell getting up from the couch and running to my room, "Just leave me alone!"

I slam the bedroom door behind me. The room closes in as if I'm Princess Leia in a Death Star trash compactor; not literally, but it *feels* like that and I know I can't stay here. Without prepping, or planning, or really giving it much thought at all, I palm the two objects on the corner of my dresser and quietly slip out of my bedroom window into the dusk, running along the road and into the woods with a weird combination of adrenaline and sleep medicine pumping in my veins.

CHAPTER THREE

ROCK BOTTOM

It doesn't look like much, my spot in the woods – a pine tree almost hard to see as dusk gives way to night. I drop to the cold damp dirt, releasing myself to the smell of pine and pitch and green growing things around me, my hip complaining about the jackknife wedged in my pocket, the one I grabbed from the dresser on my way out of the window.

I move my hand toward the knife.

Will I ever be strong enough?

It's a question I've asked myself *every* day since mom died.

I slide my hand into the pocket, and instead of the knife, my fingers brush against the rough crease and peeling edge of the second item from the dresser, the last good picture of mom BEWTS (Before Everything Went to Shit)—my own twisted version of FUBAR. I can't see much of the photo by moonlight, but I've got it memorized – the outline of my mother's lips, smiling, her face framed in a messy champagne bob; she's happy & healthy and unaware of her looming death sentence.

I wipe tears from my cheek, lean my head back against the tree behind me, and close my eyes. Sleep is my friend, and dreams my conduit to slide me to the other side; my inner eyelids fill with images—a periwinkle & taffeta sky and a rainbow light dancing like an Aurora Borealis. Maybe it's heaven, maybe it's mom reaching out to me, if it is I'd like to *see* her this time.

I let myself drift deeper until I'm immersed in marigold light—*marigold, like the liquid in Olivia's bottle*—visited by the strange girl who has come to be a regular in my dreams since mom's death—this girl, with her chunky body contorted into a side lunge, hovers midair. She never stays long. She greets me in a sing-songy voice that breaks up words in odd places.

"Faith," the girl calls to me. Her olive-skinned face shines. She's exotic and perfect except for two strange things—there's a pink hibiscus bush growing from the top of her head with one flower tucked behind her right ear, and her body is not clothed but painted to mimic a bold print sarong. I can never look away when I see her; she's mesmerizing. So why is it the memory of her fades every time I wake up? This girl wants me to do something. I haven't figured out what.

"Let me show you the way," she says. With a wave of her arm, the girl pulls marigold light from the air and forms it into a gelatinous cloud the color of congealed butter. The mass is so hot and steamy that a line of sweat instantly forms under my breasts and in my armpits, and so bright it's hard to see, so I squint. The thick cloud blocks the sky and the ground below me; everything seems to disappear except me and the girl.

My body tilts weightlessly to the side. I claw the air trying to right myself, but dizziness starts in my head as I begin to drop upside down. I look to the girl for help—*I don't want to leave yet, I just got here*—but her eyes have turned into suns, and she doesn't respond. I slip away from her, and in seconds, the girl is only a tiny speck in the air above me, and then everything turns black as charcoal, and a second later I'm completely knocked from the dream.

I know I'm back for sure, because I can smell the pitch, and feel a root digging into my calf. I remember her this time, the girl; it's at this point that I usually start to forget, but this time I remember.

With my eyes still closed, there's another bright light streaming into my brain and for a second I think maybe the girl is returning, or still there at the surface, but it's not her—the light is different—so I open my eyes and squint as the sun hits my face, streaming through the branches above me.

Was I sleeping all night? It seemed like minutes.

I reach to my pocket feeling for the bulge of my phone, but my phone isn't there; I pat my jeans on both sides, but find only the bulge of the knife. I jump up, nearly slipping on the dried pine needles, and it's then I remember that Eddie *took* my phone. There's a steady echo of cars from the highway in the distance. Daybreak has broken, and if I don't get back before Eddie gets up, I'm dead.

I snatch the picture, stuffing it deep into my pocket, and run over the soft and spongy ground blanketed with old leaves. I have to go the long way home, the-nobody-better-see-me way, because all I need is a picture of me, like this, circulating at school in my bright pink, low-cut pajama shirt, jeans, and no bra.

I veer off the main path, heading into the thick of the woods while the knife does jumping jacks in my pocket.

Hiding behind the bushes—the ones mom gave to Eddie five years ago as a housewarming gift—I can see the house a few feet in front of me, a small white ranch with a red door and black shutters. The house is dark. I duck out from behind the bushes and walk up the driveway, passed Eddie's black Camry—the same one he got when he graduated high school six years ago—to the front door, and press my ear to the oval glass window. It is quiet, which means I still have a shot at getting back in unnoticed. I turn the knob, but it slips in my hand, locked.

I head to the back of the house to my bedroom, where the window frame starts about eye level. I push the rickety window up the channel nearly to the top, and with a little jump heave myself up, but it's not enough lift and only my chest balances on the edge with my feet dangling down; a sharp lip on the window casing digging into me. There's no way I can pull myself up from this position. I let go and jump back down to the ground; I say jump, but really, I fall, and not gracefully. I look to the neighbors' houses on either side hoping not to see faces in the windows. Nothing yet, but I'd better do this fast before someone gets curious. I get up and approach once again. This time I grab the inside of the channel, walk my feet up the side of the house, and pull myself up, but instead of balancing on the casing I push myself over and fall inside to the floor, my foot snagging a piece of the frame and pulling it with me. I hit the floor hard—head first, my body piling up on top of itself and the window piece on top of me. The whole house shakes when I fall.

And then the bedroom door squeaks.

"What are you doing?" Eddie asks. I hear his deep, hard voice before I see him. "It's not even 7:00 and you're already up to something."

"Yoga?" I answer, trying to keep the energy between us light.

He flicks on the light switch.

Eddie's husky frame fills the doorway, the crown of his chestnut topped head towers to the uppermost hinge of my bedroom door.

"Where have you been?" Eddie asks sharply as blotches of scarlet creep from around his neck, up to his cheeks.

In this moment, I can't think of anything that will answer the question to his satisfaction. So I don't say anything. I roll out of my twisted mess, pushing the window piece off, and sit up against the wall across from my full length mirror, and see what Eddie sees—my hair, usually bouncy and soft at my shoulders, atop my head like a brown mop, stringy and wild. And he probably didn't miss my dirt-stained low-cut pink pajama top covered in leaves and grass.

"You're paying for the window," Eddie says.

"It's just a little piece," I shoot back.

"Whatever it is, you're paying for it."

"Fine!" I yell.

"Don't get smart with me. You're not making this any easier for either one of us. I told you that last night. You're paying for the window and you're grounded—one week. Got it?"

"Whatever, jerk. You're my brother, not my mother. You never could be mom," I say. Eddie winces, and a hardness forms in my stomach. I immediately regret making the comment.

"Get ready for school. And since you can't seem to keep yourself out of trouble, I want you home after school working on those damn boxes in the basement," Eddie says turning and walking away.

I look at myself in the mirror as I sit against the wall, and I don't like the person looking back at me. I want to scream. And cry. And punch something. All at the same time.

CHAPTER FOUR

TURNING POINT

I want to forget – the fight with Eddie, another day of avoidance at school, the painful bruises on my ribs, this anniversary, all of it, but the world is conspiring against me and everywhere I look I see my mom, and my mistakes, and the reminders of what my life could have been. I'm seventeen but I feel like seventy, with the weight of the world on my shoulders. And now I have to face the hardest thing of all, on the hardest day of all—a day where all I want is to crawl into a ball and sleep.

Staring down the dark stairs toward the small unfinished basement, I imagine I look like a bound-to-get-killed supporting actress in a horror film as I hesitate at the top. A wall of stagnant air rushes up to greet me and Eddie's voice echoes in my head—*work on those damn boxes..."*

I flick on the light switch and start down the stairs, each one creaking beneath the weight of my feet. I step off to the gravel floor, yanking the pull string of the single exposed light bulb above me. The basement comes to life.

This is all I have left of my mom, seventy-eight cardboard boxes of her stuff taped closed and piled on top of each other. I walk the line of boxes.

Where do I start?

Placing my hand on a random box, I shimmy it off the top—careful not to pull my still-tender ribs—and drop it to the ground sending a plume of dirt billowing up around me, starting me coughing and sneezing as my nose and eyes fill with particles. I step out of the dust cloud and move closer to the stairs, nearly knocking over an overflowing shelf packed with folded up boxes, rags, cleaning supplies, and bottled water. I grab a flattened box and fan the air, directing the dust cloud to the other side of the basement.

After a few sips of water and a splash to my face, the sneezing and coughing finally stop, but my chest and ribs are left aching. *My life sucks.* I grab a rag, saturate it with water, and wipe down the boxes on the top row like I should have done in the beginning.

Once I start, the boxes go fast; the first few are easy, filled with stuff I don't hold much attachment to. I'm up to box number four now, pulling it out after wiping it down. Something inside rattles like two cups clinking against each other. I slide my finger under the tape holding the box shut, and open the flaps. Picture frames, photo albums, scrapbooks & knickknacks are all thrown together, unwrapped and unorganized. *Eddie can't pack a box for shit that's for sure.* I'm drawn to a silver frame in the center—wedged between two large albums—with an intricate floral design carved into metal, it's the picture that stood next to mom's casket at the funeral, a candid shot from our mother and daughter trip to the mountains a couple summers ago. *This* makes me want to stop, but I force myself to go on anyway, force myself to look at the picture still wedged in the box; mom looks up at me from the center of the frame smiling, her hair caught in the breeze and a bunch of fresh-picked wildflowers cradled in the crook of her arm. I pull the picture out carefully, and kiss the glass over mom's cheek.

"I love you. Now and forever."

I hug the frame, wishing it could be mom instead of this cold piece of metal.

I'm not going to cry—NOT going to cry—no – no - no.

I bite my lip to dam the tears inside, and then I quickly move the picture so it rests face-down on a sheet of poly on the ground. The tears come anyway, welling in the corners of my eyes.

I can't force myself to be o.k. with this. Not yet. Why would Eddie ask me to do this today of all days?

I breathe in and release, pausing for a moment. And then I force myself to continue. Eddie told me to go through the boxes, but that doesn't mean I have to look or touch or feel every item of every box. I know what this box is. It will keep for later. I grab the sharpie from my pocket and scribble the word "PICTURES" across the outside edge of the box, replace the frame from the ground, re-tape the flaps, and move the box to the 'keep' row.

A familiar, mechanical version of Beethoven's Fur Elise plays in a row to the left. I locate the talkative box and pull it forward, gently easing it to the dirt, opening the cardboard flaps and throwing semifolded linens to the ground. Mom's cedar chest music box sits nestled in the middle of a down comforter, the sight of its worn wooden exterior feels like a recovered security blanket.

I move the comforter to the ground and scoop the music box into my palm. The top flips open and something falls out into the now empty cardboard box below, hitting the bottom with a thud; it's a silver chain necklace, with an opal pendant framed in sterling silver filigree. I don't recognize it.

I lean down to scoop up the necklace, extending my hand toward the pendant, but as I get close enough to touch it, the pendant comes alive with flashes of red, blue, green and orange. The hairs on my arm shoot to attention and my head crackles with static, and then the pendant moves toward me, as my fingers are forced to lock on it. I didn't pick it up, but now the pendant is stuck to me super glue tight. I shake my hand to free myself, but my hand goes numb and the pendant doesn't budge. I drop the music box to the ground, using my now free hand to pry the necklace loose.

Idiot

Now both hands are stuck to it.

The room swirls around me—dizziness and stomach churning. I feel weird. Everything is blurry. I feel myself falling; I try to catch myself, but the cardboard box is the only thing to break my fall, and it gives away underneath me, the cardboard grazing the spot where Olivia rammed her wrist into me. Pain needles itself across my chest. I gasp for breath once, twice, three times. Falling. Ready to hit the ground with outstretched hands but I don't feel an impact other than the cardboard, I just keep falling and spinning, the air around me crackling. I fall into darkness. And black out.

Darkness. My eyes are open, but I can't see anything—no basement, no hanging light bulb, just dark everywhere—it's so dark I'd swear my eyes are closed except I can feel my lids flutter every time I blink. Did I hit my head when I fell? I don't remember. Maybe I'm unconscious. I feel light, weightless, numb, and my ribs no longer ache—*which is a nice reprieve*—but I don't know if I'm right side up or upside down. I can't tell, because I'm not standing, I'm floating. My brain is floating too, like I've had a few drinks and I'm buzzed and everything is numb. I like the feeling, it's a good feeling—a feeling I haven't felt in a very long time.

Am I dead? My hands are running down my torso and over my legs; I'm whole and in physical form, even if I can't see my limbs in the dark below me. Or are they above me? I don't know, they're here, that's what matters—torso & chest, *check*, hands, *check*—no necklace, *perfect*. I turn my head searching for a landmark, something in the dark to orient me, but there's nothing. I flap my arms—probably looking like a bird learning to fly—and kick my legs to see if I can move around to a new vantage point. This isn't air, it's more like a thick gel, and I still can't tell which way is up or down. Or even how long I've been here, how long I was out. I start counting. I don't really know why, but it feels like something I should do to mark time. One-one thousand, two-one thousand, three-one thousand…one hundred twenty one-one thousand, one hundred twenty two-one thousand.

O.k., that got old real fast. No more counting.

"Hello!" I yell to the darkness. "Hel-looooooooo!" My voice repeats, spreading around me in a ripple until it fades in the distance, swallowed by the dark.

"Can anyone hear me?" I yell again.

A single pinprick of light blinks on, and then another, and another until the horizon is full of shimmering, yellow light. *Marigold* light. I try to flip my body to face it, moving my hands in a freestyle stroke and kicking as if swimming in the atmosphere.

The lights continue to grow—spreading and overtaking the dark and changing hues into a multi-color shimmer like the flashes in the pendant, and they're getting closer. I reach out to them. In an instant they are at my hands, the light skimming my fingertips; a tingle quickly spreads up my arm and through my body. And then the voices start, muffled and hard to understand at first, until I hear one word—*Sister,* then two words—*Sister World.*

"Hello?" I call out again. Gibberish follows. Undistinguishable words. A new voice in a whisper. This voice is full of alarm, and repeats one word. *Here—Here—Here—Here*

"I don't understand!" I yell. More gibberish. And then a voice I recognize, a sing-songy voice that breaks up words in odd places. It's the girl with the hibiscus plant growing from her head. She calls my name. *Faith*

"I'm here," I say, and wait for her response, but all sounds cease and silence surrounds me, and then the atmosphere begins to move, flowing like a tide, moving me *away* from the light.

"No! I'm not ready to leave!" I shout.

The current pushes me like a wave kicking the middle of my body—my shoulders, head, and legs wrap around my stomach. My hair stands straight with static, my hands go numb, and my head spins. Dizziness. Nausea. I'm going to puke; half-digested food spills from my mouth...to solid ground beneath me. Gravel. Light. Stairs. A crushed box is flattened under me, and by my hand, peaking from under a bit of cardboard, sits the necklace—dull and no longer glowing—illuminated not by its own radiance, but by the reflection of the single exposed light bulb above me.

❧

CHAPTER FIVE

KNICK KNACK PADDY WHACK GIVE THAT DOG A BONE

The opal stone of the pendant glistens with reflected light as if taunting me to pick it up again, but instead I reach for a red, paisley bandana sticking out from the pile of scattered linens on the ground. I grab the bandana and throw it over the pendant, and then nearly jump out of my skin when my brother yells my name from upstairs—"Faith!"

"Here," I answer mechanically, shifting myself over the crushed box and the gravel of the basement at my feet as I move to get up.

"Why didn't you answer when I called your name the first *ten* times?" Eddie yells from the kitchen, his footsteps making their way to the stairs.

He's coming down—what do I do with this thing?

I drop my hand toward the bandana covered necklace saying a silent prayer under my breath while I scoop it into my hand, and then shove it into the front pocket of my jeans.

"Sorry, I didn't hear you," I reply, scrambling to tidy the mess of stuff around me. I toss the mangled box behind the row, kick some dirt over the puke pile, and brush the dirt from my clothes as I turn toward the stairs once they start to creak.
Eddie stops halfway down, and scans the basement.

"Did you do what I asked?" I shake my head yes.

"Kept you out of trouble?" He asks.

"Uh, yeah," I answer. *I guess it depends what you consider trouble.*

"How many?" Eddie asks.

"How many what?" I ask.

"How many boxes?"

"Oh. Um, seven I think," I say.

"That'll do. Come upstairs for dinner, I picked up sandwiches on the way home," Eddie says turning to head back up the stairs. He's stoic and emotionless, and I want to shake him and ask him if he knows what today is. He pauses as if reading my mind, and then with his back to me, he asks, "You got my note?"

"No. What note?" I ask shadowing him.

"The one on the fridge," he says.

"No," I say. As I exit the stairs and enter the kitchen, Eddie points to the refrigerator.

"This note," he says pointing to a piece of paper sandwiched between the menu for Ming's Garden and a hand-ripped newspaper clipping announcing a Make Money with Real Estate seminar.

"I didn't see it," I say.

"Read it," he says ripping the paper from the fridge and handing it to me. The note is handwritten and barely legible.

> *F—*
> *Called in a favor—got you a job. You start 4:00 tomorrow at the drugstore.*
> *We'll talk tonight.*
> *Don't forget the boxes!*
> *—E*

"This is important Faith. Don't screw it up," he says. I want to scream at him so bad, but I bite my lip and hold it in. Why does he assume I'm going to screw things up?

I'll show him.

As we sit down on the couch and unwrap our sandwiches, we're both quiet. Eddie stopped insisting on dinner at the dining room table after only the first week of my being here. Now we mostly eat watching TV, but today he hasn't grabbed the remote yet, and the sound of chewing is loud between us. After minutes of torturous silence, the doorbell rings, and I inwardly cheer for the distraction. Eddie doesn't make a move to answer it.

"Want me to get it?" I ask.

"No. Finish your dinner," Eddie says. He still doesn't move, chewing the remaining food in his mouth, swallowing and wiping his lips on his napkin. The doorbell rings again. This time, Eddie lifts himself from the couch and heads to the door; as he opens it, I hear Kiara greeting him on the other side—*Kiara is here*—asking Eddie if he's lost weight.

Smooth move starting with a compliment.

I jump up, but Eddie shoots me a look as he steps outside and closes the door behind him. *WTF.* I stay put, but the wait is killer. I strain to hear anything from outside, but the windows are closed and the voices are too low.

Finally the door opens—a breeze rushes through the house—and Eddie calls to me.

"Coming," I answer, meeting Eddie just inside the front door as he closes it. My stomach drops; the door is closed and only Eddie is inside.

"Kiara *was* here," he says.

He said 'was'.

"Why was Kiara here?" Eddie asks.

"I don't know," I answer.

"You're grounded, remember," Eddie starts. It's then I remember my conversation with Kiara yesterday, but we missed our call and I forgot she was coming. I shrug my shoulders and lie, "I didn't know." Then I stay quiet. So does Eddie. It's only seconds, but it feels like an eternity. Then, I take a chance.

"Since she's here, can she stay?" I ask.

"No," Eddie says without hesitation. My heart drops again. I feel the anger building inside me.

"But she drove two hours to get here," I plead.

"I'm sorry. I don't care she drove two hours. You are grounded."

I run to the living room window, pull back the curtains, and watch Kiara's car inch away from the curb.

"You know what TODAY is, right?" I yell at Eddie.

"I know what today is, I haven't forgotten. I won't forget. But we have to move forward."

I turn away from the window and scream at Eddie—"You are an *ass*, you know that?"—and I run to my room, slam the door, and drop myself into bed.

❧

CHAPTER SIX

KIARA

Staring out my bedroom window, everything is a blur through teary eyes—the sun sinking low on the horizon, the woods filled with maple & pine trees...and then, Kiara's face as it pops up out of the dark from the other side of the glass. I jump like a startled cat.

"Jesus Christ, you scared the shit out of me!" I yell, wiping tears from my cheeks, jumping off the bed, and pulling the window up the track.

"You wanna blow this popsicle stand and go for a ride?" She asks standing on her tippy toes with a Cheshire Cat smile plastered across her dark face. I look to my bedroom door, and then back to Kiara—"Hell yeah," I say.

I lock the bedroom door, quietly.

"Hold up, let me buy us some time," I say, scribbling a note to Eddie—'*Leave me alone. Don't bother trying, I won't unlock the door*—and slip it between the door and the floor.

"C'mon hurry up," Kiara whispers.

I slip my legs over the window frame, dangling over the edge just long enough to pull the window down a bit before I jump off. It's midland that I realize my ribs and chest should hurt by now, but they don't. The injuries haven't bothered me since before the boxes.

Odd, but at least it's in my favor.

And then the thought is gone as Kiara and I take off running behind the neighbor's yard, and then the next one, ducking behind shrubs, hunched as if in a tactical military maneuver, giggling and already out of breath. We curve toward the street where Kiara's eighth generation white Honda Civic sits parked. We open the doors at the same time and throw ourselves inside, letting out a huge laugh in between our gasps for breath.

"That was epic!" I scream, feeling the adrenaline pump through my body.

"Operation Faith Rescue is complete," Kiara says pushing her key in the ignition. We high five each other, both grinning.

"You didn't pick up yesterday when I called," Kiara starts, "and I got worried about you. Figured we might need a plan B."

"I like your plan B," I say still trying to catch my breath.

Kiara types a quick text on her phone and then starts driving.

"So. Where are we headed?" I ask.

"You'll see," Kiara says turning to me with another Cheshire grin, "If you thought *that* was epic, *this* will be historic."

We're on the highway for about a half-an-hour, joking, giggling, and acting as if no time has passed since our last road trip—a few weeks before mom was diagnosed. It feels like a time warp, as if this is BEWTS, as if we are just leaving after school activities, heading to a movie or on one of Kiara's preplanned adventures; spontaneous and wild, two uncaged phenoms exploring the world. That *was* us before, when Mom was still alive.

Kiara pulls off at an exit and veers right, then makes another right and drives a few minutes before we hit a small town called Rochelle. To say it's a small town is an understatement. Almost immediately we land on Main Street, we pass a post office, pizza place, drycleaner, and some small boutique storefronts all sandwiched together on a strip. A couple of the shops are dark and have handmade paper signs taped to the windows: "For Rent" and "We've Moved"; not an economically booming town for sure. In the middle of the strip there's a barber shop with an old-time red and white spinning pole on the outside. And then, as quickly as the town started, it stops, and the strip is replaced with trees, and the street forks into two small winding roads that lead away from town.

Kiara slows the Civic and veers to the left onto the smaller of two roads following the GPS instructions to 'turn left now'. The car jerks as the pavement changes to dirt. A hand-made wooden sign nailed to a tree at the mouth of the road reads, "Kinderkamack".

"This is where we're headed?" I ask.

"Yep," she says. She must see the confused look on my face. She winks at me.

"Have a little faith, Faith," Kiara says playfully, knowing full well I hate that play on my name.

"Shut up," I say. She smiles.

Kiara eases the car slowly onto an overgrown driveway with grass and weeds springing up in a long row between tire ruts. A giant rock equaling the size of the Civic blocks our view, and the driveway curves around it in a hairpin turn like a roller coaster. A tiny one-story, run-down camp-style house emerges, the sun falling low on the horizon behind it. The house is overtaken by weeds, grass, and overgrown plants reaching skyward, so high that the foundation below the window frames is hidden. Faded green wooden shutters hang askew, and a couple have fallen off and lay decomposing on the ground. On the roof, shingles are stripped by a fallen tree branch frozen in its deed, stuck standing straight up in a deep gash at the apex of the slanted roof.

"It's a dump," I say getting out of the car. We both stop and stand beside the Civic, hands in our pockets, looking at the sun-faded, weather-worn exterior of the cottage.

"That's kind of the point," she says, "It's out of the way, we have privacy, and no one will come snooping around."

"And what exactly is it that we're going to be doing here?" I ask.

"Partying," she says, "Drinking, smoking, being teenagers. Forgetting about stuff," she says. Kiara heads to the back of the car.

"Help me with these," she says. The trunk is loaded with overflowing plastic shopping bags; I see a bright yellow potato chip bag sticking out of one and the neck of a 2 liter soda bottle out of another. This pattern continues over several bags.

"Is this all for us?" I ask as I grab a couple of bags and thread the handles over my arm.

"Us, plus two," Kiara says as she threads the rest of the bags onto her arms.

"Who two?" I ask as we walk up to the front door.

"You'll see," she says again, flashing a mischievous smile in my direction.

"Kiara Lee Blackwell what are you up to?" I ask. She laughs, and gives me the don't-try-to-get-it-out-of-me-because-I-ain't-budging look. This girl is definitely up to something, but the smile also says change the subject 'cause I ain't spillin'.

"Sooooooo," I say looking over the rundown house, knowing if I change the subject I might be able to work my way back to the original question, "how the hell did you find this place?"

"My mom..." Kiara starts.

"Your mom!"

"Shut up and let me finish, Miss Nervous Nelly," Kiara says.

"Does she know we're here?" I ask.

"Seriously. Do you think I'd tell my mom we were coming *here*? She'd flip out quicker than your brother, and you know they both have each other on speed dial. So, no, I didn't *tell* my mother, but, I did go through her real estate file and found this gem of a house in me mum's pot o' gold pile," Kiara says finishing the sentence with an Irish accent.

"Irish?" I ask.

"They're magically delicious!" Kiara sings.

"Ohhhhh. Um. Lucky Charms," I say. It's a game we play sometimes. Out of the blue one of us will throw in an accent or a quote in the middle of conversation, and the other person has to guess where it's from.

"Ding-ding-ding," she says, "You are correct." We both laugh, walking up three concrete steps to the front door, putting our bags down on the small concrete landing. The railings on each side are coming unattached and are tilting outward.

"This baby is in foreclosure. It's been abandoned for years," Kiara says.

"Obviously," I say.

"My mom has this weird habit of putting houses she's shown, that haven't sold but have gone into foreclosure, into a folder she calls 'Pot of Gold'. I don't know why. Anyway, I found this place in that folder.

Kiara's phone rings. "Hold on," she says, moving the phone to her ear. "Yeah, we're here, where are you? Uh-huh..." Half listening to Kiara's conversation, half looking around at the trees and foliage all around the house, I spot some chickadees in the trees above flitting from branch to branch and singing. I only track them for a few minutes, because I lose sight of them as the setting sun gets in my eyes.

"We'll wait for you. See you in a few minutes," Kiara says hanging up her phone. "They're almost here," she says turning to me.

"They?" I ask hoping she'll crack and tell me. Nope. She just smiles at me again.

"So how do we get in?" I ask.

"The boys will take care of it when they get here. We just wait," Kiara answers.

Kiara and I talk about the latest gossip at school. She gets me up-to-date with the dating scene and the latest teacher rumors, who is dating who and which teachers are secretly hooking up—the stuff we don't usually talk about in our short day-to-day chats. She updates the list of friends who got accepted to college, and where they've decided to go. I haven't thought about college for months. I missed my SATs. It's not like I could afford college this year anyway. Next year, probably not. It would be nice to have a ticket out of town though.

I kick rocks and bits of branches off the concrete landing, kicking them over the edge one at a time. It keeps me focused so I don't think too much about missing the chance to get out of Eddie's house with college, and my friends from the old school, how much I miss having Kiara next to me like this, how much I miss having someone to talk to girl-to-girl. Yeah, we talk on the phone, but it's not the same as having a side-by-side pow-wow. When I start thinking about everything I miss, it's depressing, and that's even before adding my mom into the mix. When I get in this zone, it's a path that's dark and dangerous. I even have a name for it. It's my Hamletdom, and it's not a very healthy place.

It's nearly dark when I look up again. The bright orange sun barely peeking over the horizon; the trees look black against the blazing skyline and the air is cooler.

A sound echoes nearby, echoing off the trees through the quiet—tires, slow and steady. The vehicle is close.

"It's them," Kiara says.

I look down the driveway through the dimming light of dusk. A truck emerges—easing past the boulder into view—and comes to a stop next to Kiara's car; a giant and a dwarf, a burgundy Ford F-150 with a four wheel ATV in the flatbed casting a shadow over Kiara's Civic. I don't recognize the truck, and the cab is dark so I can't see who is inside, until the dome light flashes on and I see Michael cracking the passenger door open. I look to Kiara, and then back at Michael as he steps from the passenger side door.

"Michael? Oh god," I say rolling my eyes. I suddenly feel very agitated. Michael is Kiara's boyfriend, and he's also an ass; rude & arrogant. We don't get along.

"Give him a chance," Kiara tells me, giving me a hard stare. I turn back to the truck. Michael is now perched on the running board staring at himself in the side view mirror, smiling at his reflection, moving his hands through his hair. He jumps to the ground, and instead of just walking like a normal person, he struts as if he's a modern-day John Travolta in Staying Alive—my mom loved that movie—in slim fit jeans and a fitted shirt. He pulls a pack of cigarettes from his back pocket, flicks the pack so that one cigarette sticks out from the top, and approaches us with the cigarettes extended in our direction.

"Anyone want a cig?" He asks leaning onto the first step of the house, as he pulls out a lighter from the side of the pack.

"Do you have to light that thing?" I snap.

"Good to see you too," he snaps back.

"Babe, you want one?" He asks Kiara as he lights the cigarette dangling from his lips. He moves up to the top of the landing and sidles up next to her.

"Kiss first," she says with a pouty face. He takes in a drag and exhales, moving his cigarette arm around Kiara's shoulder, and then he moves in for a kiss. They connect like two magnets, their lips moving in rhythm, a full mouth get-a-room kind of kiss. I imagine it tastes like smoke. My stomach turns. And then Michael grabs Kiara's ass.

"Seriously," I say. Kiara pulls away.

"Is this why you wouldn't tell me where we were going?" I ask Kiara.

"No. I didn't bring Michael to annoy you. I brought Michael so someone else would come," she says.

"Who?" I ask.

"You'll see," she says, "meantime, you two have to play nice. Tonight is about letting loose, forgetting about the past, and just having fun. Ok?" Kiara says to both Michael and me.

"I always play nice," Michael says, "It was nice for you, right babe?" I feel a heave of stomach acid pushing up my throat. Michael makes me want to puke. And then I notice a flicker of movement from behind him.

"Hi guys." It's Paul Donaldson. As he moves out from behind Michael, I see he's wearing his signature flannel shirt over a fitted tee shirt, jeans, and Timberlands. He's carrying a large cardboard box in his arms.

"Paul?" I ask. We know each other; lab partners at my old school right before mom's death, right before I moved. We kissed, once, in my room, well it wasn't exactly a full kiss because Eddie walked in on us and freaked out. That was the last time I saw Paul, because Mom died the next day.

"Faith," Paul says, leaning in for a half hug, balancing the box in one arm, "You doin' ok?"

"Yeah," I answer, coming out of the hug.

"Sorry about your mom," Paul says, with an arm lingering on my shoulder.

"Thanks," I say feeling awkward. We probably would have hooked up in a full blown relationship if I'd stayed in town, if circumstances had been different.

"Alright boys, get us in," Kiara says like a general releasing troops to war. Michael and Paul take off in a sprint, racing and knocking into each other, their flashlight beams jumping off the surrounding trees and the dilapidated exterior of the house.

"*Now,* are you o.k. with my secret?" Kiara asks.

"Good secret," I say.

The boys disappear around the corner toward the back.

"How do we know the place is safe?" I ask turning to face the house.

"The house is fine. You worry too much. Stop worrying about the house, and start thinking about what you want to do with Paul. Me, I just want them to find a way in, because it's getting dark," she says moving closer to me.

"Here, hold the light," I say. I squat down next to Paul's box looking for another flashlight. Instead I find blankets, a case of beer, and bottles of water.

"Hey Paul, any more flashlights?" I shout to the back of the house. He doesn't answer. Neither does Michael when Kiara shouts his name.

"You know they're going to prank us, right?" I say to Kiara, she shakes her head in agreement, and no sooner have the words left my mouth when Michael pops out of the dark in a full out run, lunging for us.

"Gotcha!" he yells grabbing my arm.

"Jesus Christ!" I scream. "You crazy shit!" Kiara rockets off the concrete steps toward Michael and punches his shoulder, playful but hard.

"You scared the shit out of me!" Kiara yells.

"Sorry babe, it was just too easy," he says, taking Kiara in his arms.

"I thought you were supposed to protect me and my black ass," Kiara says, her voice dropping into a pouty whine mid-sentence.

"Always," he says planting a kiss on her lips. I roll my eyes.

Behind me, the door to the house opens on rusted hinges that creak and groan. I twist around, fisted hands in front of me ready to punch whatever comes through the door.

"It's just me," Paul says with his hands in the air, his frame and face highlighted by an upwards-facing flashlight planted at his feet. I relax my arms. Paul drops into a bow, changes his voice to a medieval twang, and announces with a flourish, "Come in, m'lady!"

What a dork. I smile at him anyway. He smiles back, and urges me inside with a sideways nod toward the room. I catch a hint of his cologne as I pass—spicy & earthy with a hint of citrus, expensive, though I can't name the brand—which strikes me as odd, I don't pin him as a cologne kind of guy, but the smell works on him. It really works.

The cologne is nice, but it's quickly overpowered by the smell of must and rotting wood as I step further inside the house. I cover my nose and mouth with my hand; kicked up dust swirls around me—I can see it dancing in the path of Paul's flashlight beam and feel it tickling my throat. It's obvious the house has been untouched for some time. Paul moves up beside me. I follow his flashlight beam around the interior of the house, catching glimpses of decay—bits of faded, green flower wallpaper hang in strips, window frames are covered in dirty-white cracked paint, an old couch with faded red fabric is pushed awkwardly against a bookshelf of dust-covered, ragged books—some lying flat, some—and trash is strewn along the floor—cans, candy bar wrappers, grocery bags, a dingy boot with frayed laces, bits of mismatched clothing, and lots of indistinguishable garbage.

"Gross," I whisper to Paul.

"Guess we're not the only ones who have found this place," he says.

The air continues to fill with dust, and my eyes are paying the price. I rub them with my fingers, trying to get to the itchiness that persists just below the surface. The more I rub the worse it gets. And now the dust is attacking my mouth, assailing my palate with tiny particles bombing the back of my throat. I clear my throat to try to quell the urge to cough, but it only makes it worse. I can't hold it back anymore, and once the cough starts, I can't stop it. I can't get to the tickle in my throat.

"Are you ok?" Paul asks, turning toward me, putting his hand gently on my back.

"The dust," I say in a voice like a croaking frog.

"Maybe you should stay by the door for now, until the dust settles a bit. I think I have some masks in my truck."

"Masks?" I ask.

"Dust masks. You want one?" he asks.

"Yeah, maybe," I say.

"Alright, wait here. Take the flashlight so you're not in the dark," he says.

"How are you going to see?" I ask looking at the barely-visible truck.

"Flashlight app," he says holding his cell phone in the air. He turns the app on and jogs to his truck, his body in a spotlight of muted cell phone light, his short tapered light brown hair just barely visible moving in a controlled bounce. I watch him open the driver-side door and the cab of the truck floods in light. He pushes the bucket seats forward, grabs some things from the back, and then returns the seats in place. I probably shouldn't be staring, but I can't help it. He closes the door and jogs back, a sleeping bag in each hand and a pack of unopened dust masks dangling from his lips.

"Voila!" he says after tossing the sleeping bags to the floor, opening the package of masks, and handing me one. "Here let me put it on you," he says. He places the mask over my nose and mouth, moving the elastic strap over my head, and gently pulling my hair away from my neck and through the strap. My neck is tingling where his fingers brush my skin. He puts his hand on the small of my back—for the second time today—and there's something in the way he touches me, it makes me quiver.

"You cold?" He asks, feeling my back shake.

"I'm ok," I say, but I feel weird, good weird. Giddy.

"You wanna keep exploring or you wanna wait here?" Paul asks. I can hear he's anxious to check out the rest of the house.

"I'll go with you," I say my voice muffled behind the mask.

The next room is obviously the kitchen, an old rusted stove sits to the left with counters covered in dirt, debris, acorns, and bits of tree branches. A few small plants have taken root in a crevice around the sink, the cabinets are dirty and weather-worn. Moonlight is streaming in from the roof like a natural skylight, through the hole where a tree limb punctured it, the hole we saw from the front of the house.

"Find anything in this pig sty," Michael says as he and Kiara walk into the room holding hands.

"This room is a little iffy," Paul says.

"Hey, nice look. What is it, end-of-the-world couture?" Michael says to me as he pushes passed me hand-in-hand with Kiara.

"Don't be such an ass," I say with a muffled voice.

Paul bends down and grabs a long branch from the floor and extends it to the low ceiling, pushing the pulpy wood, testing the ceiling's stability. Debris showers us.

"Seems o.k.," Michael says wrapping his arm around Kiara's waist.

"Hold on," Paul says as he steps to the floor below the damaged ceiling where moss and ferns have taken root. The floor is soft and pulpy and weak from water damage. Paul's foot pushes through the wood as if pushing through thin ice.

"I think we should avoid this room. I don't trust the floor or the ceiling," Paul says.

"O.k. chicken shit, we'll stay out of this room, but I call dibs on the next one," Michael says as he pulls Kiara in front of him and playfully thrusts his hips toward her.

CHAPTER SEVEN

MICHAEL & PAUL

Why does Michael get under my skin so much? And yet I know the answer. Michael is disgusting; d-i-s-g-u-s-t-i-n-g. Disgusting with a capital D.

Kiara talks nonstop about all the wonderful things Michael does for her, how sweet and charming he is, and thoughtful. Michael? Really? I never see that side of him, he acts like such a jerk in front of me. I have to assume it has something to do with the fact that he asked me out long before Kiara: in 6th grade, 7th grade, 8th grade, and 9th grade too. I said no every single time, not because I thought he was a jerk back then, I just didn't like him as date-material. Now he's a vindictive son-of-a-bitch, at least that's my theory; he'd never come out and admit it now that he's one half of MiKiara and famous in school. Yes, Michael & Kiara are tagged like a celebrity couple. All because of Valentine's Day last year when Michael had ten dozen roses delivered to Kiara in the middle of Biology. I don't think Principal Baxter appreciated it, but it was the topic of hallway gossip for days. And then there was the cheer that Kiara convinced the Cheer Squad to perform during homecoming, *Michael-Michael he's our man, he's the dude with the tan, Kiara's love —tall and cute, have you seen him in a suit? Wooooooooo!* The bleachers went wild and Michael ate it up, stood like a king amongst his adoring subjects, the only thing missing was a crown and scepter.

I told Kiara as long as he's good to her, I'll butt out, but the second that changes, I'll turn his ass upside down quicker than a scared grasshopper jumps. I don't think Kiara sees it, the way he acts toward me, she doesn't see the pointed remarks or the innuendos; he can dislike me as much as he wants as long as he makes her happy—it complicates my life, which I especially don't need right now—but hell, it's one of those friendship sacrifices.

"You ok?" Kiara mouths to me, her face projecting an odd mix of shadow and cell phone light.

I shrug. She puts an arm on my shoulder and leans in to me with an awkward tilt, still holding Michael's hand on the other side.

"Are you having a good time," she asks. I shrug again. She leans in closer and whispers, "Is it Paul?" I shake my head.

"Michael?" I shake my head yes.

"Is his mouth getting away from him again?" she asks.

Oh yeah, that's it.

"I just want *us* to hang out, you and me," I say.

"I know. Me too. And we will, just a few minutes with Michael, then I'm all yours the rest of the night. I promise. We'll grab a blanket and a couple beers. K? I invited Michael so Paul would tag along. I want tonight to be special. For you. You and Paul, what do ya think?" I shrug yet again. That's Kiara, Miss Social Butterfly, solving problems with a party.

"Maybe you two can pick up where you left off? Might be good for you," Kiara says. I smile.

"That's my girl," Kiara says squeezing me in a one arm hug. "You deserve this," she whispers. Michael pulls at her arm, and jumps up in the air, moshing to imaginary music, rattling debris from the walls, tugging on Kiara again still hand-locked to him.

"What are we waiting for, let's explore bitches!" Michael yells slapping Kiara's ass again.

It is a classic Michael move, totally oblivious to how offensive he can be. Or maybe it's not oblivious at all, maybe it's all on purpose.

We split into two teams behind two flashlights, Kiara follows Michael and I follow—at his heels like a blind kitten to its mother. I can barely see anything in front of me. Paul is moving the flashlight around the ceiling, the walls, down the hallway, and everywhere except where our feet are. He stops and I nearly run into the back of him.

"You said next room is yours," Paul says turning to Michael, "that's the room you claim?" It's a small bathroom with a half-closed door and a strong smell of mold and mildew.

"Ha, ha, very funny," Michael jokes, then nudges Kiara forward and into an adjacent room, "This is our room." It's a bedroom I would guess by the size of it, how appropriate. Paul flashes the light inside. The room is empty except for peeling wallpaper and a closet that sits oddly preserved to the left. Graffiti crowds the walls. Michael bends and whispers something in Kiara's ear. Kiara giggles. I roll my eyes, knowing no one will see me do it in the dark but it still makes me feel better somehow. I ease past the room behind Paul who also seems eager to go—the floorboards creak as we walk—past another empty bedroom with sections of its wallpaper hanging in strips; the floor is covered in beer cans, shopping bags, and discarded clothing. If I had to guess, I'd say some less than savory things have happened in this house; thinking about it makes my stomach turn.

Paul leads us back to the main room just inside the front door. This room is less flop-house and more straight up abandoned property, which is oddly comforting after seeing the rest of the house. Paul gets busy setting lanterns in each corner, and the room is magically alight; it almost feels like we have electricity, *almost*. Then he sets to work unrolling one of the sleeping bags on the floor.

"Wanna sit?" He asks.

"Thanks," I say. I drop to the sleeping bag, thankful for its softness and warmth against the hard, cold floor. I slip off the mask from my face, holding it up to Paul.

Thanks for this," I say.

"Hang on to it, you might need it again. And you're welcome." Paul grabs a blanket from the box and wraps it around my shoulders.

"You looked cold before," he says.

"Thanks," I say again, blushing, remembering that it wasn't the cold that made me shiver.

"Want a beer?" Paul asks.

"Sure," I say.

Paul grabs two beers from the box on the floor.

"So. Kiara says you're living with your brother now?" Paul asks, popping the top off the beer with a key chain bottle opener and handing it to me.

"Yeah," I say taking the beer from him.

"What's that like? Living with *your* brother?" he asks slipping himself down beside me on the sleeping bag.

"Hard," I say taking a sip.

"I bet."

"He's a jerk."

"I get that," Paul says.

"You did see Crazy Eddie that day," I say.

"Yeah it got weird fast," he says.

"Yeah. It's really been hard—my mom, the move, new school, everything."

"Losing your mom, I can't imagine. I mean, I never knew my mom, but that's totally different."

"Really? I didn't know that. It's just you and your Dad?"

"Me, my dad, my older sis who lives in California now—my whole life. I mean there have been girlfriends, but none ever stuck."

"How many girlfriends?"

"I don't know, a lot. My Dad kind of bounced from one to the other for a while," Paul says.

"Oh, are we talking about *your* girlfriends or your Dad's?"

"My Dad's. You thought I was talking about me?" Paul laughs and scratches the barely-visible stubble on his cheek.

"What's so funny?" I ask.

"You thought I was talking about *my* 'lots of girlfriends.'"

"Yeah. Well. Since we're on the subject, how many 'lots of girlfriends' have you had?" I ask.

"Not lot's, that's for sure. Not many," he says with a smile.

"How many is not many?" I ask smiling back at him.

"Half dozen, maybe. But none serious," he says.

"Whys that? Prefer to bounce around like your Dad?" I ask.

"No. Just didn't click with anyone so far. Trial and error, I guess," Paul says looking at me as if I am a Where's Waldo poster. I look away, embarrassed.

"So what happened to your mom, she left or something?" I ask looking at my lap.

"No she died when I was just a baby. She was in the army and deployed overseas. Roadside bomb. Killed instantly."

"Oh. I'm so sorry," I say.

"It was a long time ago, and like I said I was too young to even remember her. But you, you knew your mom. That's got to be really tough."

"Yeah," I say fresh out of words.

"You know, if you ever need someone to talk to I'm a really good listener," Paul says.

"Yeah?" I say flashing him a big smile.

"Yeah. You can call me anytime. You still have my number?" I shake my head. "Had to change phones when I moved. Lost everything that I didn't have written down."

"That sucks."

"Tell me about it," I say.

"I have to give you my number. You want to put it in your phone?"

"I don't have my phone with me. Long story," I say.

"Oh. Remind me when we get back to the truck. I'll write it down for you," Paul says.

"OK."

"You know, I thought about you a lot these last three months. Felt bad that I didn't call you that weekend..." I feel myself blushing. *He'd been thinking about me? Really?*

"You're sorry? I'm sorry. It was *my* brother that walked in on us and freaked out," I say interrupting him.

"It wasn't your fault. I did try to call you the week after, but you never picked up. Thought you were avoiding me. Then your box was full and I couldn't even leave a message. I wondered why you didn't call. The rumors started at school when you stop showing up; there were some crazy stories circulating. Kiara told me the real deal about your mom and the move, and at that point I knew you had bigger things to think about, so I laid low, then your name came up again when I was talking to Kiara last week. I told her I wanted to get back in touch with you. She said she had a feeling I'd get to see you again. And here we are. She must be psychic or something."

"Or something. She's a planner. She planned this," I say.

"Oh yeah. True," Paul says with a chuckle. He grabs my hand, quickly and kind of awkward as if doing it before he changes his mind. My head starts spinning, a little buzz from the beer mixed with something else, giddiness, anxiety, I don't know. Whatever it is, it's getting stronger as Paul wraps his hand around mine.

"I know you're dealing with a lot, and I know that I might not fit into the whole picture right now, but maybe we can get together sometime," Paul says.

"Are you asking me out?" I ask. Paul puts his beer down and leans into me.

"Yes," he whispers into my ear. He moves his lips across my cheek, then to my lips. He tastes like beer, and my lips must taste the same, but it's his smell that is drawing me in—that mix of outdoor fresh and citrus and something else that I can't pinpoint. His lips move softly, nimbly as if dancing with my lips, soft and insistent as if the kiss has been building and aging since the last time our lips met. We are both breathing heavily, in rhythm. His hand moves to my lower back where it holds me, and my back quivers. He adjusts the blanket with his free hand so my shoulders are covered.

Mom would like him. And with the thought of mom, I start to tear, mid-kiss. Paul pulls away and looks at me.

"Are you o.k.?" He asks.

"I'm sorry," I say.

"No, I'm sorry. It's too soon, right?"

"I just all of a sudden—this sounds stupid I know—I thought how much my mom would have liked you," I say. Paul folds me up in his arms.

"I miss her Paul," I say.

"It's ok," Paul whispers. He holds me there, his arms around me, "It takes time to heal," he says. I pull away, wiping my face with my sleeve. I look at Paul. He's looking at me.

"I am so sorry," I say, just as Michael and Kiara reappear at the edge of the room.

"And that's how it's done," Michael says sauntering out of the shadows and into the light of the living room. Paul and I are still looking at each other.

"Are we interrupting?" Michael asks.

"No," I say quickly. Too quickly.

Michael gives Paul a high-five as he passes.

"Want another beer," Michael asks.

"Hell yeah," Paul says moving to get up, but before he's up all the way, he leans back down, pushes a strand of my hair behind my ear, and whispers, "I meant what I said. When you're ready."

I watch him as he jumps up and jogs to Michael's side, chugging the last of the beer he opened with me. Michael tosses him a new one.

"Nice catch," Michael says, "Dude, we have to hang out more often."

"Yeah. I think *so*," Paul says glancing back at me. Michael follows his gaze, gives him a shoulder bump, and whispers, "Piece of advice buddy, if you're gonna try to tap that—good luck, ice queen doesn't put out from what I hear."

The thing about quiet rooms is even the tiniest sounds can be heard. I hear Michael's comment. We all do. Paul looks dumbfounded.

"What's wrong with you?" Kiara yells swinging at Michael's shoulder for the second time tonight. This time her punch lands.

"Ouch!" Michael bellows, rubbing the spot on his shoulder.

Kiara storms away from Michael, toward me, and drops herself onto the sleeping bag beside me.

"Boys can be such assholes," she says loud enough for everyone to hear.

"I'm ready to go home," I say. My calm is surprising; I'm not crying, not angry or upset. I'm just numb.

"Can I talk you into staying? You and I are going to have a couple drinks, gossip, probably giggle a lot, and that starts right now. And then, maybe later, you and Paul can get together. I saw you two talking." She nudges me.

Kiara doesn't know about the kiss I just screwed up.

"What if I get Michael to promise to behave?" Kiara asks.

"I don't know. I wouldn't want to put a freeze on the festivities," I say loud enough for everyone to hear. Michael and Paul turn to look.
Kiara gives Michael a glare. "Michael promises to behave the rest of the night, don't you Michael?"

"Yeah whatever, sure," he mumbles in between gulps of beer.

"C'mon, you and me, a couple beers, some chips, girl talk, like before—BEWTS, remember that?" Kiara says, nudging my shoulder, and then she turns and shouts across the room, "Boys, go play in the corner or something." I want to laugh. If I made a comment like that, I'd be 'the bitch' in the room, but when Kiara says it the boys go to the corner silently like whipped dogs.

I agree to stay. I don't really want to—I'm missing my pajamas and a warm bed right about now, music in my ears, blocking out the world—except I kind of want to see where this Paul thing goes, and honestly I don't have much of a choice in leaving no matter how much Kiara appears to be considering my request. It's the Kiara charm—yes she's using it on me, and even I find it hard to repel—but I've known her long enough to spot her magic at work; I just don't have the energy for the back and forth tonight, only to end up staying in the end anyway. Kiara is my ride and Kiara wants this night to go on as planned. That's that.

My head is crowded, my thoughts like a bag of marbles scattering in all directions. I need quiet to sort it all out, but Kiara just wants to talk. Sitting opposite me on the sleeping bag, she's talking enough for both of us, pausing here and there. When I shake my head or look up at her, she waits for more, and then when I don't offer more, she picks up carrying the conversation again. She knows I'll come around at some point. For now, she's got enough to say for both of us.

I can't stop thinking how I screwed it up with Paul, going over the details again and again. I mean who cries during a kiss? Seriously. Every time I get a shot with Paul it's like we're surrounded by a line of gunpowder destined to ignite, demolishing the legs that might constitute a beginning. I wonder if we'll ever get past "the first kiss".

Before tonight I hadn't thought about Paul in months, even though he was all I thought about for hours after that first kiss in my bedroom. Losing mom the next day meant there was no room for anything else, and then tonight, feeling that spark like it had never gone away, starting over again with Paul—I don't want to let it go.

Kiara has stopped talking. I look up at her.

"What are you thinking about?" she asks.

"Nothing," I say.

"Want some Fritos?" she says holding an open bag to me.

"No, thanks," I say.

"What about Pringles? I brought your favorite Cheeseburger flavored," she says.

"You found them, where?"

"Online," she says with an upturned eyebrow.

"How long have you been planning this?" I ask. She only smiles.

"Hold on, let me see which bag I put them in," Kiara says, getting up and heading to the corner where the grocery bags are spread out around the boys. She bends down and rummages through each one, all the while talking pointedly with Michael and Paul.

There are momentary gaps of silence, times when the grocery bags are still, the chip bags stop crinkling and beer is not being opened. It's in these fleeting moments when I hear the wind whistle through the house's wooden cracks, the plink-plink-plink of bits of branches and acorns falling on the roof. I sip my beer, looking into the next room at the hole in the ceiling and the stars flickering as the night clouds pass in front.

"Are you opening every single bag?" Kiara scolds the boys.

I turn back to the house and its decaying facade, back to the damaged ceiling in the next room. I scoot to the right, moving the sleeping bag under me to get a better view of the sky. *This* is what I need to get right with my thoughts. I could sit here all night in silence, staring at the sky, getting lost in the darkness—it reminds me of my spot in the woods behind Eddie's house. And mom. I slide my hand to my pocket, searching for my security blanket, but instead of reaching the picture, my hand is blocked by the wadded up bandana. I gently pull it out, careful to keep the pendant snug inside.

What do I do with it?

The balled up bandana sits on top of the shadowed lifelines of my palm. I can't stop looking at it.

Do I dare? I don't even really know what happened in the basement, it was like some kind of hallucination maybe. That doesn't explain how the rib pain vanished. Weird.

My thoughts are multiplying, rabbit-quick, crowding out all thoughts about Paul and Kiara, and tonight, and focused solely on this thing in my hand.

Maybe the gem is coated with something. No, that's stupid. Maybe I'm just simply losing my mind.

The walls start to shake and dust kicks up into the air as Michael and Paul wrestle for a bag of chips. Michael sweeps Paul's feet—sending him crashing to the floor—snatches the bag and drops himself down into a sitting position against the wall.

"Boys are like overgrown children," Kiara says muttering to herself, still looking for my special Pringles.

Michael and Paul shove hands into two separate chip bags, chomping and chewing, opening more bags and tossing them back and forth—chips spill everywhere—and they're laughing, chugging beer, spewing more chips, and egging each other on. Those damn chip bags crinkle every time they grab one and plunge a hand inside. The noise is jarring.

What if I show them the necklace? It's just a necklace, right.

Crinkle-laugh-crinkle-chew-crinkle-laugh-crinkle-crinkle-criiiiinkle-CRINKLE!

"Can you guys stop!" I say almost yelling.

"Oh, here we go," Michael moans. I toss the blanket off my shoulders and stand up facing Michael.

"Shut up. Just shut up," I say without blinking.

"You shut up. Get out of my face," Michael says staring at me.

"You are an arrogant, big mouth, ass," I say, my voice strong and unwavering.

"And you are a bitch," Michael says.

"Ok, ok, let's just cool off," Paul says getting up to wedge himself between the two of us.

"I'll cool off when he shuts his arrogant mouth, because I'm about ready to punch his ass," I say.

"Whoa—whoa—whoa, Faith. Let's calm down," Paul says.

"Calm down? What about him?" I yell.

"Michael, an apology?" Paul prompts.

"Apologize? For what?" Michael asks.

"To be the 'bigger man'," Paul says.

"Bigger man, my ass, but whatever. Fine. Sorry," Michael says looking at me.

"Faith, are we good?" Paul asks.

"No, not really," I say.

"See! I apologize, and she keeps going. She's got to cool it too," Michael says.

"Don't worry Michael, I'm going to 'cool it' outside," I say.

"You're not going outside alone—white girl in the dark—nuh uh," Kiara says.

"Yeah, I am," I say.

"I'm comin' then," Kiara says.

"I need to be alone," I say. I grab the flashlight from the floor.

"Can I borrow this?" I say to Paul.

"Of course. You sure you don't want some company?" he asks.

"Not unless you want to watch me go pee," I say.

CHAPTER EIGHT

DESTINY

I really do need to go pee.

I was too abrupt with Paul and Kiara, I know. I hear their voices inside the house, fading the further I move away, searching the perimeter with the flashlight, looking for a place to squat without being seen. Across the driveway I see it—a thicket of bushes around a too-round-to-hug oak tree. The bushes are cramped and hard to get through from the front, so I circle around the back, passing both vehicles then turning to face the house. The coast is still clear.

I slip behind the thicket, laying the flashlight to the ground—the still lit tip buried in a mixture of pine needles and dried leaves, to mask my position; I rest the necklace against the flashlight so the bandana stays closed. Carefully, I unbutton my jeans and slide them down, keeping my underwear in place until I squat, then sliding it all forward out of the way.

It's a little creepy out here by myself. I'm not usually jumpy in the dark, but from this vulnerable position every sound sets me on edge—the wind rustling the bushes, acorns dropping on the roof—either of these are better than footsteps, voices, or cars and luckily I haven't heard any of those yet. Hopefully I'll be done with this squat before I do.

The pee is still coming. Must be the beer. Through the bushes I focus on the house, light pouring out of its windows and the still open front door—like a lighthouse through the fog. Kiara, Michael, and Paul are just inside the front door. I can't hear what they're saying, I'm too far away, but they're probably talking about me in all likelihood. Kiara doesn't look happy, in fact she looks downright pissed, her arms are crossed tight to her chest as if she's holding in her anger, and her left heel is bouncing off the floor— only her left—her right leg is firmly planted, and she's biting her lip.

The pee is slowing, slowing to a trickle, and then sputtering as my bladder kicks out the final dregs. I glance to the house again. Paul is standing in the doorway.

Shit!

I duck further down, shielding myself behind the bushes.

"Faith!" He calls. Paul turns away for a second and calls for Kiara. I move to finish, yanking at my underwear and my pants, but I'm wet, and it's in this moment that I realize, I didn't bring any toilet paper.

Oh, shit.

I can't walk around like this. I shake my pelvis like a dog shaking off a bath, but it's not enough. I still feel wet.

Think—think—think.

The bandana. I grab an end and pull—spilling the pendant to the ground—and wipe, letting the bandana fall when I'm done. I pull up my underwear and jeans in one swoop, button the top, and bend down to pick up the flashlight.

What about the necklace?

Hovering, flashlight in hand with the beam trained on the pendant—it looks harmless and beautiful, and shimmery...I just want to touch it.

Pick it up. Stop being a baby and pick it up.

I could, with my sleeve even, and slip it back into my pocket.

You're going to have to touch it sometime. Just do it.

I reach out with my fingertip just above the pendant's surface, the stone's reflected light like a kaleidoscope on my hand. And then it happens again. The pendant draws my hand to it and I'm beyond decision; everything goes black instantly, accented with a sharp wind, funneling particles that hit my face and scratch my arms.

Then even that is gone.

The world around me is nothing but black.

I've pissed my pants.

I drop my hand to check my crotch but even before I get there my hand dips in a puddle, wet and warm, all around me—I'm drenched—the back of my shirt, my hair, my arms, and my legs.

Oh God, I'm lying in my own piss.

I fumble to get up, but I slip. I can't see anything. It's too dark to find traction. I should be able to make out tree silhouettes or the outline of the house—even if the lanterns are off—but I can't see anything.

I bet it's that damn necklace again.

I close my eyes—count three seconds—and re-open, hoping for a reset, and it works—*kind of*—the whole world opens up around me, the darkness disappears in a flash of marigold, and then even that clears and I can see...I am not where I was before. The air is different—warm & humid with a breeze that smells of damp wood and decaying vegetation— and the trees I ducked behind for coverage by the old house are gone, so are the house and the cars, and Kiara and Michael, and Paul, all gone; replaced with scenery that is different, but familiar, the place from my dreams—a sky that is periwinkle taffeta infused with a rainbow of dancing light, like an Aurora Borealis across a big, beautiful daytime sky. It's a sky of dreams, and somehow not quite right, and it's changing, trees are popping into view where only seconds ago there was nothing, and now seconds later there's a cramped throng of giant-sized tropical foliage—Murumuru Palms, Elephant's Ears, Monstera, Lipstick Trees, Amazonian giants I learned about in Social Studies, crowding my periphery, and moving.

The trees are moving.

No, they're not moving. I am.

I bolt up from my prone position.

Water from the ends of my hair...

It is water—Oh thank god—dirty, particle-rich water, but it's water and not piss.

...down my back, soaking my shirt that is already clinging to my skin. My head is foggy & spinning and there's a cold wave of sweat that sweeps over me—rocking back and forth, the sounds of moving water surround me—my skin turns clammy and cold and my stomach is ready to erupt; dizzy—I close my eyes again.

Something is moving in the water, dipping into it, pulling through it.

A paddle?

I open my eyes and shift, my knees bump the edge of something hard, and the dizziness is back so quick I can't see what I just jammed my knees into because I've closed my eyes already. I pull both knees in and swivel upright, determined to get past the dizziness. I take in a breath, open my eyes again, and force myself to see. I *am* in a boat, a small narrow canoe, hand carved and covered in uneven chiseled dugouts. I'm at the bottom, sitting in an inch of water that sloshes as the boat moves.

I'm not moving the boat, so how is it moving?

Just as I think the question, the dipping and pulling sound returns beside me. Straightening my back and cautiously looking over the side of the boat, I see what's making the sound—a wooden paddle crafted from a Marupa tree, dipping in, and moving the water. Up the shaft of the paddle my eyes move to two dark wrinkly hands pulling the wood across the water—I stop, frozen, barely moving—there's a nearly-naked man sitting there with his broad-shouldered back to me.

The man moves slowly and deliberately, his aged olive skin sitting in loose wrinkled rolls around his frame, his arms dipping and pulling the paddle, synchronized with another. I whip my head around. Another paddle, and another man, a near carbon copy of the first, sits stoic with his pot-bellied mid-section facing me. A small animal pelt wraps around his waist, and his feet are covered in handmade moccasins. He stares at me, expressionless, his eyes and forehead accented by bright red markings that remind me of tribal war paint from the Amazon case studies from my Social Studies book; everything around me feels Amazonian—the water, the foliage, the canoe, and the guys at the helm, everything except the sky; the sky is something completely foreign. Both men are silent.

"Hello," I say still turned toward the man in back. He averts his eyes and doesn't respond.

Don't be an ass. I said hello.

I inch closer to him, crawling on my hands and knees over the boat's bottom through the sloshing water. The canoe tilts and sways as I move. I stop, and face him, and move in closer.

"I said, hello."

He continues to stare around me, as if I'm not there or not important enough to acknowledge. I know I should be frightened, but I'm not, I'm annoyed.

I move in close and wave my hand in front of his face. The man continues to stare around me, out to open water ahead of us. I twist around on my knees, gripping the edge of the boat to steady myself, leaving the man behind me and inching to the front. The hollowed center of the boat is wet and crowded with thick rope, nets, and fish that flop end to end splashing me as I crawl. My jeans are now two-tone, darker where the water soaks them, light on the few remaining dry areas. The bottom of the boat is slippery—my knee slides, the boat lurches, my hand slips across the edge, and I completely lose my balance and fall to the bottom, my arms and legs splay out in the water. Fish flop from side-to-side hurling themselves into the air with their tails. Water, and god knows what else, splashes into my face.

The men laugh, large belly laughs that make the boat rock even more.

"Laugh, go ahead, laugh at my expense."

My tee shirt and jeans are now completely soaked and clinging. Even my bra is wet. I cross my arms. They can laugh all they want, but they aren't getting a show.

I sit at the bottom of the boat with my legs in the water and my arms crossed in quiet rebellion, knowing that all I have to do is wait. All dreams end, and this one will be no different—there's no other explanation that makes sense. I must have fallen asleep in the woods and I'm dreaming.

The laughter slows and the men return to their quiet deliberate movements. The waiting feels endless.

I could hurl myself over the edge of the boat, but who knows what might lie-in-wait—some giant prehistoric fish with fangs and a taste for human flesh.

I could wait for the boat to veer closer to land, and jump to the embankment and run—*could be a viable idea*.

I scan the bank; hordes of tropical foliage crowd the edge leaving no openings; big leaves and thick underbrush thicken before my eyes, so dense the forest beyond is obscured. And then the embankment disappears and we are out of the river and into open water, so abrupt I didn't see it coming, as if it changed right before my eyes. I turn to see the river, but a thick mist obscures everything behind us.

Ahead, the open water is endless and empty on the horizon except for a solitary land mass in the distance.

The rowing men traverse the water like Olympic athletes, and in what seems like mere minutes the island's grainy beach is just ahead, empty, and only a few feet in front of the boat. I look back to see where we came from, to understand how we traveled so far in such a short time, but the mist still shadows us and nothing beyond it is visible.

I turn again to the island. The beach is now covered with people, as if appearing out of thin air while my head was turned, and each one mirrors the men in the boat; I've heard of twins before, or even fathers & sons or mothers & daughters looking alike, but a whole village?

I grab the edge of the boat to steady myself as both men jump into the waist deep water, one man guides the back and the other the front, they push it onto the sand until it is completely beached. Then one of them, and I can't tell which, takes off through the crowd. He is quickly engulfed in bodies. I lose sight of him for a minute, and then see him again midway up the beach continuing at a quick clip towards a single thatched hut towering at the edge of the beach. The crowd follows him, matching his stride and following his path like a group of graphic clones until they all disappear inside the structure.

I push up from the bottom of the canoe leaving the water at my feet. As I straighten, a hand drops onto my shoulder. I turn, startled.

The second helmsmen of the canoe has perched his hand like a parrot. He doesn't speak, but points to the ground.

"Stay here?" I ask. He nods once. I give him a thumbs up, which seems to confuse him, because he points at me again, and then to the ground. I guess the thumbs up isn't as universal as I thought, even in dreams.

"I get it," I say & shake my head, hoping that it conveys my understanding. He nods & smiles, imitating me, and then takes off in the same direction as his partner.

I pull my tee shirt up to my nose thinking it's either him or it's me, and I nearly gag. It's me. I smell like dirty water and fish. I scramble to get out of the boat but stop mid-step. That's when I notice I am alone. The beach is empty—every soul I had seen crowd the sand is now gone—and eerily silent, no sounds: no surf, no birds, and no insects. The air is still, the water doesn't move, and everything is quiet; too damn quiet. Nervousness creeps up in my stomach. The only thing moving is the flashing of yellow and green that streaks the periwinkle sky above me. I reach my right leg out of the boat to the sand balancing all my weight on my left foot, and as I shift, the boat lilts and I teeter. For a split second there's hope that I'll recover and right myself; my leg tilts to one side and then the other; shaking I try to hold on, but then I lose my balance completely and slip over the edge, landing face first onto the beach. Sand fills my mouth; grit sticks to my teeth, wedges inside my shoes, and coats all the wet surfaces of my clothes. I spit out a mouth full of grit, pushing myself up from the sand at the same time, and then shake like a dog to get the rest off me.

"Fun-ny," a soft, feminine voice says from be-hind me in a slow, staccato rhythm as if getting used to the words in her mouth. Her voice is soft, high pitched, and lilts up at the end of each second sylla-ble. I turn quickly, and my eyes affirm what my ears have already told me, I am no longer alone on the beach, and I am standing face-to-face with the stocky, olive-skinned, hibiscus-growing girl from my dreams.

"Not a dream. It is real," the olive-skinned girl says.

My mouth drops open.

"El-ders are wait-ing," the girl says in a sweet but insistent voice. She grabs my hand like she's my best friend leading me to a day of shopping at the mall. "Fol-low me," she says coaxing me forward. And I do, I follow her, although I don't know why, except I feel like I should.

The girl heads toward the thatched hut at the edge of the beach, the same hut both helmsmen and the villagers disappeared into. The structure seems too small to house so many people.

I try to keep up with the girl, but each step I take sinks my feet into the sand with course pebbles funneling into my sneakers and wedging into my socks. The girl's feet don't sink. She walks over the surface of the sand like Jesus over water and she doesn't slow down, instead she picks up her pace, pulling at my arm.

By the time we arrive at the hut I'm hot, sweaty, and exhausted.

The girl motions for me to stop.

"Wait-here," she says with her soft voice lilting up at the end.

"O.k." I say. She has already slipped inside the dark opening and disappeared. I try to find her outline, some piece of her profile through the dark, but she's gone completely. There's nothing to see beyond the opening—no vaguely visible shapes, no furniture or decorations—I can only see blackness through the entrance, and only hear silence—no shuffling feet as the girl walks away, no voices, and no movement whatsoever—as if the opening is a black hole.

I don't dare go inside by myself.

I can wait.

I pull off my sneakers one at a time, emptying each one of sand. Pieces of dried vegetation, helpless against my weight as I lean for support, fall from the side of the hut to the sand below. A strand of hair flops into my face and I push it back in line with the rest; the strand is dry, as is the rest of my hair and my jeans which seems oddly fast.

I wait, leaning on the hut and looking over the water and back toward the shoreline already swallowed up by the mist that continues to creep toward me.

I've seen horror movies about killer creatures that lurk in the mist, I wonder what could be in this one?

I am still the only person out here. Maybe these people know something I don't. Maybe that's why they split.

I wonder if I should just go inside? But I remind myself that another rule of horror movie lure is to NEVER go into a room when you're told not to, particularly by yourself—*isn't that grounds for getting killed?*

I pinch myself on the arm.

Still here.

The girl calls my name. It sounds like an echo from somewhere behind me. I turn. The girl's figure materializes in the dark doorway of the hut, her outline first and then the shape and form of her body, and then the finer details—the pattern like a painted sarong on her skin, the pigment of her face, and the definition of each strand of hair. She reaches her hand out to me.

"Come," she says, beckoning me into the darkness.

Do I follow, or run?

I hesitate for a moment, glancing back at the beach—the shore is completely hidden behind the mist so thick and gray that nothing is visible beyond it, continuing to creep like an animal on the prowl.

I step forward grabbing the girl's hand. My foot goes numb, and as I immerse myself in the darkness the numbness climbs up my leg, my torso, and spreads over my body. Fear balls up in my stomach. The girl squeezes my hand, and the all-around darkness lightens, dissipating like a breaking mist, giving way to an endless staircase of steep stone steps that remind me of the mines in Guanjuato that we visited for our last family vacation in Mexico. The stone steps start at my feet and sharply descend to a place with no visible end. It's cooler here, but not by much.

The girl extricates her hand from mine and continues down the steps with the same ease that she traversed the sand. She isn't waiting for me, she assumes I have no choice but to follow now that I'm in the darkness, and she's already a few steps below me working her way down.

There's an echo rising from somewhere below.

Is that where we're headed?

I hold to the stone walls on either side to steady myself as I descend. The girl is putting distance between us, maneuvering the steps with familiarity, and then she disappears sharply to the right.

"Wait for me," I call to her, picking up my pace. I *do not* want to be left alone in the dark, in a place I don't know—dream or no. I take two steps at a time—hoping I don't misjudge the distance and tumble down the stairs—until I get to the spot where the girl disappeared. There's an opening in the stone wall, cast in shadows, an entryway made of more stone, and the girl waits on the other side, her arms crossed and her back casually pressed against the wall as if to make a point.

"Thanks..." I say out of breath, "...Thanks for waiting..." She cuts me off before I finish.

"We are ex-pected," she says with an edge to her sing-song voice. She pushes off from the wall and presses on, down a long expansive corridor that lights up once we step inside; the corridor dead ends at a door, a door fit for a giant with two-toned patterns etched in stone at the heart, the patterns moving as if alive. The door opens toward us, scraping the floor—the noise announces our arrival in the massive room that awaits.

The girl steps inside, I follow like a puppy dog to its master.

A massive room sprawls up and out, high as a ten story apartment building and wide as a football field, filled with rows and rows of bucket seats that look oddly out of place—it's as if I'm standing on a stage looking out to the interior of a theater that thinks it's a sports car—each seat is filled with a glowing light, only a few are still dark, and each light is unique—some are pulsing, some moving, some bright, some dull, and some represented by different colors and hues. The room buzzes with quiet murmuring...but I don't *see* any people.

The girl moves deeper into the room onto a stage like platform—the focal point of the entire space. I don't follow her, I stay where I am, close to the wall at the entrance.

The buzz in the room is like loosed electricity—the walls hum, crack, and vibrate—I can feel it in my feet, coming up from the floor. On the opposite end of the room, level to where I am, there's a short man who emerges from the darkness, walking slowly with his shoulders squarely over his body, tapping a braided wooden staff along the floor as he walks. Ghostly skin sags loose around the man's face and his shoulders are topped with long iceberg hair that falls long and straight from his head down past his elbows; a white cloak is fit to his torso and flares out from his waist, draping loosely to the floor, with small hands barely peeking through wide bell shaped sleeves. He's old but not feeble, looking less elderly and more like an ancient wise elder from a classic Kung-Fu film.

The man walks past the girl—acknowledging her with a slight nod—and continues to the front of the room. It looks as if he's about to address an audience, but there's no one here. He opens his mouth to speak, but instead of a voice there's a deep crackly sound like a Theremin mimicking a whale call, and then from the seats there's a response, a chaotic, frenzied chant of screeches and vocalizations. The room fills with light so bright I have to squint to continue to watch, and the temperature rises—my armpits sweat and a ring of perspiration forms around the base of my neck and under my breasts. I fan my face with my hands, and focus on the row of chairs across the stage. The lights in each chair spark as if building intensity, then pop into a glowing orb, and then pop again revealing a body, a person—out of thin air. The room fills alternately, each chair's light popping and then popping again. Jubilant, thunderous applause erupts as more and more bodies burst into the room. And then the room is full of people. The floor shakes as people stand, jump and cheer all the way up to the uppermost tiers. The light levels out and I look out over the crowd. Every seat is now filled, and everyone appears to be near carbon copies of the two guys in the canoe, everyone but the girl and the silver-haired man at the front of the room.

The girl drops back to me, leans in to my shoulder, and whispers, "Clear your mind."

"What?" I ask turning to her. She nods to the silver-haired man who faces the crowd. The man raises a hand to the air—the room quickly quiets—as the man starts to speak again, a low rhythmic sequence of sounds echoes from his mouth to the highest seats.

"I will tran-slate for you," the girl whispers placing her hand on my shoulder. Instantly, the sounds from the man's mouth form into words.

"...much time has passed," he says with a tight jaw and clipped words reminding me of a Scottish accent—his voice has a certain allure to it that draws me in, "our days grow shorter and we grow weak. The problem has been ignored for far too long..." he continues.

A chorus of whispers rumble through the room like a low growl.

"...*He* has been ignored and now *He* has grown strong right in front of us, and *He* grows stronger every day..."

The whispers of the room grow into a unified snarl.

"...and we are left with no choice. We *can not* ignore him any longer."

The room fills with the sounds of shifting bodies and voices that swell in pockets.

"Do not be afraid," he says attempting to calm the crowd, but it does little good as the room erupts into a chaotic frenzy; they *are* afraid, and confused...and angry sharp voices crack like whips, one after another in shouts.

What are they so afraid of?

"I know your fears. I feel them too, just like each and every one of you, but now is the time we must remain calm. I need you to quiet yourselves and listen."

And when they don't quiet, the man raises his staff to the air and yells—"Qui-et!"—in a voice that booms like a clap of thunder, echoing to the uppermost tiers and back again. When he speaks again his voice is the only one in the room.

"Thank you," he says and continues, "It is true we must talk—there *are* many questions—but our time is short, and today we must focus not just on the questions but the answers, not only on the problems but the solutions, and today I bring to you...a solution. Our survival lies in the energy of *together*, here and elsewhere. We have no choice brothers and sisters, but to break the most sacred of promises made by our elders..."

The room is quieter than quiet—as if death himself swept through—and still the man continues, he doesn't pause for a breath.

"...We must break silence with the one place we are taught not to speak about, the one place that now holds the last hope to our survival."

The man turns away from the crowd, searching the few faces that line the rear of the stage until he gets to me—his steely eyes fix on my face. I move to the side, sure that his gaze is meant for the girl standing next to me, but the silver-haired man's eyes follow me as I move.

My stomach drops.

"Come forward," he says to me sliding his staff under one arm and reaching out to me with both of his hands.

"Me?" I mouth.

"Yes," he says speaking only to me, his voice in my head; his hands beckon me forward.

I can't move. The weight of the room holds me in place, the anticipation of thousands of faces hang heavy in the air, and then I feel a gentle nudge from behind me as the girl slips her hands on my shoulders and presses me forward. The knot in my stomach grips at my insides and pulls taut. All eyes are on me. Everyone is looking, staring as if I'm some circus-freak exhibition.

I want to hide.

"What does he want?" I whisper to the girl beside me.

"Go to him," the girl coaxes.

"But that's up there in front of everybody," I say.

"Yes. They *need* to see you," she says.

"Why?" I ask.

"Go. He will ex-plain," she says nudging me forward. The man extends his hands once again. "We need your help," he says.

"My help?"

"You are Faith McDaniels," the man says.

"Yeah," I confirm, still very confused.

"You are where you are supposed to be, Faith McDaniels, be assured. This is not the first time your name has been whispered in this space. The difference between the past and the present is that now you join us in body—not just in name—and *they* need to know you exist," the man says indicating the crowd before us.

"But I don't know anything," I say looking at the man and hoping the panic I feel is evident on my face. Since mom's death I've avoided the spotlight at all costs, but somehow I keep getting dragged right back into it none the less.

"Your mom is in your thoughts," the man whispers to me, "she is in our thoughts too. It was a great loss when she died, and it is because of her death that we come to you and not her."

"My mom? What does my mom have to do with this?" I ask, but once I say the words I realize this dream, like most, has probably manifested from my thoughts, and it makes sense that my mom comes up.

"This is just a dream," I say out loud.

"Think what you must, but know it is not a dream, and the threat against us all is very real. We need your help. Without it *our* worlds will be overtaken. Yours and mine. Your mother understood that, and that is why she fled. That is why she hid you for so long," he says.

He's bringing up my mother again.

"Continue her legacy Faith. If you do not, your people will suffer just as mine will. Our worlds our bound together. Continue your mother's legacy, be a protector of both our worlds."

I need to understand what this has to do with my mother.

My heart beats fast and my head spins like a carnival Tilt A Whirl ride. My hands turn cold and clammy. At my back, soft fingers grip my shoulders, spreading heat past my shirt and into my skin. The warmth spreads down my arms, into my chest, down through my legs and into my toes until my head stops spinning, my heart slows, and everything tingles with pins & needles. Then the girl grabs at something invisible in the air and twirls it around my head. My heart picks up again, but this time it's an energized thump and not a fearful one. I feel like I downed a cup of espresso spiked with an energy shot.

"Bet-ter?" The girl asks from behind me.

"Yeah. What is that?" I ask, indicating the girl's hands and the air where she pulled the invisible energizer.

And then the man is in my head again—"That is who we are," he says.

"Air?" I ask.

"The energy of this place is what we are, the energy is everything. It is also who you are, what you have inside of you," he says.

I look at the man and hope that the panic I feel is evident on my face once again.

"Everything cannot be understood so quickly. But know this, *He* will not wait for you to understand," the silver-haired man says.

"He who?" I ask.

"*He* is a threat to us all, and if he is allowed to continue we shall all perish."

"I don't know who 'he' is, and I don't know how I can help," I say.

"You are Faith of Sister World, daughter of Elise," the man says, "You *are* the key."

"The key to what. I can't even keep my own life together," I say. The silver-haired man smiles.

"You are much more than you know," he says holding his index finger at eye level and turning away from me. He heads back to address the crowd. The girl slides in to replace him, grabbing my hands in hers.

"*I* will show you what you need to know. *You* must think about your friends back home and your brother. Think about their safety," the girl says.

"Are they in trouble?" I ask.

"They could be. If He has found you, He can find them. Every-one is in jeop-ardy. Your mom knew that bet-ter than any-one," the girl says.

"Will you tell me more about how my mom is involved in all this?" I ask. The girl nods.

"Then...yes, count me in. I'll do what I can, although I still don't know what good I'll do," I say. The girl grasps her hands together, as if in prayer, and whispers a *thank you* as she bows to me; it's then that the silver-haired man lifts his head and faces the crowd at the front of the room, raising his staff and shouting, "The girl—Faith McDaniels, daughter of Elise, has agreed to join our efforts to defeat Him!"

The reaction in the room is undeniable, loud and boisterous like a crowd at closing curtain at the finale of an award-winning Broadway performance...and then there's a noise that doesn't fit—a disturbance in the center of the crowd like the whirring of tornado winds. Screams. A kaleidoscope of lights flashing in and out.

The girl grabs me by the shoulders and throws me to the floor, covering me with her body. She snatches my hand and shoves something in, cold and vibrating—the pendant with its chain hanging off my wrist.

Dizziness hits in a wave—everything whooshes away in blackness—and as everything fades around me, the man's voice echoes in the air, "Get her to safety!" and then his voice is in my ears, "Faith McDaniels, daughter of Elise - do not forget what you have promised."

CHAPTER NINE

SOMETHING LOST

I t was a dream—*Oh thank god*—because there's the rundown house and the hole in the roof, the car and the truck, and ground beneath me. Gravel. How did I get from the bushes to here? I don't know. I don't care. I'm *here*. I'm back!

I pick myself up wiping dirt from my jeans. It's dark, except for the lantern light glowing from the windows and the open door of the house; reminds me of that old movie Monster House, the light marking a face in the abandoned facade. The light is enough for me to see my way in the dark, enough to find Paul's flashlight wedged under the front wheel of his truck. I kick the flashlight out, scramble to pick it, and flick it on.

"You are bound to your promise," the silver haired man's clipped voice sounds in my head.

"Get out of my head!" I yell.

Goosebumps travel up my arms. I shiver.

It's not real, it's just a dream – not real, just a dream, I repeat to myself standing alone in the dark.

Kiara shrieks my name and I jump. She's running at me full sprint from the corner of the house, the beam of her flashlight bouncing off the side of the vehicles.

"Oh my god! I heard you scream," Kiara yells, "You o.k.?" She tackles me in a hug.

"She's here guys!" Kiara calls to the back of the house.

"You scared the shit out of us! Why d'ya tak off?"

"I didn't."

"Well, where've you been for the last two hours? Your hands are cold," Kiara softens, grabbing my hands in hers and rubbing them.

"I don't know," I say.

"What do you mean 'you don't know'?"

"I mean, I think maybe I fell asleep or something...I guess," I say.

"How the hell did you fall asleep?" Kiara asks.

Paul runs up nearly out of breath—"What happened?"

"Nothing. I'm fine," I say, too embarrassed to even look at him.

Michael is next to arrive, rushing in like a contestant to a Pit Stop from The Amazing Race. He sidles up to Kiara putting his arm around her shoulder, "Is she o.k.," he asks her.

"I'm right here dude, and yeah I'm o.k. *Michael*," I say. I'm still annoyed with him. He's not off the hook yet.

"Your hair is different," Paul says.

"It is?" I ask, touching the top of my head, "Is it really bad?"

"No, it's just different," Paul says. He looks at me and then to the ground. I nod. Everyone gets quiet, until Michael breaks in, "Look, I'm sorry about before, my mouth got away with me—not that I'm making excuses—but I shouldn't have said what I said, and I'm sorry," Michael says.

"O.k.," I say.

"You look cold, we could turn on the car to get you warmed up," Michael says.

It's a peace offering—he doesn't do that often in front of me, never mind *to me*—I'll bite. I nod yes.

"Great idea sweetie," Kiara says, pulling at his cheek.

"Or the truck, it probably heats up faster," Paul says.

"Or the truck," Kiara says looking at me with a wink and a smile.

"C'mon, let's get you in the truck," Paul says to me.

"We might want to pack-it-up soon anyway," Paul says over his shoulder as he heads to the truck, "I have a test tomorrow first thing."

"Grades, dude, you're worried about your grades, seriously?" Michael says.

"Well, yeah, can't jeopardize college. Not at this point. It's my ticket out," Paul says.

"Aiight, I hear that," Michael agrees.

"I'm going to need help with all the stuff," Kiara says pulling on Michael's arm, "Help me with the bags?"

"Yeah, babe, right behind you."

"You guys need a hand?" Paul asks.

"That's o.k., we've got it, you just make sure Faith gets *warmed up*," Kiara says winking at me.

Kiara wraps her arm around Michael's waist, locking her index finger in a side belt loop on his jeans, and leads him toward the house.

Paul's pickup is big and bulky, and the first step onto the running board is high. Paul helps me up, opens the door and guides me in. I could do it on my own, but I let him be chivalrous. As the doors close on both sides, the cab goes dark.

Paul turns on the truck and cranks the heat, and it's not until I feel the heat on my legs, I realize how cold I was outside and how good the heat feels; the dry heat, alcohol, darkness—the combination is like an instant sleep elixir.

I lean my head back against the headrest and close my eyes.

"Feeling better?" Paul asks.

"The heat feels good, thanks," I say with my eyes still closed.

"You know, my team is playing two towns down tomorrow. You busy?"

"I'm grounded kind-of-busy," I say.

"Oh," Paul says.

"But what did you have in mind? I mean I'm grounded tonight too, and I'm here," I say.

Paul pulls a pen & notebook from the center console and scribbles something onto one of the sheets using the lights from dashboard to see what he's doing.

"Here, my number," he says ripping the paper from the notebook, "if you can get free, call me."

"What time?" I ask.

"Game ends around eight, eight-thirty."

"O.k."

"We can just talk, or go for coffee, or dinner, anything," Paul says.

"Sounds cool," I say looking at his face in a weird mix of shadow and dashboard light. Reminds me of a song my mom used to listen to by some dude named Meatloaf, and that gets me thinking - what if Paul is expecting some of that "paradise by dashboard light". My stomach flips. I glance at my reflection out of the side view mirror, and there I see that Paul was right about my hair, it looks like a neglected airdry. Damn. Probably how it looked after I was soaked in the canoe. Wait a minute, even I'm mixing up dreams and reality.

The voice of the hibiscus-girl is in my head, "It was real. You only have to be-lieve, you only have to have faith."

I can't take it, these voices—"Shut up!" I say out loud.

"What did I say?" Paul asks quickly.

"No, no not you. Sorry. I was just thinking out loud, about other things," I say.

"Oh. Because if I said something wrong..." Paul says.

"No, it's me. I'm all over the place," I say.

My attention is torn between Paul, and the thoughts in my head. I'm trying to ignore what might, or might not, have been a dream. Did I fall asleep, or didn't I? These voices are making it hard to ignore. Maybe it was real?

I kick off my shoes, and try to see through the dark to the floor of the truck.

Sand. Every time I've ever gone to the beach, there's always sand for days; if the beach was real there should be sand.

It's too dark.

"Can we turn on the light for a sec?" I ask.

"Sure," Paul answers.

The light turns on, but it's still hard to tell—my feet are in shadows. I bend down.

"Here, need some light," Paul says. He turns on his flashlight app and angles it at my feet.

I pick up a shoe and shake it, and there at the bottom are a few granules of sand. I gasp before realizing I'm doing it. The realization leads me to one thing, and one thing only. I need to find the necklace.

"What's wrong?" Paul asks.

I drop my hands to my pockets searching for the necklace, but it's not there.

"Um, I think I, um, dropped something outside," I say to Paul. I push my shoes back on.

"Ok, I can help you look. What are we looking for?" Paul asks.

"A necklace, with a long chain. The pendant looks like an opal," I say.

"Ok, well, let's look for it," Paul says. He jumps out of the truck, crosses in front of the vehicle to my door to open it for me. If I wasn't so weirded out right now, I might be enjoying all this attention from him, but honestly I'm starting to freak out, thinking about everything that happened from the beach to the stage—the silver haired man, the girl, the 'He' they kept referring to, and the promise. I made some kind of a promise.

Ah shit, I'm screwed.

Paul offers his hand to steady me as I step down from the truck, and then he asks, "Could it be inside, maybe Kiara picked it up with the rest of the stuff?"

"It's not in the house, I had it in my hand when I went outside," I say.

"Do you know where you last saw it?" Paul asks.

"In the bushes, over there," I say pointing to the spot where I crouched to pee.

"Want one?" Paul asks holding a flashlight out to me.

"Thanks. Listen, if you find it, let me pick it up, please..." It sounds weird the second it leaves my mouth, but what am I supposed to say? I don't know what will happen if he touches it. Hell, I don't know what happened when I touched it. "...It's just (*I have to think of something so it doesn't sound so weird*) it was my mom's and it still has her smell, and...

"It's ok. You don't have explain. I won't touch it," Paul says.

Even with Kiara and Michael joining the effort, we come up empty—no necklace, no pendant, no chain, no nothing. I hate to leave it, but everyone's getting tired. Maybe I can somehow get back here tomorrow. Or maybe I don't find it all and I can forget about this weird shit.

We leave, and head home. I'm quiet most of the trip. Thinking.

Kiara pulls up on the side of the road half-a-block from my house, and cuts the lights.

"Need any help getting back in?" she asks.

"Nah, I got it," I say.

"Sorry it was a bust tonight," Kiara says.

"It wasn't. I got Paul's number," I say as I pull out the folded piece of paper from my pocket and wave it in the air. Kiara looks like she might burst out of her skin as she high-fives me and squeals—"You, —yes!"

"All you," I say to her. I lean over to her and she meets me with a hug.

"Thank you," I say, squeezing her tight.

"Awe shucks, don't make me tear up now," she says from my shoulder.

"Shut up," I say to her.

"No, you shut up," she says.

"We are some weird kind of friends, aren't we?"

"The best kind of weird," Kiara says.

"Yeah, the best kind. Well, I better get inside, let me not push my luck," I say pulling away.

I open the car door, slide out of the seat into the dark, and close the door gently behind me. Kiara rolls down the window.

"Bye," she whispers.

"Bye," I say as I wave to her through the dark.

Kiara pulls off and I make my way to the back of the house in the pitch black, stopping under my bedroom window. This time—learning a lesson from the last bedroom return—I make sure to dismount softly into my room.

After changing for bed, I lay awake, thinking. My brain is going, and going, and going; thinking about the kiss with Paul, the fight with Michael, but most of all about everything that happened after I touched the necklace tonight. The promise is prominent in my thoughts, and the fact that I lost the necklace – my only means of getting answers.

❧

CHAPTER TEN

THE JOB

I guess it was bound to happen one day, me getting a job. There's no sense dwelling on why or how I'm standing here in front of Main Street Drug, because none of that matters right now. Today is the day I start my job—with no sleep, another crappy day of school behind me, and my stomach growling.

I'm trying to psych myself up for this and it isn't helping.

I've been inside the drugstore countless times before; I buy my Tampax down the aisle to the left, toothpaste and floss two aisles to the right. In the back, there's a rack of magazines—I don't think I've ever gotten anything from there, but I know it's there. Somehow it feels different walking in now—

past the three registers to the left just inside the automatic door—I guess because going forward I'll be an employee instead of a customer.

I have to look for—I check the piece of paper with Eddie's scrawled notes—Mr. Ang, the manager. "Excuse me," I say to a sixty-something, slightly overweight grandmother type dressed in khakis, a dark blue polo with a bright blue smock over the top.

"Can I help you find something?" she asks.

"I'm looking for Mr. Ang, I'm supposed to be starting today," I say.

"Oh you must be Faith, I'm Felicia," she says extending a hand to me.

"Hi," I say shaking her hand.

"Follow me," she says, leading me to the back of the store and through a door to a room.

"This is the break room," she says motioning to a small square table and four folding chairs, "Have a seat. I'll get Mr. Ang."

Felicia exits out a second door that leads outside. I sit, and wait, fidgeting with a loose piece of plastic at the edge of the card table.

The outside door opens after a couple minutes and a short Asian man with graying hair and an identical blue uniform steps into the break room. He doesn't offer his hand.

"You're Faith," he says.

"Yes, my brother told me to come today, to start work," I say.

"Eddie is a good boy, I don't mind doing him a favor. Have you had a job before?" Mr. Ang asks me.

"No," I say.

"Alright, well first we have to fill out some paperwork," he says.

He opens a file cabinet and grabs a manila folder from the front, pulls out a half inch packet of papers and plops it onto the table.

"You need to fill out the first two sheets today, read through the Code of Ethics & Business Conduct and the rest of the pamphlets in there. Did you bring ID?" He asks.

"I have my school ID," I say.

"Let me see it," he says. I hand it to him. He sighs. I don't know if he's sighing at me or if it's a habit. He opens a small closet door and pulls out a blue smock and hands it to me.

"Dress code is khakis, blue polos, and this smock. I see you're in jeans and a tee shirt today, we'll let it go since it's your first day and you're training, but don't show up to work like that again," he says.

"Sorry, I didn't know..." I start to say.

"Put the smock on," he says, "I'll get a name tag made up for you for your next shift. Make sure you fill out the Availability Sheet so I can add you to the rotation."

"O.K," I say.

"Any questions?" he asks.

"No," I say.

"Alright, then go ahead, get to the sheets. I'll give you a tour when you're done and then you can shadow Felicia for the first hour until she leaves," he says.

The grand tour, narrated by Mr. Ang, takes all of five minutes—"Here are the bathrooms—make sure you clear it with me before you leave your post; back room where you take your break; this is the pharmacy—never go back here unless a manager or the pharmacist approves it; this is Rick—one of our pharmacists (we shake hands, and he welcomes me aboard); registers—I'll have one of the girls train you next time; the blue bins with the flaps are how we get inventory so never throw them out—we swap them when new inventory arrives; here's the closet with cleaning supplies—we do a thorough cleaning each night after we lock up so the store is fresh when we open in the morning."

Mr. Ang continues, "Take this bin and add these items to the inventory on the shelves, new stock in the back, old stock up front, then go through and make sure all the stock is front facing, straight, and neat. Once we lock-up you'll vacuum and dust the shelves. Questions?"

"What's 'front facing'?" I ask.

"Go along the shelves and make sure the front of the product faces out," Mr Ang says sounding annoyed.

"OK," I say.

"So get to it," he says rushing me along.

The first three-and-a-half hours of my shift crawl. I must look at the clock on the wall a million times. I hope this goes faster once I'm trained. I can't wait to get home.

"Faith!" Mr. Ang yells.

"Over here, Mr. Ang," I answer. He rounds the corner to the aisle where I'm dusting.

"I need you to vacuum the store—the front, the back, the entrance mats, everything. You've got to start now or you won't get it done. You remember where the vacuum is?" he asks. I shake my head.
"I have to run out to make the deposit," he says lifting the large blue zippered industrial envelope from under his arm, "Doors will be locked, Rick is outside in the back if you need him. I'll be back in fifteen minutes. Remember, the whole place squeaky clean, got it?" he asks.

"I got it Mr. Ang," I say. He sighs again, turns on his heels and heads to the front door, locking the door behind him as he exits.

I walk to the backroom to get the vacuum; the back door to the outside is open, so I guess that's where Rick the Pharmacist is. I leave the door open, and drag the vacuum to the front.

Once the vacuum is on it's hard to hear much over the motor's deep growl—it revs up as I push, and slows as I pull. It's almost hypnotic. Grvv—Grrvvv. Grvv—Grrvvv. Grvv—Grrvvv. Grvv—Grrvvv. And then bang! A noise from the back, louder than the sound of the vacuum. I jump, then turn the vacuum off. The noise stops. *Probably the Pharmacist.* I turn the vacuum on again and fall back into a hypnotic rhythm. And then another bang, and another. I turn off the vacuum. The sound is coming from the backroom, and through the break room door as air whooshes and whistles like a wind tunnel, knocking the door open and then closed, open and then closed again. I crane my neck to see if anyone is out back, and that's when the weirdness escalates. A blast of air swoops from the backroom into the main area of the store, its clear pigment turning dark and condensed as it moves, sweeping into the pharmacy, sending empty rust-colored pill bottles plinking to the walls. Now dark and thick like molasses, it picks up full bottles of medication from the counter—hard pills shaking inside plastic bottles, sounding like maracas—and sends them flying and then falling with a thud—thud—thud.

"Rick. Mr. Pharmacy!" I yell to the back, but Rick doesn't answer.

The dark, thick mist moves over the counter into the aisle below. I duck behind the vacuum. Boxes of hair color fly from the shelf, into the air, and then to the carpeted floor until the shelf is bare and all contents lay haphazardly below.

The wind stops whistling and the mist is still. I can't help but stare at it. It feels alive, as if it sees me, and then, it condenses into a dark cloud that hovers in place. A voice booms from it, and says only one thing, my name.

Then the cloud explodes like a sonic boom, the shelves in all the aisles shake with product teetering and falling onto the floor. I drop to the carpet, holding my hands over my head.

"Holy shit!" Rick exclaims walking in from the back, standing in the open doorway clad in his white lab coat and mouth agape.

The dark misty cloud thins so fast it's as if it dissolves into thin air, and then it's gone, completely, and all that's left is a store with all its inventory knocked over, scattered, and thrown to the carpeted aisles.

"What the hell happened here!" Mr. Ang screams, charging inside the front door, walking over mascara tubes, eyeliner pencils, and lipsticks that had once been on the display units by the front register, now scattered on the floor.

I can't move. I'm frozen, both hands over my head, still ducked behind the vacuum cleaner.

"Where's Rick!" Mr. Ang yells.

"Um"

"Back here," Rick says popping his head up from behind the Pharmacy, "there's medication all over the floor."

Mr. Ang looks as if he's about to explode, his cheeks are turning fuchsia—a pressured red, as if he's about to burst.

"Sorry," I say, though I don't know why I'm apologizing. I didn't make this mess.

"Sorry? You're sorry? *You* vandalized my property?"

"I didn't..." I start to say, but Mr. Ang won't let me finish.

"You are not leaving here until every last thing is picked up. Do you hear me?" Mr. Ang screams, "And today's paycheck, no paycheck—it's paying for the damage."

"So I don't even get paid?"

"Paid? Paid! Do you know how much damage this is?" Mr. Ang screams.

"But I didn't do it!" I scream back, heading to the front door. Mr. Ang moves to block my exit.

"You're not going anywhere missy. You will pick up every last piece of product on this floor, and you will make a list of everything that is damaged and you WILL pay for it."

"Now you sound like my brother," I say.

"Maybe your brother has it right. He told me you've got issues, but who does this? Seriously. What the fuck!" The manager yells again, clearly his emotions are all over the place. "I'm not picking this shit up. You're picking it up, even if you're here all night!"

Mr. Ang pulls out his phone. He's either calling Eddie, or he's calling the police. Neither option benefits me.

"I have to go. I really am sorry," I say. Since the front is blocked by Mr. Ang, I make a dash for the back door, jumping over a jumbled wall of 24-pack toilet paper packages. Mr. Ang screams from somewhere close behind me.

"Get back here! I'm calling the police."

I yell back at him, "Check the cameras! I didn't do it!" I slam the backdoor behind me, and duck behind the giant green dumpster overflowing with the trash I'd taken out earlier.

The backdoor opens on squeaking hinges, and Mr. Ang sprints through it and yells to the dark, "You're fired!"

I strip off the blue smock and toss it into the garbage, and wait for Mr. Ang to go back inside, then I hightail it to the other end of the lot, ducking behind cars as I go, headed to the 7-Eleven at the entrance to the shopping mall. They have a pay phone outside. I hope it works. With only fifteen dollars and a few coins in my pocket, and no cell phone, I don't have many options, and I don't think I'll be going home with Eddie tonight—not tonight, and probably not for a few days until this blows over.

That *thing* in there was more than just the wind, it was more than something normal. It spoke and said my name. What the hell was it? All that crap about saving the world and keeping me safe, I don't feel so safe. I think I'm even more screwed than I thought.

I dial Paul. "It's Faith. Can you call me back at this number...," I say leaving a message, clutching the receiver of the pay phone to my cheek and reciting the number posted on the box. This town is so dated there's still this single working pay phone, but I guess I have to be thankful for that, there aren't many pay phones left and I'd be up Shits Creek right now without it. Not that I'm out of the woods yet, Paul is Plan A but he hasn't picked up my call.

From this vantage point I can see the front of the parking lot and the main road, and the entire shopping plaza including the drug store. The lights are still on, Mr. Ang and Rick are picking up products and shoving them into the blue-flapped bins. And here comes Eddie, his Corolla stopped at the light on the main road—his turn signal on—getting ready to pull into the parking lot.

My stomach drops. I am so dead. I duck around the other side of the pay phone as Eddie moves the Corolla into the parking lot. My plan right now is to just not get caught. Eddie either knows, or he will find out about the mess in a matter of minutes, he'll side with the manager, and I won't be able to go home for a while. He'll probably think I did this to get back at him for making me take the job in the first place. Everything is always about him.

Maybe I can try to get back home before he does, pack a bag, and be out before he gets back, but what if he hightails it home? I'd have to leave now and catch the bus, and then walk the rest of the way. If he does make it back before me, I'd be stuck. No phone to have someone pick me up. Best to get someone on the phone first, then make the decision to chance it or not, especially with nowhere to stay, because all my friends are at least two hours away—two hours one way, two hours the next, and parents that would ask questions. Paul said he was going to be close by today. I'll wait and hope he calls back soon.

Otherwise I'll call Kiara. I know she'll come to get me. I just have to stay unseen for now.

Eddie pulls up in front of the storefront, car running and headlights on. He doesn't get out of the car right away, but I can see his dark shape moving inside. I don't think he knows what happened yet. He's waiting for me to come out. After a few minutes, his door opens and he's steps outside, walks up the glass of the front window and peers in. It looks like he's wrapping his knuckles on the window. Mr. Ang walks to the front door, unlocks it and lets Eddie in. Hand motions, *big hand motions* from Mr. Ang, while Eddie stands there, with his hands at his side, listening. I can't see his face, but I know that Eddie's neck is probably getting red by now, his eyes about to pop from their sockets. Eddie picks up something from the floor and throws it against the wall, the something shatters and liquid bursts into the air like a wet bomb. Mr. Ang yells, I can tell, his hands are in fists now. He's pissed that Eddie broke one more item of his inventory; friends or not, it still comes down to money. Then Eddie collapses to his knees, his body shaking as if he's weeping—I've only seen Eddie cry one other time before, and that's when Mom died—Mr. Ang drops down with him, and now I can't see anything because they've dropped out of site.

Guilt. Heavy, heavy guilt at the pit of my stomach. I must be the worst sister in the world, and I didn't even do anything to deserve it this time. That stupid thing did it. I'll bet it has something to do with that pendant. Maybe I can fix this if I find it.

Where is that damn pendant!

∂

CHAPTER ELEVEN

GOING BACK

A car approaches, a souped up candy apple red Civic. It inches toward the pay phone, even though this is the most remote part of the 7-11 parking lot. I grab the receiver and duck my head to the side, trying to catch a glimpse of who is in the car, but the windows are tinted and the interior too dark.

The car pulls up beside me and the driver's side window rolls down.

"Hey. I thought that was you. What are you doing out here?" It's Tomas, the jerkwad who got me in trouble on my first day at MHS.

I ignore him, and pretend to be on the phone. He continues anyway, "I just picked up some pizza, want a slice?" he asks.

"I'm on the phone," I mouth.

"No you're not, you didn't put any money in," he says. I glare at him, and hang up the receiver.

"I was on the phone before. Just so you know. Besides, why are you talking to me," I ask.

"Why wouldn't I?"

"First day of school, you nearly got me suspended," I say sarcastically.

"Well, that was just a joke—initiation. Nothin' personal," he says with a smile. It's a nice smile. I don't think I've ever taken the time to notice how perfect his smile is.

Stop it. He's not your friend.

"You know I hate the school because of you," I say turning away from him, looking at the phone, trying to will it to ring.

C'mon Paul, call me back.

"You waitin' for a call? Need a ride or something?" he asks.

I don't answer. My brain is turning over his offer. Do I wait for Paul to call? Maybe he won't and I'm stuck here all night. There's always Kiara, but that would be a two-hour wait, minimum. Or I can take Tomas up on his offer and go where? He can drop me at home and I can pack a bag. Maybe I can grab my own phone. I can't imagine my brother taking my phone with him considering it didn't look like he knew about what happened before he got here. Besides, Tomas owes me. This could be partial payback for the crap he pulled that first day.

"O.k.," I say.

"Hop in," he says.

The interior of the car smells like a combination of hot cheese, grease, baked pepperoni, and the coconut air freshener that hangs from the rear view mirror.

"Let me get that," Tomas says picking up the pizza box from the passenger seat, "Here grab a slice while it's still hot."

I *am* starving. I didn't eat dinner before I left to go to work because I was running late, and even on break I only had a bag of chips. Still, I don't go for a slice.

"Is this all for you?" I ask sliding into the leather seat, over the hot spot where the pizza sat.

"Yep. Tuesday is pizza night. I work at the pizza shop..."

He nods toward the shopping plaza.

"... I take a pie home for myself on Tuesday because no one is home. Mami has bingo, Papi works late. Just me. Plus it gives me a break from Spanish cooking. Who doesn't love a good slice of pizza, right?" he asks.

He sounds like such a normal person, unlike the monster I'd painted in my head since the incident. Honestly I've avoided him at all costs at school.

"Where we headed. My place or yours," he asks.

The hairs on the back of my spine stand up.

"We're not hanging out, and nothing is happening here," I say motioning between the two of us. I make a move to grab the door handle.

"Relax. It's just a joke. I wasn't implying anything," Tomas answers.

"You don't exactly have the best track record with me," I release the door handle, "and it's been a helluva night," I say relaxing back into the seat.

"No problem. I do kind of need to know where we're going though," Tomas answers.

"Chestnut Ave, at the end," I say. As he moves the shift to drive, I look back over my shoulder at the drugstore. Eddie's car is still parked outside. I turn away.

"Tomas' Taxi at your service," Tomas says pulling out of the 7-11 parking lot.

"Can I borrow your phone," I ask.
Tomas grabs the steering wheel with one hand and pulls his phone from the front pocket of his jeans.

"Here," he says extending his arm and phone to me.

"Sorry to ask. I left mine at home," I say.

"No big deal," he says.

I pull out the paper with Paul's number from my jeans and dial. Voicemail, again. I don't leave a message. I hand the phone back to Tomas.

"Seriously, grab a slice of pizza. Most of it will just sit in the fridge until tomorrow," Tomas says.

I hesitate for a second, and then decide this is just more payback, so I open the box. The smell is amazing. The cheese thins as I pull a slice from the pie. I fold it over, careful to keep the oil from dripping on me or Tomas' seat.

"Want me to grab you one?" I ask Tomas.

"Yeah, hand me a slice," he says.

"Did you make this pie?" I ask.

"Yeah," he says.

"It's good," I say with the tip of the pizza in my mouth.

"Thanks. It's pizza, not a gourmet meal, but at least I can say I make a good pizza," he says smiling, his lips glistening with oil.

"It's more than I can make," I say.

"Seriously?"

"I don't cook. My mom used to. She was a great cook. I should have learned," I say.

Tomas is weirdly easy to talk to.

"It's never too late," Tomas says.

"It is for me, I'll never be able to learn from my mom. She died," I say.

"Yeah, I kinda heard that. Sorry she died," Tomas says.

Nothing like 'death' to halt a conversation. Neither one of us talks for the next few minutes. I focus on eating my pizza, and Tomas does the same.

After we finish our slices and wipe the grease from our fingers, Tomas is the first to break the silence. "Maybe you could come by the pizza place one night and I could show you how I make a pie," Tomas says.

"Yeah. Yeah, maybe," I say, and then, "I'm just over there, you can drop me off here," I say.

"You live here," Tomas says pointing at the brick house to the right.

"No, I live a couple houses down, but drop me off here," I say.

"My name is not going to be splashed across the newspaper as being an accomplice to a crime, right?" He asks.

"Don't worry about it. I live down there, just leave it at that, o.k?" I say.

"It's just a joke. You've really got to loosen up. Want me to walk you to your door?" he asks.

"No!" I yell.

"Hey, fine by me. Don't let me pry. I was just trying to be nice," he says.

"Sorry. I'm not getting along with my brother right now, and I don't really want to make things worse," I say.

"Fine, it's none of my business," he says with his hands in the air, "I'm not asking you to explain."

I slide from the passenger seat and out the door, closing the door quietly. Tomas rolls down the window.

"It was nice sharing a pie with you," he says.

"Yeah, it was nice. Thanks. I appreciate it," I say.

"Want another slice for the road?" Tomas asks.

"No thank you. I'm good. Thanks for the ride," I say.

"See you around," Tomas says sliding the Civic into gear and doing a U-Turn in the street in front of me. I watch him drive away, slow to a halt at the stop sign at the end of the street, and then he's gone, and I focus myself on the task at hand.

I beat my brother. I'm the only one here. I throw some stuff into an overnight bag, rescue my phone with only 12% charge from my brother's nightstand (*he didn't charge it—what a dick*), swipe the fifty dollars hidden under the coins in the change jar in the closet (*yes, I know you hide the money there Eddie*), throw on a hoodie, and I'm out of the front door again. I'm not sure how long I'll be gone or even where I'm going, but I know it will be over-night at least.

Walking past the shrubs, I slip the hood over my head and walk away from the house. My cell phone rings just as I move past the boundary of the property, almost as if I've triggered some homing beacon—it's Eddie, I can tell by the ringtone. He's probably guessed I've made my way back home, guessed I've commandeered my phone, guessed I'm not staying put to face him, and he's right, but he should know I'm not going to pick up the phone ei-ther. Not yet. I grab it from the side pocket of my backpack and reject the call.

Then I dial Paul again.

"Hello?" He answers.

"Paul?"

"That's me," he says.

"It's Faith," I say.

"Hey. You called. I wasn't sure if you were go-ing to, I kept trying to call *you* but it went straight to voice mail, and then I called that number you left but the call wouldn't go through. Anyway, I started hav-ing deja-vu."

"Sorry. I didn't have my phone on me," I say, but what I really want to say is that my stupid ass brother swiped my phone, but I don't, I keep that to myself, because Paul has already experienced the psycho side of my brother, and I don't want him thinking the apple-doesn't-fall-too-far-from-the-tree.

"Where'r you at?" he asks.

"Are you still in the area?" I answer with a question.

"Game just ended, about to grab some food with the guys. Wanna join us?" he asks.

"I hate to ask, but I'm in a pickle. Could you pick me up instead?" I ask.

"Yeah. Sure. Now?"

"If you could. Only if it's not a hassle, hate to pull you away from your dinner," I say quickly.

"What? No, I want to pick you up. We were supposed to hang out anyway, right? Just tell me where and when," he says.

"There's a bridge near my house at the inter-section of Thompson Court and Wyatt Street, do you know where that's at?" I ask.

"No, but hold on I'll plug it into GPS. Hold on."

I hear Paul call out to his friends—"Hey guys, go on ahead. I'll catch up with you tomorrow"—while I veer off the road walking down the embankment that will take me under the bridge. Eddie doesn't usually drive this route, but tonight is not a usual night and anything is possible. I can picture him pushing the accelerator just to get home and catch me there. I'm not taking any chances, it's best to stay out of sight.

"Yep, got it. I can be there in 25 minutes," Paul says.

"Cool. I'm nearly out of juice, so we'll talk when you get here? Call me when you're close, k?"

We hang up.

I'm alone.

Alone under the bridge in the dark. The crickets are chirping; their songs echo off the metal support beams. I've been pushing myself all night, keeping on the move, keeping my mind occupied so I wouldn't dwell on what happened back at the drugstore. Now I have no choice but to think about it.

How the hell did that thing know my name?

Six missed calls, two messages—all from Eddie—and twenty-five minutes later Paul's name pops up on my screen.

I rush to pick it up.

"Paul?"

"I'm close, about 2 minutes out," Paul says.

"O.k., I'm coming. Wait for me by the bridge," I say. I pick myself up from the ground, and gather the water bottle, food wrapper, and phone scattered around me, using the phone's light to scan the ground for anything I missed. There's a little water left in the bottle. I pour it on my hands and then run my hands through my hair to tame any out of place strands. I wipe debris from my pants, straighten my shirt, and then scramble up the embankment, phone tucked between my ear and shoulder.

"I'm coming," I say again into the phone before disconnecting the call. Paul's truck is parked at the top, edged to the side and off the road. I waive to him.

"Hiding from someone?" he asks through the window as it rolls down, "Hope it's not me."

"No," I say with a chuckle pulling on the passenger door, "it's been a weird, unexpected night, and you are a life saver," I say.

"Fight with your brother," he says nodding at the backpack slung on my shoulder.

"Something like that," I say.

"So where to?" he asks.

"I've got to go back to the house," I say.

"Alright, so how do we get to your house from here," he says.

"No, not my house. The house from last night," I say.

"Why do you want to go back there?" Paul asks.

"I have to lay low tonight," I say.

"Yeah? But why *there*?" he asks.

"I have to. I have to go back for the necklace," I say.

"Is that what you were fighting about with your brother, a lost necklace?"

"No. I wish. It's more complicated than that," I say, "You got a charger, my phone is about to die."

"Glove compartment," he answers.

I'm sure this wasn't what Paul had in mind last night when he suggested we get together. In fact, if I had to bet, this scenario didn't even cross his mind; this is more like a rescue than a date. Our track record is still abysmal.

The house looks even creepier than last night as we pull up in total darkness, the headlight beams of the truck casting shadows to the corners where the light can't reach.

"The place gives me the creeps," Paul says, "Let's look for your necklace and get the hell outa here. You don't plan on staying here tonight, right?"

"I don't know. It's an option," I say.

"No way. I'll take you where-ever you need to go. Crash at my place, or I can drop you at Kiara's. Not here," he says.

He's worried about me, how cute.

"I don't really have a lot of options," I say.

"I just gave you some options, there are always options, so let's find your necklace, and then we'll talk. I'm going to check inside, make sure there's no one hanging around. You o.k. out here while I look?" Paul asks.

"Yeah. I'm going to start hunting around in the woods."

"Don't wander off, o.k.?," Paul says.

"I'll stay in the front—flashlight on so you can see me."

"Why don't you take your phone too. Call me if you see anything weird," Paul says.

"O.k." I say grabbing the phone looking at the screen: 30% charged. Enough for now.

I need to understand so many things, and the questions are circling in my head. I'm trying to piece it all together but it's not making sense—the thing in the drugstore, what the silver hair man referred to as Him or He in his speech, how the pendant works? I'm sure there are questions I don't even know to ask yet. So many questions; I'm hoping I can get some answers once I find the pendant. The pendant is the key—I just know it is. I have to convince Paul to let me stay, alone. How else am I going to test it? There's no way I can explain this to him, to any of them— Paul, or Kiara, or Eddie for that matter. No one's going to believe me. Not about this.

There's something glowing in the weeds off the side of the driveway. I step toward it. It's as if the sky from that other place was captured in a bottle and uncapped in this dense cropping of weeds. A shimmering light of pinks, yellows, and blues hovers in a cell phone size patch over the overgrown grass.

"What's that?" Paul asks coming up behind me. He walks passed me, shining his flashlight to the spot in the weeds. He drops down and fishes through the grass.

"Hey I think I found it, is this your necklace?" He says, picking it up by the chain and dropping it into his hand. He touched it. *Shit.* I take in a breath and hold it in my chest. But nothing happens—the pendant is clearly in his hand.

"Is this it?" he asks walking toward me.
"Yeah, that's it," I say, but I hesitate because I don't want to touch it. Just because nothing happened when Paul touched it doesn't mean the same will be true when I do.

"Here," Paul says moving the pendant closer to me, "Sorry about touching it. I forgot."

"It's ok. You hang on to it for a bit, so I don't lose it again," I say to him, but I do need to figure out how I'm going to get it back from him without touching it. I don't have the bandana anymore.

"So how much trouble are you in?" Paul asks.
"What do you mean?"

"You were worried about this necklace, we found it, and you don't even want it; you're not even happy we found it. What gives?" He asks.

He's perceptive.

He walks to the cement landing at the front steps.

"Wanna talk?" he asks.

I hesitate for a moment. I can feel the trilling in my stomach already.

"Have a seat, mi'lady," he says placing the still-lit flashlight to the concrete. I sit down next to him, with the flashlight in between us facing up. His face is awash with light. It's not the only thing the flashlight catches, it also spotlights his still-taut, after game muscles peeking out from under his short sleeved shirt. I can't help but notice.

"So what gives," he says.

"I tanked the job tonight," I say.

"No biggie," Paul says, "It's just one job, right? There are millions of jobs out there."

"It's a biggie to my brother," I say.

"He'll get over it. If you ask me, your brother is wound a bit too tight," Paul says.

I sit quiet for a few seconds.

"The drugstore got trashed," I blurt out before my brain has a chance to filter my words. Paul looks at me, puzzled, his face squished around his nose.

"Trashed. The whole place," I say.

"I'm trying to understand how this equates to you losing your job. I can't picture you trashing the place," Paul says.

"Finally someone takes my side. Can I just say how much I love you right now," I say before I realize I'm saying it. I'm not sure I was ready to say that.

Paul's face does a complete 180, and he looks like he's about to lean in to me, but I'm not sure.

"What else can I say that will make you *love* me even more," he says playfully.

I can't help it, I chuckle...and now I'm grinning a big full toothy grin.

"I like your smile," he says smiling back at me.

And then he does lean in—this time there's nothing to distract me, no thoughts of my m-o-m., *shut up brain, shut up,* no Michael to convince me I'm not worth it. Paul thinks I'm worth it, he thinks I'm kissable; he moves his lips to mine, pressing our lips together, moving across my mouth gently with such care and ease I know he's done this before. He's a pro. He pulls back looking at me, searching my face for something, a sign maybe. I kiss him back, pressing my lips in and my chest up to his so there's no space between us. I can feel his chest rising and falling with each breath. His smell is intoxicating, just as much as last night and three months ago, it envelopes me and there's no place I want to be but here. Forever.

Paul's hand moves to my lower back, pushing me into him and knocking the flashlight over at the same time, it falls off the edge of the landing and onto the ground. We're in the dark, and somehow I feel safer than I have in many months.

I don't know how long we kiss, it feels both long and short, but when Paul pulls away my lips are numb, my arm pits sweaty, and I cannot stop smiling.

Paul grabs my hand, interlocking his fingers with mine.

"Let's get out of here," he says, he can't stop smiling either, "Let's grab something to eat."

He guides me down from the landing, and then holds my face in his hands, looking at me in the dark. He kisses me again, and we're off for another marathon.

Now I don't know if I even have lips because I can't feel them. I never knew kissing could leave you breathless. I guess it just takes kissing the right person.

Paul pulls up to a 24-hour diner two exits off the highway and eases the truck into a parking spot in a dark corner at the far end of the lot, the only empty spot big enough to accommodate the truck's girth without boxing us in. I reach out to open the door.

"No, no—wait," he says.

He jumps out and runs to my side, opening the door for me.

"You don't have to do that," I say.

"I know. I want to," he says stretching his hand up as a guide so I can balance while finding my footing on the running board.

Is he always like this? I never got the chance to hang-out with him much in school.

The diner is packed with people: teenagers sipping from straws in over-sized glasses of soda, a travel-worn elderly couple with bags under their eyes and diner-coffee-cups on saucers filled with coffee, and lots of mixed-aged groups with breakfast food piled on plates. The smell of bacon grease and toast fills the main room as we walk to the "Please Wait to Be Seated" sign.

"How many?" the thirty-something-with-blond-hair-in-a-hair-net waitress asks us.

"Two," we both say in unison.

"Jinx," I say to Paul.

"Punch buggy," Paul says to me as he gently hits the flesh between my elbow and shoulder.

"What's punch buggy?" I ask.

"I heard someone say it after jinx one time," he says.

I give him a questioning look, "I think that's supposed to be when you see a VW Beetle on the road."

"I don't know," he says, shrugging his shoulders.

"Follow me," the waitress says, grabbing two thick menus from the side of the counter, and leading us inside the restaurant.

"Here ok?" the waitress asks motioning to a table by the window.

"Fine," we both say in unison again. He looks at me. I look at him.

"Punch buggy," I say quickly, punching Paul's arm before he does it to me.

"I don't see a Beetle anywhere," he says.

"Touché," I say, sliding myself into the booth opposite Paul.

The waitress hovers over us. "Do you know what you want," she asks, pen to pad, and ready to write our order.

"Know what you want?" Paul asks me.

"Um, breakfast, I think," I say.

"I'll order first, give you a minute," Paul says to me, then to the waitress," I'll have a cheeseburger with bacon, side of fries, and a strawberry shake."

"Mmmm, that sounds good," I say to Paul, then to the waitress, "I'll have the same, except make mine chocolate."

"How do you want your burgers," the waitress says, scribbling our orders on her pad.

"Well-done for me," Paul says.

"Medium-well," I say.

"Very good. Coffee or water while you wait?" The waitress asks.

"Water," I say.

"I'll have coffee," Paul says.

After the waitress leaves, Paul slides out of the booth opposite me and stands, shoves his hand into his pocket and pulls out the necklace - he extends his hand to me with the pendant flat in his palm.

"Here," he says, "it keeps jabbin' my thigh." The center of the pendant lights with a soft glow.

"How's it doin' that?" Paul asks moving his finger to the pendant to touch it.

"Paul, don't..." I say quickly. He touches the stone anyway - lights swirl inside following his finger, refracting out of the center of the pendant...but that's it, nothing else happens. I half anticipate Paul disappearing before my eyes as he touches it.

"Hm," I say, not realizing I'm voicing-it-out-loud until it's out.

"What?" Paul asks still offering the necklace to me with his extended arm.

I reach out to grab the necklace from Paul's hand, the pendant slips from his hand to mine, and I feel it instantly - the surge of energy from the neck-lace to my skin, the hairs on my arm lifting like soldiers snapped to attention. Paul may not have been affected by the necklace - he didn't disappear as I feared, but I have a feeling I'm about to. The air in the room swirls, but no one in the room seems bothered by it.

Am I the only one who can feel it?

The room disappears, swirling away with the wind - a magician's trick as the booth, the waitress, Paul, and the smell of bacon and toast fade from me, replaced by a veil of darkness, disorienting me...

...light-headed...

...ready to faint...

...as one room quickly leaves another slowly comes into view to replace it, the details fuzzy and distant - gray sides, big space, and someone calling my name in the distance. I see my hand - one second it's in front of me, and the next it's in back - twisted at an abnormal angle. Time and distance distorted. And then I see bucket seats, stone walls, and a big room stretching up and out - THE room, that place, and just like that I'm back there again.

CHAPTER TWELVE

෬

ENERGY. EN.

The room is empty, and quiet except for a low monotonous hum that whirs like an over worked air conditioner straining during a heat wave - the sound of it echoes off the empty chairs and the stone walls, ricocheting around the room; the sound is important, but I don't know why. I don't even know where it's coming from, but I do know that it's connected to the energy that pulses through everything here; I can feel it coming up through the floor and into the soles of my sneakers, vibrating in my palms, clinging to my hair as static. I just know. *You know when you just know?* I know. They say a woman's intuition is strong. Mine feels really strong here.

I'm standing in a half-digested puddle of To-mas' pizza (that's vibrating too); bits of bile at the edges of my mouth and a burning sensation in my throat. My feet are unsteady beneath me. My body does not like whatever this is, this move from where I was (the diner) to where I am now (*what do I call this place?*); the pendant like some device that moves me from one place to the next - reminds me of that big round gate on that show my brother used to watch, Stargate I think it was, except this "gate" fits in my hand and takes me one place only. Here. But where exactly is here? The only thing I know about this place is what I've seen, the water, the ca-noe, the island, the doppelganger-people, the hut, and this room underground under the beach. It all *looks* normal, but it makes me uneasy because it's "off" in places - the sky that flashes with light, this room with its bucket seats and theater design too complex for these aboriginal people. The "people" make me uneasy, they flash in-and-out like magical lightning bugs and talk in screeches and sing-songs for language.

And now I'm back, gone only a few hours re-ally - not long enough to forget everything that happened or the promise I made.

"Faith," hibiscus-girl calls to me over the mo-notonous hum. I jump and turn. The girl is nowhere, only her disembodied voice in the air around me.

"I'm glad you are safe, and you made it back to us," she says, the end of her sentence lilting up in her usual sing-song cadence.

"Where are you?" I ask.

"I am here," she says.

"Where?" I ask looking around. Her body takes shape in front of me, a shadow defining its features - filling in the details of the thick green leaves and pink delicate flower of the hibiscus growing from her head, each strand of her long dark hair spilling neatly over her shoulders and down her back, perfectly styled as if hair-sprayed in place. And again, the brightly printed floral pattern painted over her body.

"How did you do that?" I ask.

"Eas-ily. And you shall too," she says.

"I don't know how to do that."

"We *are* dif-ferent from you, but you are not so dif-ferent from us," she says.

"I'm telling you right now I don't know how to do that," I say.

"Not to worry, all will be an-swered soon," she says.

"Good because I have a lot of questions like what the hell was that thing back in the drugstore? Do you know what I'm talking about? That was from here right?"

She moves closer to me, but doesn't answer my question.

"So much de-pends on you," she says, "I am glad you made it back to us."

"I don't know how I got here, except this thing is somehow connected to it," I say holding the pendant up to her face, level with her eyes.

"Yes," she says.

"Why does it keep bringing me back here?"

"You are meant to be here," she says.

"The whole 'I made a promise' thing or because of what happened at the drugstore?"

"Part-ly both," she says.

"Do you know what happened in the drugstore?" I ask.

"Yes," she says.

"Then tell me, because I'm still trying to figure it out," I say.

"You have less time than we thought," she says.

"What does that mean? Was it *Him*?" I ask.

"You..." she says moving closer to me and putting her hand on my shoulder; I wait for her to finish but she doesn't, she lets the word hang in the air around me.

"Me what?" I ask, "You're not answering any of my questions."

"We should start. The answers will mean nothing with-out the know-ledge," she says.

"Isn't that the same thing?" I ask.

"No," she says, "Answers are on-ly facts. Know-ledge is what you need to stay a-live."

The girl's face turns serious.

"Let's start with some-thing ea-sy," she says.

"You want to get-to-it, get this over with and get me back, right? I can appreciate that. So what do I have to do, take some magic pill or something?" I ask.

"No," she says, "I will learn you."

"Teach me? Is that what you mean?"

"Teach you. Yes," she repeats, "You must know us first. And you must know you," she says.

"Yeah, well, I'm nothin' to brag about so don't get your hopes up too much."

"Sit," she says motioning to the floor. I follow her instruction, stuffing the pendant in my pocket and sitting with my legs bent under me.

"We are not flesh like you," she says dropping herself opposite me, copying my pose.

"You're not?"

"No," she says.

"So what ARE you?" I ask hesitantly, almost afraid to hear the answer.

"We are a bas-ic form of en-er-gy" she says, "we do not have bod-ies un-less we cre-ate them; we can-not be seen, or touched, or felt. Those things can be made from en-ergy, but our en-ergy can-not be cre-ated by us. It is limited."

"But I can see you."

"Yes. To save en-ergy we stay in pure form, we do not us-ual-ly create a physical form, but for you, we do," she says.

"Why?" I ask.

"So you could know us in a form that is ea-sy to re-late to. We chose im-ages from your mem-ories and thoughts," she says.

"No, I mean, why do you have to conserve en-ergy?" I ask.

"When our en-ergy is gone, we are gone. For-ever," she says.

"So you can't get more or make more? How did you get it to start with?" I ask.

"You," she says.

"What do you mean?"

"Your people. You give off en-ergy that we use to sus-tain our-selves, but it is no lon-ger e-nough," she says.

"Seven billion people aren't enough?"

"You have more people, but the en-ergy is less us-able," she says.

"Why?"

"As you ad-vance, we dim-in-ish," she says.

"Because of technology?"

"Part-ly," she says.

"Because we're doing less work ourselves?" I ask.

"Part-ly," she says.

"And you can't get it anywhere else?"

"No. And *He* is blocking en-ergy too, from you to us, so we get an even smal-ler amount," she says.

"This is the same *He* I need to worry about?"

"Yes, the one you need to defeat so we may survive," she says.

My stomach tightens.

"What do you mean 'defeat'?"

"It is the pro-mise you made," she says.

"I promised to 'help', not 'defeat'," I say, and then continue, "I think your world is doomed if you think I'm your savior. I'm not great at anything. Not anymore," I say.

"You doubt your-self, but I see your power," The girl says.

"I don't think so. I can't even save my own mother, can't even fight a stupid bully in the bath-room. I don't think your world has much of a chance," I say looking down to the floor.

The girl doesn't answer.

"And besides what does my mother have to do with all this? That man before, he kept mentioning my mother, even knew her name."

The girl doesn't speak, but her eyes don't leave my face.

"Maybe you should just return me—send me back—there's still time, I can make an excuse to Paul—not sure how I'll explain disappearing in the middle of the diner, but I'll come up with something," I say.

Neither her voice nor expression changes as she starts talking again.

"We have no more time. You are our fin-al hope," The girl says, her voice as even as before, but her eyes boring through me like Superman through steel.

"For the record, you're making a mistake," I say taking in a full breath and exhaling.

"We are not," the girl says.

"If you're not going to send me back, and I don't know how to get back myself—I don't even know where I am—I guess I have no choice. Right?"

"You have a choice. Al-ways," the girl says.

"How do I have a choice? If I ask, will you send me back?"

"Let me show you some-thing first," she says.

With a wave of her arm the room disappears, quickly replaced by a marigold cloud; the ceiling is still barely visible, but it looks as if it's suspended midair without a foundation. I squint and adjust my shirt as it sticks with sweat.

The girl sits across from me, cross-legged, and now suspended in air. I look down to my legs quickly and find I too am suspended with nothing below me but yellow air.

A tinge of vertigo hits, and there's nothing to focus on to correct it. All I can do is to fight it, fight through the dizziness building in my head.

I look at the girl again, her eyes closed in concentration, and see her as a steady and still point of reference, something to focus on to calm the vertigo. I focus on her. And it's then that everything changes again around me, the yellow morphs into a mix of colors and shapes that then morphs into mountains and trees and endless blue sky; a picture perfect landscape fit for a nature poster, with a sloping terrain that rises past the confines of the ceiling into a mountain, the peak capped with a crown of white snow glistening burnt orange from a setting sun. Rocks, hillocks and massive tree trunks sprout from the ground reaching like fingers to the sky as branches stretch and fill with leaves. Other branches reach down, just outside my periphery vision, stretching from the outside in, filling the base of the mountain with a forest of weeping willows swaying to a breeze that sweeps through them. Grass and wildflowers pop up around me, the grass tickling my ankles as it emerges below me. I can feel my ass and legs on solid ground now. Nothing remains of the theater, the stage, the yellow canvas, or the ceiling; everything is now landscape.

"How did you do that?" I ask. The girl has opened her eyes and is looking out to the mountain.

"En-ergy," she says.

"What about all that yellow before, what was that?" I ask.

"En-ergy," she says again, "Re-fined, with-out form."

"So how do you..."

"It's all en-ergy. I on-ly changed its form," she says.

"How?" I ask, genuinely curious.

"It is the same en-ergy, I trans-lated its physical appear-ance. Do you un-der-stand?"

"Translated? Like we do with language?" I ask.

"Ex-plain," the girl says.

"We have several languages where I am from, well more than several, it's like thousands, but a lot of languages—essentially we are all saying the same things, the meanings are the same, we're just saying it in different forms," I explain.

"Sounds close," she says.

"What do you call it, just energy? Come to think of it, I never even asked your name either—do you have a name?" I ask.

"No, at least not one that trans-lates into your words, it's more of a sound."

"Is it like that for everything, here?" I ask.

"Al-most. Our world has a name, one that trans-lates, we've had to use it to mark our-selves in the uni-verse. En-litra, this is Enlitra—sister world to Earth," she says.

"En-light-ra?"

"Yes."

"I like it," I say, smirking, "looks like I'm going to have to start nicknaming things though. I can't keep calling you 'the girl' in my head."

"You can call me TheGirl. I'm fine with that. It's what I'm used to you cal-ling me," she says.

"I don't think I've ever called you that," I say.

"In your thoughts, you have," she says.

"So you *are* in my head!" I shout.

"Yes."

"Stop doing that. It's rude!" I shout again.

"It can-not be helped. Thoughts read like speech in the en-ergy plane. It can be hard to sep-arate them. Sor-ry."

I guess I can get used to calling her TheGirl. I mean I used to have a cat I called HiName; couldn't find a name that fit and just started calling to her — 'Hi No Name' then shortened it to HiName. I never changed it. I guess this is the same idea.

"You know 'Energy' sounds so geeky. Can we shorten it; call it En, or something? Sounds better doesn't it?"

"You may call it what you like, it is the same trans-lated dif-ferently," she says with a smile.

"Did you just make a joke?" I ask.

"I tried to," she says.

"Not bad, not funny but not bad," I say.

"We must con-tinue. We have much to cover. This is on-ly the be-ginn-ing of your un-der-stan-ding," she says, her smile dropping back into a seri-ous countenance.

"So you're really not sending me back, even if I ask?" I say, my face matching her seriousness.

"I will. I prom-ise. But first I have more things to show you," she says.

She promised—that has to count for some-thing. Hopefully promises are the same on Enlitra as they are on Earth, and hopefully I'll find an explana-tion for Paul that will make sense. Not sure how I'll explain disappearing right in front of him, this might just be another instance of 'fucked it up again'; every time with him.

Love and the end of the world, as if I didn't already have enough on my mind.

"It's your turn," TheGirl says.

"My turn for what?" I ask.

"I want you to feel en-ergy..." TheGirl starts. I look at her, debating whether I should correct her or not, and then I do, "En, you mean," I say.

"...En," she repeats.

I nod.

She continues.

"I want you to feel En tran-slation," TheGirl says.

"Me? How am I supposed to do that?" I ask.

"I will guide you," she says.

"Anyone can do this?" I ask.

"No," TheGirl answers.

"So why do you think I can do it?" I ask.

"I know," she says.

"You are just full of answers, aren't you; I thought you were supposed to "learn" me. How am I going to learn anything, if you don't tell me?" I ask.

"We don't have time, you must *listen*," she scolds, and then continues, "and close your eyes."

"Why do I have to close my eyes?" I ask quickly.

"If you do not, the dizzy-ness will re-turn," she counters back.

Good reason, I guess, although the idea of closing my eyes right now isn't sitting well with me—there's a trilling anxiety in my gut, but I dislike the vertigo even more, so I do—I close my eyes...but when I open them a few seconds later, I'm in a tree—

not a regular backyard oak or maple—a giant tree, a Sequoia or maybe a Redwood.

"What the hell!" I shout looking frantically for something to hold on to.

"Hang on to the trunk. And do not fall," TheGirl offers as advice.

"No shit Sherlock," I reply, moving my hand to the right, feeling the soft, fibrous bark of the trunk, then wrapping my arms around it in a death grip. My arms barely reach a fourth of the way around the massive trunk, my fingers searching between thick cords of peeling reddish bark for finger holds in the crevices.

I peer around the trunk and down, the ground looks as if it's a mile below me. The vertigo smacks into me and my head swims.

"What are we doing up here?!" I yell hugging the tree tighter.

"I am learning you," TheGirl says sarcastically. If I could see her face I imagine she's saying it with a half a smirk.

"Shut up. Get me down. Get-me-down!"

"Learn what I teach, and you shall get yourself down," she says.

"You know this is really messed up. Seriously!"

"Trust En," TheGirl says, her voice steady and with no lilting cadence. I turn my head away from the trunk to look at her. She's standing beside me on the branch like a seasoned gymnast on a balance beam.

"What does that mean?"

"Look down," she says.

"No!" I say, afraid if I look down my body might think that's the direction I want to go.

"Trust the en-ergy," TheGirl says again.

"I'm not looking down," I say.

"You will. You must." TheGirl says.

"What kind of lesson is this—Suicide 101?"

"It is the les-son you will not for-get," she says, "give me your hand."

"I'm not moving," I say resolutely.

"You want to re-turn to Earth? You want to see Paul? You want to go to your friend, your brother? Now give me your hand," she says sternly like a mother to a child.

My stomach lurches at the thought of moving, even releasing one finger from its finger hold sends my head swimming again and a cool wave of sweat washing over me.

"Trust me," TheGirl says. There's something in the way she says it—a truth in her tone that re-minds—if I am so important to these people, why would they put me in any danger? They wouldn't, right?

Maybe I do need to trust her.

So I do. Slowly, I release my left hand from the bark and move it behind me toward TheGirl.

"Don't let me fall," I say, my right arm still wrapped around the tree.

TheGirl covers my hand with hers, not to steady me on the branch, but more for reassurance.

"How is that going to stop me from falling?" I ask.

She doesn't answer, instead she pumps her hand once and a warmth radiates from her to me; more than just skin to skin heat, this is something more intense. The warmth spreads up my arm and down the other, like alcohol in my bloodstream, up and down my torso, down my legs to the tips of my toes; it chases away the cold sweat and the dizziness and replaces it all with a strange sense of calm and confidence. The fear in my gut is numbed.

"Did that help?" TheGirl asks.

"Hm?" I say still focused on the changes in my body, only half listening.

"I will take it back if you can-not con-cen-trate," TheGirl says.

I don't want her to take it back. I like it.

I shake my head in a barely perceptible yes, not wanting to move too much for fear of losing the buzz.

"Now listen and under-stand what I say. En is every-where; you need to know where to find it, and you need to know how to change its form—its appearance, its use, its strength. Under-stand?"

"Um, I understand what you're saying, but I don't understand how to do it," I say.

"I will show you now. It will be dif-ferent where you are from than here, you may not be able to trans-late as eas-ily or exact-ly in the same way, but that I can-not help with. I can-not teach what I do not know. You will need to learn that on your own," TheGirl says.

"Ok?" I say, still not entirely sure I under-stand what she's talking about.

"So you are ready now; yes?" TheGirl asks.

"Ready for what?"

"Let go of the tree," TheGirl says.

The warmth from TheGirl's hand pulses again in my veins, and again her voice has a truth I cannot ignore; it urges me forward, numbing fear and doubt. I push back carefully from the tree—my hand lingering above the bark, ready for a desperate grab for stability—and stand upright on the branch.

"Good. Now let go," TheGirl says.

"I did," I say.

"No, like this..." She says pushing off from the branch with her feet, diving into the air.

"Oh hell, no way!" I shout after her, watching her career toward the ground, moving my right hand back to the trunk to steady myself.

"Trust me. Think of some-thing that flies. I will help you," TheGirl says, her voice now part of the air around me.

I can't look down anymore, I can't see where she is or even if she is still falling. If I look down, the dizziness and fear will clench me in its grip and no amount of warm fuzzies in my body will help; I am sure of it. Instead, I grip the bark, and listen & hope not to hear a thud from the ground below.

"When you jump, tran-slate your energy to be that which flies," the air chirps with TheGirl's voice.

"But I don't know how to do that!" I yell to the air.

"All you must do is think, and con-cent-trate on that which you are think-ing of," she says.

I'm still listening for a thud, but there is none, instead I hear and feel only the wind that has picked up around me, rustling the leaves from all directions.

"Jump, quick before the tree is no more..." TheGirl says, her words trailing off as the wind be-gins to swirl more intensely around the tree.

"Get me down!" I yell.

My branch creaks and sways, pieces of the tree pelt me from above while the wind changes, in-creasing velocity and direction like a gale with a motive; leaves tear apart around me into leaf con-fetti, and the bark is stripped from the trunk.

"You will fall," TheGirl coaxes, "Jump!"

"Falling, jumping, isn't that the same thing? Are *you* doing this!" I yell, frantically digging my fingers in deeper as my finger holds disappear with the stripping bark.

"Jump," TheGirl says calmly, her voice in my ear. I turn, thinking she's standing on the branch beside me, and as I turn I see it—the branch disappearing in front of me as if being erased and replaced with only air.

"No!" I shout, "No, no, no." I grab the trunk desperately trying to get hold of the bark, but it continues to shred beneath my fingers.

"Heeeeeelp!" I scream.

"Just let go," TheGirl's voice whispers in my ear, and all at once the tree is gone and I'm falling. The wind whistles loud around me, it's the only sound I hear beside the sound of my ears popping and my arms flapping frantically beside me.

"You have wings – fly!" TheGirl's voice echoes over the whistling wind.

"I'm not a friggin' bird!"

"Make yourself into one," TheGirl says.

"I don't want to die, I don't. I changed my mind. I don't want this!" I yell, tears forming at the corners of my eyes.

"Then use your wings."

"What wings! I don't have fucking wings!" I scream so forcefully I feel the sound strip my throat.

The scream is like a released stopper of emotions building over the last three months—I see my mom's face flash in my head, not a death picture of her but one of her smiling and giggling with me; my brother at thirteen with jeans rolled up to his knees, wading through a stream behind our house searching for frogs and freshwater snails; fast flashes—driving to the movies with Kiara, a lunch room food fight in the eighth grade cafeteria, a spelling bee ribbon ceremony—random memories; and then Olivia Johnson's hot breath in my ear, her palm jammed into my chest and her two friends giggling and laughing as they exit the bathroom. I can feel the tips of my ears hot with anger.

"Use that," TheGirl's voice whispers in my ear, "Emo-tion will give you a boost. Think of something that flies while you are still angry."

The ground is close now. I can see the tops of normal sized trees and grass below that. I can see how the landscape changes into small hills and hollows. Soon I'll be part of that; splat on the ground if I don't do something.

"An ani-mal, first one you think of that flies, what is it?" The wind sings with TheGirl's voice.

"A bird," I say out loud, barely able to push the two words from my mouth.

"Which one, think of what it looks like, how it moves. Quick-ly."

"An eagle."

"Pic-ture it in your mind, move as if you are that ea-gle," TheGirl says.

I picture an eagle, the same one Mom & I spotted on our last mountain hike, perched on a branch above us while we stopped to rest our legs and drink water. We nicknamed her Private-I, because she was watching us just as much as we were watching her, cocking her head from side to side, deciding if we were friend or foe. I picture her now in my head, and I move my arms as she did when she took flight from that branch, capturing wind beneath each wing—and it's then that I see my arms are no longer arms but wings, twice as long as my arms and covered in chocolate brown feathers.

I scream.

The scream is not my scream but a long deep screech that rides my larynx, and my chest is not my chest but a mound of muscle; my feet are gone, my sneakers now grasped in two yellow talons tucked back near a fan of long white tail feathers.

I have wings.

I am a bird.

But I am still falling.

So I flap; one wing at a time, which is kind of like rowing with only one paddle. The wind resists me. I flap harder, and sync my wings until they flap together and the air catches beneath each limb.

Instead of down, finally I'm moving up and forward. I am flying.

The air in the clouds is thin, so I take several shallow breaths until my lungs are full. My wings shift automatically to catch a warm current that nestles beneath me and I push myself into; it carries me straight for a few yards and then down towards a small rivulet carving a winding path through the landscape. The water is still and mirrors the large dark body that glides gracefully over its surface, a body of chocolate feathers white and dark, a muscular neck that swivels in short jerky motions, and wings that stretch and pivot and move in flight.

I see the eagle, and me, in one.

In my veins my blood burns, the warmth from TheGirl surges to my muscles, my skin, and my bones – everywhere.

I catch an updraft and ride it high, surveying the landscape below, and the view is spectacular. The landscape is boundless, not confined within walls or boundaries, it is a world stretched in all directions with no seeming end, and topography as varied as it is endless—hills and valleys, flat fields, bodies of water, and mountains. I feel liberated with the wind gliding over my body—alive; everything around me looks and feels more vibrant, as if I'm seeing for the first time. Trees are everywhere, mammoths as big as the first tree and smaller varieties of oaks, maples, elms and many more I can't name, and flowers that dot the canopy with patches of color.

Even so, as immense and detailed as the scenery is, it's not perfect, there's a flaw. If I look at it just right from the corner of my eye, I can see the image shake and distort slightly, like a mirage that makes you believe in the idea of it until you go to touch it and it evaporates in front of you. It's not really real, it's not earth, and it's not home.

If this is all translated energy, I can see why someone would want the power.

"Not just anyone," TheGirl's voice returns whispering in the air around me, "Him."

I guess she heard me.

"What does *He* want with it," I say to the air, consciously forming the words so they don't come out as screeches again.

"He is tak-ing it for him-self," she says.

"And doing what with it?" I ask.

"Get-ting stronger," she says, "while we get wea-ker."

"So that's the plan, he just wants power?" I ask, picking up another current and riding it with my wings outstretched.

"That is a question for Him. I do not know," TheGirl says, her voice tinged with emotion; she's trying to cover it but I can hear sadness in her words.

"Do you know him?" I ask.

"It's e-nough for to-day. Come down. There's some-thing else I want to show you," she says evad-ing the question. I really want to ask again, but I can tell from her voice that I shouldn't push the subject, there's sadness and warning in her tone.

I tilt my body, wings slicing air to cut through the current and head down, and it's then that I real-ize I don't exactly know where I'm going or how to land.

"I am here," TheGirl says as she illuminates herself with a bright yellow glow on the ground be-low me.

"I see you. Now how do I get to you?"

"Land like the bird," she says.

"There's got to be an easier way. I've seen you change things."

"There is, but first you must learn to fol-low through on that which you cre-ate?"

"Why? Why can't you just abra-ca-dabra me down?"

"There are reas-ons," she says.

"They are..."

"You need to learn con-trol..."

"I think I've already done that. I'm flying for Christsake."

"...con-trol through fear, un-cer-tain-ty. You need to learn de-tails—they can help if you are trying to stay con-cealed, you may need it. I've been help-ing you so far, but this you need to try on your own. Try to keep the rea-lity of what you have formed. Fin-ish this. The slight-est crack in your con-cen-tration can break the co-hesion. So land. Like an ea-gle," TheGirl says, her voice now coming up from her highlighted figure on the ground directly below me.

It's then that I feel my body jolt midair as the girl pulls her "help" away. It's just me now. No won-der it came easily to me before, I wasn't doing it, she was. And now that I'm up here by myself, I feel na-ked. I don't know what I'm doing.

"What if I fall?" I yell down, my voice revert-ing back to a screech.

"You have not fal-len yet," TheGirl whispers in my ear.

Doesn't mean I won't.

"If you think you will, you will," TheGirl says, "And if you think you won't, you won't. What you fo-cus on is what will be trans-lated. So, think like an ea-gle and land."

The wind is rushing past me now; wings above my head, my body on point to the ground. I've stopped flapping, and I'm dropping like a brick.

Concentrate. C'mon I can do this.

"Fas-ter," TheGirl says.

"I'm going as fast as I can!"

"If you can-not learn this, we are all doomed. I have faith in you Faith," she says.

I can feel the tips of my ears growing hot even as the cool air whips around them; why did she have to say that to me?

The ground is coming up fast.

Think like an eagle.

Be an eagle. An eagle knows how to fly and how to land.

I can see treetops now.

I thrust my legs out beneath me and fight with the wind to bring my wings parallel. The wind is strong and my muscles ache as I pull against the current. I have to keep my feathers slicing the air or I could break a wing. I fold both wings halfway with the tips pointing to the ground like fingers; the position like a parachute, capturing air beneath my cupped wings, but the ground is still fast approaching.

Too fast.

I pull up aborting the attempt, picturing my mangled body on the dirt splattered into a million little pieces.

"Again. Trust the en-ergy," TheGirl reminds me.

"I could die down there!" I scream.

"You could have died every day for the last three months. But you didn't," TheGirl says.

"How the hell do you know that?"

"Isn't that why you keep the knife in your pocket?" she taunts.

"Yeah. It is. And I haven't done it yet. When I do, it will be on *my* terms, not yours!" I yell.

"Good. Use the anger. AND LAND," TheGirl yells in my ear.

I try two more attempts and both times I swerve away from the ground at the last minute. TheGirl has stopped talking to me. Instead I see her glaring as I pass overhead.

I swing around for another attempt—my wings cupped to slow me down—but instead of continuing to drop like this the whole way, I outstretch my wings and fly parallel to the ground dropping closer in small increments like a plane approaching the airport. I keep my eyes trained on the target—a flat runway patch of ground with lots of grass just past TheGirl. I move my head in quick swivels side to side checking the air for obstacles.

And then the wind changes and I'm thrown to the right and down, out of the current and pummeling toward the ground. A second wind swoops up under me, knocking my tail feathers upwards, and I tumble in the air head over tail like an air somersault...like I used to do on the mats in gymnastics...when I was five...my coach reminding me to tuck everything in.

"You have lost con-trol, get it back. Change your En to what you need. Quickly now!" TheGirl yells from where she stands only a few feet below me. My voice is stuck in my throat; I can't answer her and I can't scream; frozen in this moment, lightheaded from the somersaults and hardly able to breath.

I can't get control.

The ground is almost here, so close I can smell the earthiness of the soil and the green of the grass. I can't just let my body break the fall.

Survival.

In the last seconds, I search the ground for something soft, something to target. There's a patch of dense grass just a foot to my right, nearly beneath me. I flap a wing hoping it will propel me close enough, and then concentrate on the grassy patch, remembering TheGirl's advice; picturing what I'd like the grass to be—each blade thick, soft, and bouncy like a spring in a mattress, and then I close my eyes repeating *thick-soft-bouncy, thick-soft-bouncy, thick-soft-bouncy,* and hope for the best.

Impact.

My chest hits, cushioned first on a soft pillow of grass and then smacking the hard soil below—the breath in my lungs forced out just like when Olivia smacked my chest, until there's no more breath left. My heart squeezes, stops, and then pumps quickly to catch up.

A rib tears away and snaps.

My head jolts up and back, so far back I can see my tail feathers, upside down, as they metamorphose back to my naked ass that jiggles with the movement of impact.

And then there's lightness. Numbness as I bounce back into the air. The heaviness in my chest loosens. My head snaps to the side. Hair flutters around my face, and then I'm back down again, on the grass, but this time it cradles me like a giant goose down pillow. I don't dare move. I know the pain is coming.

TheGirl's face appears over me.

"Nice look," she says to me.

I move my head to scan my body. I'm naked, head to toe.

"Shit!"

I move to the side—trying to cover myself with the tall grass that pokes up around me – and pain rips through my chest and down to the muscles around my ribs, just as I expected. I wince and clench my teeth. It's a familiar pain.

"You let your fear take over..." TheGirl says, "...as I exp-ected. We have work to do. But. Still. Good job on this." She points to the grass below me.

"You could have killed me! Was it you that made me fall?" I yell.

"You are a-live," TheGirl says calmly.

"Alive? I friggin' broke a rib and who knows what else!" I yell. The pressure from yelling sends a shooting pain through my chest. I try to breathe through it, but I really want to scream.

TheGirl sweeps her arm over me.

The warmth returns to my body, numbing the pain that plagues my muscles.

"Bet-ter?"

I shake my head.

"Where were you when I needed that after Olivia pummeled me?"

"If you re-call, your pain *was* tak-en away," she says.

"So it was you, in the por-tal, that first time?" I ask.

"Yes."

"You have a funny way of keeping me safe. Do you mind?" I say indicating my nakedness.

"It is noth-ing more than a form of energy to me," she says.

"Yeah, well, to me it's my body. Do you mind?"

"Here," TheGirl waves her hand over me again, and my clothes return, the same ones I was wearing earlier. She offers her hand, and lifts me upright from the ground.

"Thanks," I say, wiping grass and dirt from my backside.

My feet are a bit unsteady now that I'm back on the ground, my legs wobbly and my hands shaky, but all the pain is gone.

"You may find some after effects since you are not used to it," TheGirl says, and then continues, "We must keep going, please listen and try to focus. I can-not share with you every-thing you need to know in such a short time, but I can share with you the most im-por-tant in-for-mation. *He* knows you and *He* knows where to find you now. He will try to get the pow-er from you, and he will do any-thing to get it. He would like noth-ing more than to see En-litra gone, and if he can sus-tain him-self on Earth, he will take steps to make that hap-pen."

"How can one person, one "entity" decide the fate of a whole world?" I ask.

"Poor de-cisions have given him access; that error has sealed our fate," TheGirl says.

"So he'll cut you off from the En you need to survive?"

"Yes," she says.

"So where do I fit into this?" I ask.

"*You* are either the bridge or the barrier. We hope you will be the barrier, be-cause if you are not, we will cease to ex-ist that much quicker. You have the abil-ity in-side you and you must guard it with your life. Give me your hand, let me show you why," TheGirl says.

I give her my hand.

The world changes around me. Details flash so quickly my vision blurs; trees morph into buildings, hills into storefronts, a city grows from an empty space with buildings popping up around an oversized lawn, and a large latticed steel structure grows into the sky, instantly recognizable as The Eiffel Tower.

But then something isn't right.

Large girders at the base of the tower twist and groan as if the hand of God plucks the structure from the ground; it sways and rocks on the foundation and then it topples like a felled tree, crashing down with a massive thud.

The landscape completely changes again.

Sand blows in wiping the city away as if shaken like an Etch-A-Sketch clearing the screen, and now sand is everywhere—several shades of brown and moving in a wave—gaining speed and leaping into the air, and behind the course sand and fine dust are the outlines of familiar structures—pyramids and stone temples with statues cut to match ancient pharaohs.

The wind whips harder; the sand eddies and then crashes to the ground, smacking the earth with such force that everything shakes and crumbles. Structures fall; the sand levels everything.

The landscape changes again, and again, and again, and again. Images flash quickly, places strange and familiar, but each change ends the same. Destruction. And now it's flashing, again, and this time what stands before me is very familiar; it is home, the buildings and streets and people that I know from the town where I grew up. The old house, the one mom died in, is perched on the hill at the end of Montgomery Street, the exterior paint peeling in weather worn spots. Power lines crisscross in the backyard and stretch to the end of the street. A bright red tricycle lays on its side, thrown to the grass near the sidewalk. The white fence, erected by one of mom's old boyfriends, skirts the yard. Down the street, Mr. Cooley unlocks the front door of B&B Bait & Tackle. The shop sits at the edge of the river, the same river that winds through the center of town and powers the old historic water wheel that draws tourists during the summer. And my favorite smell wafts from the open window of Mrs. Bulbulia's house to the right, her famous colossal blueberry muffins. A few more houses down an elderly man works in his front yard. He looks familiar, but I can't remember his name. Other people are around too; running errands, pushing baby carriages, jogging, walking dogs, and chitchatting with neighbors; some look familiar, and some don't. The traffic on the narrow rural street is minimal, but an occasional car drives by. This is a place I love, a place I miss, and my stomach is twisting into tight knots because every image before this ended the same.

Without warning, the high noon sun flares a burnt orange and bleeds into the sky. A blinding flash of white follows. And then BOOM!—an explosion. Everything convulses.

People look up at the blast and then at the things that begin to fly in all directions—shingles, wooden beams, the red tricycle, uprooted trees, whole rooftops, cars, halves of houses, and people— Tommy Kay from my old Trig class, Mr. Cooley and bits of the Bait & Tackle, and Mrs. Drouan from the checkout line at the Pic 'n Save. Things rise and fall. Bodies hit the ground like giant rain drops on a tin roof. I cringe each time I hear the sound.

The white fence, around the perimeter of my old house, bursts into flames, sparked by the power lines that rip from the poles. The smell of burnt wood and paint, rubber and flesh fill the air. I try not to gag, but bile pushes up from my stomach and into my mouth.

Rain, black as oil, falls from the sky. It plunks off of Mr. Cooley's body as he lays motionless on the ground, missing a limb, his head crooked unnaturally under him. I used to buy worms from Mr. Cooley in the summer when I went fishing. Now the dirty rain beats upon his lifeless body.

People are dead everywhere.

The elderly man from the house down the block is frozen in place, hunched dead over a bush. Bodies from the center of town slide down the river behind the Bait & Tack. Moans and wails echo from a few survivors, but nothing moves except for a lady who hobbles down the middle of the street—hair singed, shirt shredded, arms coated with soot and her face full of divots and shards of glass; it is Mrs. Bulbulia. I drop to the ground at the sight of her and sob; I can't stop the whimpering that sits in a tight pouch at the back of my throat. Mrs. Bulbulia is the neighborhood mom, the one who hands out hugs like Halloween candy. Now she looks like a zombie from a horror movie with bloody gashes and glass lodged in her face. It doesn't make sense, none of it, all these people dead or dying.

I wipe tears from my face and look up to see the end of the blast—remnants of white as it flashes to oblivion—and the flare of the sun as it fades into nothing. The sky turns an overcast periwinkle as if bruised by the blast, and a cold current moves in, followed by a murky shadowless form, black as ink with dark edges that leach into the air like the thing from the drugstore.

I hold my breath.

Everything around me begins to blur as if the landscape is about to change again, but I'm still here.

Something has changed but it's not the place. It looks as if time has elapsed, like I've moved forward as smoke rises from the scattered debris that fell before. The air is clogged with smoke and with the smell of death and decay. I retch; I can't stop the puke that jets straight from my stomach to my mouth and then out to the ground. Chunks of my last meal cling to my lips, I wipe them free but the taste of bile sticks to my throat. I heave twice more. My stomach churns. I cover my nose with my hand to block the putrid smell of rotting flesh.

The old house is now a crumbling foundation with a few scorched wooden supports that stand upright like dirty bones of a weathered skeleton. The town itself is nearly unrecognizable, like a war zone from a third world country.

How could anyone survive this?

And then movement. I turn to it.

Huddling under the crumbled remnants of a structure I see them, the gaunt faces of survivors—dirt streaked cheeks and matted hair. Fifty, maybe sixty people cower together in the space of a small room. They share a wild-eyed stare toward the sky. I follow their eyes, and there, suspended, as if grasped by the dark shadowless form is a person; too far and too high to know who, except to guess it is a man by his silhouette against the bruised sky. His head is thrown back and frozen in place, while the rest of his body convulses, arms & legs flail untethered in the air. A swell of twinkling, daylight dust rises from his body and funnels upwards toward the black mist; the mist pulses and then darkens as it absorbs the twinkling light. The man's body then drops to the ground with a thud.

A young girl, nine or ten years old, is thrust up into the air next. She hovers for a few moments, just above the group that cowers in the rubble; hands reach out to her, but none can stretch far enough. The girl claws the air trying to break free from what holds her, but her hands connect with air only. She is yanked toward the same spot the man had plummeted from, and the girl screams a high pitch hysterical cry that whizzes through the air with her body. The screams continue even after she jolts to a stop, where a black misty hand plunges down from the darkness above, into her chest. It pulls back. Twinkling rose colored dust billows into the air like diamond dusted smoke, and rises upwards.

The cloud darkens and pulses as it absorbs the girl's energy.

The girl's screams stop. Her body is still, stretched lifeless in the air, and then released. She crashes to the ground below.

I cringe.

I understand. THIS is the danger that he poses to *my* world.

He is harvesting energy, and these people that cower in the rubble will be sucked dry one by one, and then thrown to the ground like gnawed cobs of corn, and none will survive if He is left to his plan. He will take their energy, he will take the Earth, and he will take Enlitra.

Bodies tower over me, piled high, cast aside and left to rot as if garbage; limbs bend in awkward positions, ribs jut from bloated bellies, skin glued to bones, and eyes pop from stricken emaciated faces. The darkness churns and twists overhead, alive, snaking around the dwindling periwinkle sky, choking out the sun, turning day into night.

My world, Enlitra, and none other are safe. Everything goes black around me, and for a minute I think He has reached out with his inky hands and grabbed me, but then I hear TheGirl's voice, "Now you un-derstand," and I see the pendant glowing blue through the pocket of my jeans, and I know it's TheGirl keeping her promise.

CHAPTER THIRTEEN

෮

BREAKING THROUGH

The return home from Enlitra is quick, no nausea or dizziness this time and only a slight jolt moving me from there to here, and then into the hard square booth from the diner, my left knee knocking into the table's leg underneath. A nearly full glass of water topples onto a coffee cup. Both water and coffee spill onto the table.

"Oh geez!" Paul exclaims as he jumps up from his side, dragging napkins over the spill.

I'm a little dazed, and trying to acclimate—I'm back at the diner, Paul is here, and gauging by Paul's reaction it doesn't look like much time has passed.

How is that possible? I was gone for at least a few hours.

"Faith, are you o.k.? Any coffee get on you?" Paul asks.

I force myself to move back from the table, sitting deeper into the booth.

"No, the coffee didn't get me," I say half dazed.

"Here, lift your plate," he says dragging a second napkin to the center of the table.

"Can we get some extra napkins over here?" Paul calls to the waitress across the room.

"Be right with you," the waitress answers turning toward the kitchen.

I lift my plate so Paul can clean, and the smell of burger, bacon, and greasy fries hits my nose. My stomach growls.

"Just when our food arrived too," Paul says. I think he's been talking nonstop since he started wiping down the table, but I'm only catching bits and pieces.

"Yeah," I say, offering little to the conversation but a response.

The waitress arrives with a stack of white napkins that she plops in the middle of the table.

"Anything else?" she says looking at the mess she'll need to clean before sitting the next guests.

"No, we're good. Thanks," Paul says, and then to me as the waitress leaves and he sits back down wiping the last of the spill, "Where were we?"

"I don't know," I say. What I really want to say is that I was literally somewhere else, Enlitra to be exact. Yeah, I don't think that would fly. Not really.

"What are you thinking about?" he asks.

"Uh, how hungry I am," I say, picking up a fry and popping it in my mouth.

"Me too," Paul says.

I move a hand over the front pocket of my jeans under the table, checking for the pendant; it's there. I don't dare stick my hand inside the pocket, not when I just got back, but it is reassuring to know the pendant is there and safe. I have lots of things I need to sort out. First of which is seeing if this En thing works here like it does there, but I'll leave that for tomorrow. For now, I think I'll enjoy this burger and fries. And get to know Paul just a little bit better.

"If I drop you anywhere tonight, it has to be somewhere safe—it's one-thirty," Paul says climbing back into the driver's seat, "and I'm NOT leaving you at that place, alone."

*Now that I have some answers, maybe I don't need to go back **there**, but I do have to go some-where.*

"Just bring me home then. I'll deal with my brother in the morning," I say resigned.

"I'm not saying that, I'm just telling you I don't feel comfortable just leaving you anywhere. I can't bring you home at this hour, my Dad would flip."

"Yeah, Kiara's mom too," I say. *Particularly if she's talked to my brother.*

"Well, let's go for option D then," Paul says.

"Which is?"

"Let's make a night of it," Paul says.

"Which means?"

"There's that 24-hour bowling place in Susquehana. We could bowl a few rounds, get a couple drinks, some nachos for the late night munchies, coffee, I don't know...whatever you want. We'll be tired in the morning, but who cares. Sleep is for the weak, right?"

"Yeah. Sleep is for the weak," I say putting on my seat belt.

The key is dangling in the ignition, but Paul hasn't turned the car on yet. He's staring at me. It's dark inside the truck's cab besides the glow from the nearby overhead parking lot lights, but there's just enough light to see his face focused on my face.

"Or. We could pick up where we left off," Paul says reaching over and releasing the seat belt I just clicked in place.

My cell phone rings and it's that special ring I assigned to only one person.

I look at Paul.

"It's my brother," I say.

"Are you going to pick it up?" He says leaning back. I can't see his face anymore as he's moved back into the shadows, but I can see disappointment in the way his shoulders drop back against the seat.

I pick up the backpack jammed into the space at my feet and fish out my cell phone, holding it in my hand. I slide my finger over the Reject option.

"No. I'm not picking it up," I say tossing the phone back into my bag.

"Isn't he just going to keep calling?" Paul asks.

"He has been calling all night," I say, grabbing the phone again and dropping the volume to mute, "Now, we won't hear it." I toss the phone back into the bag, and lean over to Paul.

"Where were we?" I say.

The corners of Paul's mouth curve up.

"I think you were just about to kiss me," he says smirking.

I lean all the way over the center console and push my lips to his like a magnet drawn to metal. Paul fishes for the seat lever and the seat kicks back. Without taking his lips from mine Paul crawls to me, his body pushing in, and his hands now inching up my shirt.

Eddie wouldn't approve. I block Eddie out of my thoughts; it's not what Eddie wants, but what I want.

Paul's hands are cold. He moves up the back of my shirt and nimbly releases the clasps. My bra falls. Paul is breathing hard. He pulls my bra out from the bottom of my hoodie and tosses it onto the seat, then slides his hands back up the front of my shirt, groping my breasts as he kisses me.

"Don't take my shirt off. What if someone sees," I say in between breaths.

"I'm not taking it off," Paul says releasing his mouth from my lips and ducking his head inside my shirt, his mouth onto my right side.

A fire ignites inside me, my dark areas tingling inside my jeans and I can't stop breathing in rapid breaths.

The temperature inside the truck is like an inferno, and I'm burning up.

A car alarm sounds next to us. I jump but don't stop.

"Paul," I say.

"Ignore it," he says.

Then there's another to the left, and another across the parking lot.

"What's going on?" I ask.

Paul stops and removes himself from my shirt.

He looks up and around.

"Car alarms. Someone probably set them off. Don't worry about it," he says ignoring the commotion, moving his lips back to my lips, and his hand down the outside of my pants and between my legs. I'm about to burst—that's what it feels like; Paul has sent my body over the edge, every nerve is tingling and the space between my legs is burning.

And that's when the car alarms explode around us—every car in the parking lot screeching in alarm like popcorn kernels in the microwave.

"That's not nothing," I say.

The truck shakes and lurches—as big as the truck is it's hard to imagine what could have moved it—the front swerving kitty corner, jumping the concrete lip of the parking spot and banging into a light post. Paul flies into the air, his lips and hand plucked from me. I'm airborne for a few seconds and then I land back to the seat.

Everything stops

"Are you o.k.?" Paul asks reaching his hand up to my shoulder.

"Yeah, I'm o.k.," I answer.

All the lights have disappeared.

Paul props himself up from the gap next to the seat; once up, he offers his hand pulling me up from my prone position.

"Let's see what's going on," he says grabbing a flashlight from behind the seat.

The parking lot is dark. Paul moves around with his flashlight like a detective solving an elusive case. Cars are set sideways in their spots; many strewn kitty cornered, some bumped into the cars next to them. Paul's truck is the only vehicle free from damage, unless you count the dent on the hubcap where it collided with the light pole; other cars are not so lucky.

"Earthquake?" Paul asks.

"We don't get earthquakes around here," I say.

"Yeah, well whatever happened, it's a mess," Paul says.

"Paul, let's just go," I say.

"Hold on, let's make sure no one got hurt."

"I don't want to be here when the cops show up, in case Eddie reported me missing or something," I say.

"You don't want to stick around and find out what happened?"

"Not if the police show up," I say. It's not just Eddie I'm worried about. What if Mr. Ang called the police too? He did threaten to do it.

"Things are never dull around you, are they?" Paul says.

No they're not, and you have no idea.

I wonder. Did this have something to do with me? Or Him?

"Please. Can we go," I plead, jumping into the truck.

"Yeah, I'm coming," Paul says.

And then sirens start in the distance. Paul glances around the parking lot one more time before jumping into the driver's seat; he readjusts the chair, turns the ignition, and maneuvers the truck around the littered parking lot, and away.

We drive for a while without a real destination—at this hour not much is open—and then we head toward Madison and decide to pull off the road to nap for a bit so we can both function in the morning. Paul grabs the sleeping bags from the rear seats and we use them as blankets. We cuddle up together in the dark...and start to talk...and then we talk for hours, until Paul stops talking at some point and I hear the sounds of him sleeping.

I'm wide awake—not because I don't want to sleep, or because of everything that's happened so far tonight, both of which would be reasonable reasons to be up. No, I'm wide awake because I've been trying to hide my hands under the sleeping bag since Paul and I started talking.

Something is wrong with me.

My fingernails are glowing—it's faint, but noticeable, particularly in the dark.

I don't think it was an earthquake that caused those cars to go crazy in the parking lot. I think it was me.

Something changed in my body when I went to Enlitra this last time, and now my body is going haywire and I don't know how to control it. This is something TheGirl never warned me about, then again, maybe she didn't know.

I lay awake, and think, until the alarm on Paul's phone sounds at six.

"Paul, wake up," I say shaking him with my shoulder, my hands back under the sleeping bag.

"Huh," he says rolling toward me under the sleeping bag.

"I'm going to walk to school," I say.

"You're still going to school? I'll drop you off. I'm awake," he says wiping his eyes.

"I can't just go on the run. The first step to setting this right with my brother is not missing school. But I don't want *you* to get in trouble, if someone sees you dropping me off..."

"So," he says.

"I know my brother, he's already alerted the school, Mr. Ang from the drugstore probably called the police, which means once they know I'm at school—they could check security cameras and see your car," I say.

"Seems like a bit of a stretch—I didn't do anything wrong, you didn't do anything wrong. What are you worried about," he asks.

"I didn't go home last night, remember?"

"Lots of teenagers don't show up at home at night," he says moving his fingers through my hair.

"If Eddie associates you with me, I won't be able to see you again. If the cops pin you anywhere near this town last night and they connect you to me, you become an accessory. That's what I'm worried about," I say.

Well, and the fact my fingernails are glowing, but I'm keeping that to myself.

"Alright I got it. Let me at least drop you off closer. It's still a bit of a walk," Paul says.

"You've got to drive back to school in time for your own classes, and the walk helps me think," I say.

"You have it all sorted out, don't you? What if I say no? What if I lock the door and don't let you out."

The lock on the door snaps shut.

"Open the door," I say to him.

"Let me at least drop you off closer," he says.

"First you won't let me stay at that house last night..."

"For your safety," he interrupts.

"...now you won't let me walk to school," I say growing in aggravation.

"Again, for your safety. You are so worried about getting caught, or someone seeing me with you, but don't you think walking on the side of the road makes you vulnerable. And visible," he says.

"Fine. You can drop me off closer, but not all the way," I say.

"Fine," he says sitting up in the driver's seat, turning the key in the ignition.

"You are very complicated," he says.

We drive off in silence.

❧

CHAPTER FOURTEEN

BACK IN THE SADDLE AGAIN

66 Let me know how it goes with your brother—
call him," Paul says as I slide over the leather
seat and toward the door, "and Faith...I had a
nice time."

"Me too," I say looking back at him as I open
the door, strategically hiding my hands.

"Call your brother, he's probably worried
about you," Paul says.

"You're probably right," I say closing the door
behind me. Paul rolls down the window.

"I know I'm right," he says, and then he continues, "How about dinner and a movie over the
weekend?"

"If I'm not grounded for life," I say.

"One way or another, I'm seeing you this weekend—if not sooner," Paul says with a smile.

He purses his lips and smacks the air with a kiss in my direction—one more kiss for the road— and I blow him his own kiss. He grabs it from the air and places it to his heart.

"You've got me under your spell Faith McDaniels," he says.

I don't think I could love him anymore than I do right now; I'm grinning like the Cheshire Cat.

We waive to each other as he pulls away.

When the truck is fully out of sight, I slip from the road to the woods, and head toward the back of school, toward a utility shed at the border of school property and the neighbors land. I've got an hour before doors open; an hour to get my fingertips back in order and an hour to practice this En thing before it gets out of hand, but before all of that, there's one other thing I need to take care of first. I *need* to call Eddie. I don't really want to talk to him, but I do need to let him know I'm alright, and let him know I'm here. I hope it's enough to keep him from flipping out completely, and if I time it just right, I can call when he's in the shower. Eddie is a schedule guy, and he sticks to his without deviation.

I check my watch. It's Eddie's shower time. If I call now it should go right to voice mail. I grab the phone from my backpack and dial, rehearsing what I'll say in the message while the phone rings.

(*Voicemail, thank god*)

"Can't get to the phone, leave a message at the beep."

And then I'm on...

"Eddie. It's me. I know I messed up not coming home last night. Sorry. I know you're pissed about that and the job—it wasn't my fault, I didn't do it, I swear—but I wanted to call you so you know I'm o.k. I'll be at school today. Please don't do anything crazy and I'll be home tonight, and maybe we can..." "Press 1 to save your message, press 2 re-record", the voice mail's female auto attendant interrupts.

There's more I want to say, but I press 1 and hang up. I hope it's enough. My attempt at school is a peace offering, I hope he gets that. I hope he doesn't show up and make a complete ass of himself. And me.

Now I need to make sure I don't make an ass out of myself either, I have to figure out what the hell's going on and how to control this thing that's happening.

I flash my fingernails in front of me as if examining a new nail-job. In the light they look normal, but who knows if they'll still glow in a classroom with the shades down for a video. It would be just my luck that today would be the day we watch

Shakespeare in English or some video demonstration on Thermodynamics in science. Yeah, my luck. I cup my fingers around one set of nails, looking to see if they glow when there's less light—nothing. It's true I don't feel any different. Maybe it's gone, whatever it was.

Something in my favor, finally?

It's quiet this early at school, even quieter back here where the sounds of the cars from the main road are dulled. The quiet is nice, gives me time to think, time to figure it all out— figure out what I'm doing, figure out if this En thing is real and what it means here, because already its feeling distant like a dream.

I close my eyes, take in a deep breath, and try to remember what TheGirl did and what she said. The first time she told me to close my eyes and open them and everything had changed, so I open my eyes now to see if anything happens, if anything changes, but it doesn't, everything is the same; of course, she's not here to translate things for me.

I remember her saying, "All you must do is think, and con-cent-trate on that which you are think-ing of," so I have to *think*, but right now that doesn't make much sense. Think about what?

I guess I should just pick something and try to change it? I open my eyes and look for something small. There's a bed of acorns strewn around me on the ground. I bend down and pick up one acorn, and place it in the palm of my hand.

What could I do with this? Change it into something else...like a leaf, or pencil, or an apple. I could use an apple right about now, I'm starving. *Would it taste like an apple or an acorn?* I don't know.

"Change this acorn into an apple," I say out loud. Nothing. If the acorn was animated it would probably stick its tongue out at me and call me stupid because an acorn cannot change into an apple. *Idiot.* Who do I think I am, Hermione Granger with a wand?

TheGirl said something about *finding* En. TheGirl's voice returns to me as if I've rewound a recording, "En is every-where, you need to know where to find it, you need to know how to change its form— its appearance, it's use, its strength."

So this is an acorn. It has some kind of energy, I need to take the energy and change it into an apple's energy. How do I know the difference? I stare at the acorn and picture an apple in its place, and repeat, "apple-apple-apple". Still nothing. I close my eyes and say it, "apple-apple-apple."

I open my eyes in a squint, hoping to see an apple in my palm, but the acorn is still there.

"I don't know how to do this. I give up," I say to the air.

"If you think you will, you will," TheGirl says, sounding as if she's right next to me, "And if you think you won't, you won't."

"Awe shut up. I don't know why I even believed this to begin with. It's not real. Stupid dreams," I say to the air.

I move my backpack off my shoulders and pull out my cell. I killed thirty minutes, thirty more to go. I walk to Dunkin Donuts for a coffee and a bagel.

I was here early, so why is it I'm rushing to get in the front door before the late bell? Typical me, lately. Why am I such a fuck up?

I get through the door and no one stops me— no note for me to see the main office because Eddie has called and flagged me missing, no cops waiting to question me on the drugstore mess from last night—so I breathe a sigh of relief, as cliché as that sounds. It means I'm going home tonight. Eddie didn't wig out. I need to keep my end of the bargain.

Once the day gets started it turns out to be a fairly typical day, I make it through AP Biology, Calculus, Creative Writing, AP World History, Spanish, and Sr. English, and now I just checked in to study hall and I'm heading to the bathroom to kill the rest of last period. I have to think about how I'm going to handle Eddie tonight. This calls for a plan, maybe dinner and an "I'm sorry" note on the front door.

I round the corner, and standing in front of the bathroom door, as if waiting for me, is Olivia Johnson. I turn to leave, hoping to avoid her before she sees me, but as I turn, her two beauty queen Stepford sisters block my escape. They nod toward Olivia. I could make a run for it, but they're probably faster than me with their soccer athleticism and endurance. I'd be out of breath before I'm even halfway down the hall.

"Going somewhere?" Olivia says as her sidekicks push me toward her.

"Just going to use the bathroom," I say.

"Good. So was I," she says and pushes me inside the bathroom as I walk past her.

She nods toward her posse, "wait outside."

This is not good.

"I'm going to kick your ass this time," I say to her as I turn on the balls of my feet to face her.

"I don't think so," she says. She moves her arm in the air over me as if wiping away a fart or casting a spell.

"What the hell was that?" I ask.

"Oh nothing," she says.

I move in close, and match her stare.

"You don't scare me, you or your Stepford sisters," I say.

And that's when I see it, her eyes change in
front of me, from brown to black, dark as a midnight
sky.

"New contacts?" I joke, trying to buy time to
think.

She chortles, smiling at me.

"No they're not contacts," she says.

My chest tightens mid-breath.

"Are you scared now?" She asks with a voice
not her own, in a deep rasp like a sixty-year-old
smoker – the altered voice is similar to last time, but
not quite the same—and the words slither off her
tongue. I want to sprint to the door, but I can't, not
just because Olivia is blocking my exit, but she has
somehow frozen me in place, literally. I can't move
anything but my eyes and my mouth. I guess this
time, 'she' sees me as a threat.

"What did you do to me?" I scream.

"I have a message for you, a message that He
tried to deliver to you yesterday. Go to the house. He
waits for you," Olivia says in the not-her-own voice.

"What are you talking about?" I scream.

"Scream again and I shall make sure you can-
not," she says.

"Let me go!"

The muscles in my mouth clamp shut. I can't talk or breathe unless it's through my nose.

"I warned you," she says. She step up close to me.

What does this bitch have about invading my personal space? *Move bitch, move!*

"If he could be here himself he would, but soon that won't be an issue. When that time comes, you will know him fully, and you *will* give him all he needs," Olivia says.

Olivia turns toward the door as I hear my name outside in the hallway, just outside the bathroom door; it's a male voice with an accent, "Faith, are you in there? Are you o.k.?"

It's Tomas.

The door to the bathroom pushes open.

"Get out of my way," he says, pushing past the two Stepford Sisters standing guard at the door.

"That's the *girl's* bathroom. You can't go in there!" one of them shouts pulling at his arm. The other girl shouts down the hallway, "There's a boy in the girl's bathroom!"

"Faith?" Tomas calls.

I can't answer him. I can't move.

Olivia swipes her arm over me as she twirls on her heels.

"I was just leaving," she says, her dark eyes flashing back to normal.

"Are you o.k?" Tomas asks placing a hand on my shoulder.

I suck in a big breath.

"How did you know I was in here?" I ask.

"Saw Olivia push you in, then I heard you scream," he says.

"Thank you," I squeak out.

"You're o.k., right?"

"I'm good. Thank you," I say.

"O.k. I gotta run, if they catch me in here it might be hard to explain," he says.

"Yeah, thank you, *really*," I say.

"See you around," Tomas says as he pushes through the door. He turns back to me at the last minute, "Hey, you want a ride home after school?"

"No. Thanks though," I say.

"It's just a ride," he says.

"O.k..." I say with a chuckle, "...sure."

"Meet me by the entrance to the gym, my spot is right there. Three o'clock?"

"I'll be there," I say.

Boy was I wrong about him, very wrong—I guess first impressions aren't everything.

~

CHAPTER FIFTEEN

TAKEN

I find Tomas' Civic parked two spots to the left of the gym's entrance, but no Tomas. I check my phone. I'm early. I lean against the building and scroll through the messages that have piled up since yesterday—13 missed calls and 12 voice mails.

Eddie: "Drugstore. 4:00. Don't be late. I'll pick you up at eight."

Paul: "Faith, it's Paul, sorry I couldn't pick up I was on the court. Call me back."

Eddie: "I'm outside the front door, come on out."

Eddie: "What the hell is wrong with you! You trashed the place? Seriously? I told you this was important. You have been nothing but a pain in the ass since mom died. God damn it. I can't believe you did this!"

Eddie: missed call

Eddie: missed call

Eddie: missed call

Kiara: "Hey girl, you called, buzz me back."

Paul: "Me again, call me."

Eddie: missed call

Eddie: missed call

Eddie: "God damn it Faith, pick up the phone!"

Eddie: missed call

Eddie: missed call

Eddie: missed call

Eddie: "This is it Faith, seriously this is it. I don't know what else to do. Where the fuck are you?"

Eddie: missed call

Eddie: "Get your ass home. You better be there by the time I get back or you won't be getting in tonight. I promise you that."

Eddie: missed call

Eddie: missed call

Eddie: missed call

Eddie: "Sorry I lost my cool. Just call me—let me know you're o.k."

Eddie: missed call

Eddie: "Call me. Please."

Eddie: "I got your message. I called the school and they told me you signed in today. Come home tonight. Please."

Paul was right. I made the right decision to listen to him.

I'm going home tonight.

The phone vibrates in my hand, and Eddie's picture pops up on my screen.

"Hi Eddie," I say picking up the call before I talk myself out of it. *I hope he stays calm.* Eddie is silent on the other end.

"Eddie?" I ask.

"You're o.k.?" He finally asks in a small voice.

"Yeah. Yeah, I'm o.k. I'm still at school, on my way home in a few," I say.

"Can we talk, I mean, when you get here," he asks.

"You're home?" I ask.

"Yeah. I couldn't go to work today," Eddie says, "I was too worried."

I want to say sorry, in that moment I want to yell it through the phone, but something stops me— my brain is thinking it but my mouth won't form the words—and I know Eddie is waiting for me to say it.

The silence between us stretches into what feels like an eternity.

Eddie sighs. I'm on the verge of blurting out an apology, when he says, "Hold on, there's somebody at the door."

Eddie drops the phone to the counter, I can hear it hit the marble, and then I hear his feet pad the linoleum. He greets whoever is at the door in the distance. I can't tell who is there, the conversation is too inaudible and the voices too distant.

As I wait, Tomas exits the gym and lights up when he sees me leaning against the wall.

"Hey beautiful," he says.

I give him a look.

"Can't a guy give a girl a compliment? I'm just stating a fact," Tomas says.

"I'm on hold with my brother," I say pointing to the phone.

"At least it's not your Dad," he says giving me a wink.

I cover the phone's receiver with my hand.

"I don't have a Dad," I say, looking down to the ground, thinking about mom, and trying to cover the emotions bubbling up.

"Sorry. I didn't know you lost your Dad too," Tomas says looking crestfallen.

Still covering the receiving, I whisper, "I never knew my Dad. My mom was both. And now my brother is. Big shoes to fill. Best to look out for my brother because he can get a bit 'fatherly'," I say.

"Take your time," Tomas whispers unlocking the car, throwing his backpack in the rear seat, and sliding into the driver's side. He looks like a sad puppy dog waiting for me.

With the phone back to my ear, I push off from the wall and move toward the passenger door. Tomas rolls down the passenger window.

"I'm really sorry," he says in a low voice through the car.

"It's o.k.," I say opening the door, sliding my backpack off my shoulders and placing it at me feet as I move in.

The phone is hot on my ear, but I keep it in place. On Eddie's side, a door closes and footsteps knock on the linoleum as they traipse across the kitchen floor, and I wait, but the seconds grow longer, and still no Eddie.

"Same spot as yesterday?" Tomas asks backing the Civic out of its parking space.

"Yeah, thanks," I say looking up from the phone.

"You got it," Tomas says.

On the other end of the phone, several footsteps sound against the linoleum in quick uneven strides, then stop abruptly with a smack, and then a loud thud as something heavy falls.

"Eddie?" I call through the phone, but instead of an answer, the phone on his side jostles around against something hard and then lands with a clunk.

"Hello?" I say.

"Hello?" Eddie responds, sounding a bit out of breath and disoriented.

"Yes, I'm still here. What the heck was that?" I ask.

"Nothin'," he says.

"Doesn't sound like nothing. Who was at the door?" I ask.

"Faith?"

"Yeah, it's Faith, dude, what is up with you?" I ask.

I wait for his response but he doesn't answer - I can hear him breathing in an exaggerated inhale and exhale.

"Eddie?" I ask.

Then a voice comes through the phone—it's not Eddie's voice—it's a voice that is deeper and raspier with breaks like a teenage boy going through puberty, "Eddie can't talk right now."

"Who is this?" I ask—I can hear the desperation in my voice as I talk.

"I told you to come to the house, but you did not. Now you will," the voice says.

"What happened to my brother? Put him on the phone," I say.

Tomas slows the Civic.

"What's up? Everything o.k.?" he asks.

"What have you done to Eddie!" I yell.

Tomas pulls the car to the side of the road, and puts his hand on my shoulder.

"What's going on?" Tomas asks.

"I don't know, I think someone broke in to my house," I say.

"I'm calling 9-11," Tomas says picking up his cell from the center console.

"Alone," the voice instructs through the phone.

"No police Tomas, he says I have to come alone," I say.

"I don't think that's a good idea. Think about it."

"Alone, Faith—you can bring the boy, but if you bring anyone else, your brother will not be whole again," the voice instructs.

I cover the phone's mouthpiece.

"Oh my god, he's going to kill my brother. What do I do? He says no police, Tomas, so no police."

"Who is this guy, someone you know?" Tomas asks.

"I don't know," I say.

"Keep him talking. That's what they always say on police shows," Tomas says.

"What do I say? I don't want to say the wrong thing," I say to Tomas.

"Tell him you want to talk to your brother," Tomas whispers.

"Where's my brother? Let me talk to him. Please. I want to know he's alright," I say, my throat dry and tight.

"He cannot come to the phone. The important question right now is, where are *you*?" the voice asks.

"I'm coming," I say and turn to Tomas, "Step on it, please, faster."

The phone goes dead, the call disconnects.

"Hello? He hung up on me," I say turning to Tomas.

I redial the number. Busy. I try again. Busy. And again. Busy.

"Faster, please, faster," I say to Tomas, my legs moving up and down nervously.

From behind us, blue lights and a siren sound, and a voice bellows in the air telling us to "Pull over."

"Oh my god—oh my god—oh my god," I say, freaking out in my seat.

"Calm down," Tomas says angrily.

"I don't know what's happening to my brother and we just got pulled over, and you want me to calm down!"

Tomas reaches across my legs to the glove compartment, and pulls out the vehicle's registration.

"If you make a scene, then the cops will detain us longer. Right now you're acting like you're on crack or something, do you want them to suspect something other than speeding?" Tomas asks.

"No," I say.

"Then calm down. He'll write the ticket, and we'll be out of here," Tomas says rolling down his window.

A big burly fifty-something white cop in a neatly pressed uniform saunters up beside the car, and a second officer—thin and younger—moves up to my window.

"License and registration please," the burly cop says to Tomas. Tomas hands both to him.

"Any drugs, alcohol, or weapons in the vehicle?" the cop asks.

"No sir," Tomas says while the cop looks around the interior of the vehicle.

"Pop the trunk for me please," the cop says.

The burly cop nods to the thin cop and the thin cop disappears around the back of the vehicle. We can hear him rustling through the contents of Tomas' trunk.

"Do you realize how fast you were going?" the cop asks.

"No sir. I wasn't paying attention, we were talking. Sorry," Tomas answers.

The younger cop returns to my side and taps on the window.

"Can you roll down the window please miss," the burly cop says, "Officer Burton would like a word with you."

I fumble with the buttons beside me.

"I got it," Tomas says.

The window moves down.

"How are you doing today, miss?" Officer Burton asks.

"I'm o.k.," I say quickly.

The cop stands poised with one hand on his hand gun and the other hand on his nightstick.

"Can you get out of the car for me miss," the cop asks.

"Do I have to?" I answer.

"Yes please, ma'am," he says.

"Go," Tomas encourages me.

"Step over here, please," the officer instructs indicating the back of the vehicle where the trunk is still open.

"Do you know this young man in the vehicle," the officer asks pointing toward the front.

"Yes, we go to school together," I say nervously.

"And is everything o.k. with you and him, you look nervous," the officer asks.

"I'm fine, just had a rough day, and he's giving me a ride home," I say.

"Where do you live Miss?"

"Chestnut Street," I say.

"O.k., back in the car," the officer says.

"Thank you officer," I say and I rush back and close the door behind me.

The burly officer has Tomas' license and registration in hand, and he's headed back to the parked police car where the younger officer is already inside.

"Just stay calm," Tomas says.

"Yeah," I say.

"You're sure you don't want to say something to these nice gentleman about your brother, before they send us on our way," Tomas asks.

"No. No police."

"Guess it's going to be up to me then," Tomas says straightening in his chair.

"Up to you, what?" I ask.

"To be your protection detail," he says.

After a few minutes, the burly officer approaches the vehicle again.

"You were clocked at 20 over the speed limit. In the future, please obey all posted signs. Here's your ticket. Pay by the 24th to the address on the back," the officer says, "Have a good day."

"Let's go," I say rushing Tomas to drive after the officer leaves.

"Hold on, they're watching us," Tomas says.

I grab the seat below me with my hands to stay my anxiety.

Tomas rolls up both windows.

"What the hell was that?" I ask Tomas.

"Which part?" Tomas asks.

"The third degree for a speeding ticket?" I ask.

"It's called being Spanish in a small town," Tomas says.

"Here," he says handing me the ticket, "how much is it?"

"Ninety-five dollars!" I yell.

"There's goes next week's paycheck," Tomas says.

"I'll help you pay for it," I offer because it feels like the right thing to do.

"Don't worry about," Tomas says, "Let's just see what's up with your brother. Agreed?"

I shake my head and focus on the road, counting down the streets until we reach the house.

CHAPTER SIXTEEN

౨

EX VI TERMINI

"Which house exactly," Tomas asks as he approaches the spot where he dropped me off the night before.

"Go a little further, up there, the house behind the two bushes," I say.

Tomas eases the Civic into the driveway, and parks behind Eddie's car. The front door of the house is open a crack.

I jump out before Tomas even turns off his car, and I run to the front door. I hear Tomas calling after me, "Wait Faith, don't just go in. Maldita Sea!"

Of course I don't listen, I need to get to Eddie.

I fling open the front door, leaving it gaping behind me. I don't have to go far to find something, something that stops me in my tracks. To the right, the room is filled with papers floating midair, as if all of Eddie's bill piles are charmed to lift and float and suspend themselves. I take a step to grab the nearest sheet, which looks to be an electricity bill, and all the papers drop to the floor covering the kitchen's linoleum.

Tomas slips in behind me.

"I told you to wait. Puta Miedra, what a mess," he says, "What are all these papers? And what's that?"

I turn to him to see what he's referring to. He nods to the corner wall, which had been obscured by suspended paper moments ago. It's the only open wall space in the kitchen. Spread between the left wall and the right is a message scrawled in black; inky and dripping to the floor—*Go to house to see your brother.*

I stare at the scrawled writing. It's Eddie's handwriting.

"Eddie!" I scream and move to check the rest of the house, but Tomas grabs my arm.

"Wait here," Tomas says, "Listen this time, please. I'll look for him."

Why would Eddie write this? Why would Eddie fake something happening to him? No. *He* made Eddie write it. *He* found me at the drugstore. *He* found me here, but I wasn't home—Eddie was. It's the only thing that makes sense. But what doesn't make sense is the message—I'm here—at the *house*—and the message is telling me to 'go to house'.

Tomas runs down the hall and back to the kitchen, "It's empty. There's nobody here."

"It doesn't make sense," I say out loud.

"What?"

"That," I say nodding toward the wall, "It's telling me to go to the house, but we're in the house," I say.

"Maybe he means another house," Tomas says, "Do you guys own another house?"

"No," I say.

"A relative's house, maybe?"

"I don't have any relatives," I say.

"None?" Tomas seems surprised.

"No, just my brother now," I say.

"You should see my family, I have more relatives than I need. I could rent some out to you," Tomas says trying to lighten the mood, "Or maybe you can come over for a holiday meal when we cram thirty people into our tiny apartment. You'll probably appreciate your small family after that."

"Yeah, maybe..." I say distractedly. I'm trying to figure out this message.

"Did you see any other clues in the rest of the house, anything out of the ordinary?" I ask, desperate to understand.

"I didn't see anything, but then again it's the first time I'm here," he says.

Tomas walks to the scrawled writing, and runs his finger over the wall through one of the drips.

"What is this, it's very oily," Tomas says rubbing the substance over his fingertips.

I step up to Tomas and wipe my index finger over his, spreading some of the oily substance between my fingertips, and in that instance the pocket of my jeans explodes with light and grows hot against my skin.

The pendant.

I reach in the pocket—careful to touch the chain only—and pull out the glowing pendant. In the stone's face is an image against the glowing flecks, faint and easy to miss, but I see it.

"What is that?" Tomas asks.

"I know where we need to go," I say ignoring Tomas' question, "Can you take me there?"

"Give me an address and I'll get you there," Tomas says as we exit the house and head to Tomas car.

I don't have the address.

"Damn," I say thinking to myself out loud. I've been there two times already, but I don't remember the exact route, never mind the address—being a passenger is different than a driver—honestly I didn't pay enough attention to know the route.

"What?" Tomas asks turning his attention from the road to me as he eases away from the curb.

"I don't have the address," I say stuffing the necklace back into my pocket—the glow, the heat, and the image have all disappeared, "Shit, we have to get there. Hold on, I know who to call to get it," I say.

I dial Kiara and get her voice mail, "Hey. I need the address of the house we were at the other night. Can you call me back? It's urgent," I say.

"Which direction should I go," Tomas says pulling up to the end of the road.

"Hold on, one more person to try," I say, scrolling through my address book for Paul's number.

"Take a left to the highway, I think," I say hitting the phone icon on the screen.

Paul picks up.

"What's the address of that abandoned house?" I ask.

"Well, hi to you too," Paul says.

"Sorry," I say, and then with as much enthusiasm as I can muster under the circumstance, "Hi Paul."

"Why do you need the address?" he asks, he sounds slightly annoyed.

"I have to go there," I say urgently.

"Another fight with your brother? Did you call him?" he asks.

"It's a bit complicated. My brother's in trouble. What's the address?" I ask pushing again to get the information.

"I can come pick you up, if you can wait for me..." Paul starts.

"I'm already on the way," I interrupt, and then continue, "I just need the address," I say.

Paul is silent on his end.

"Paul?"

"Who is taking you?" Paul asks.

"A friend from school," I say.

"Which friend," Paul says.

"Tomas," I say.

"Really? And does Tomas know who *I* am?" Paul asks.

"Um, I don't know. Probably not," I turn to Tomas, "Do you know anyone from Raymond High?"

"No, I don't think so," Tomas answers.

"That's not what I mean," Paul says to me.

"Does he know you have a boyfriend?" Paul asks, and then continues, "Now might be a good time to tell your friend Tomas who I am."

Boyfriend? When did he make it official, just now? Not that I'm complaining, under any other circumstance I'd be insuppressible right now, but this is so not how I thought I'd get confirmation. Keep your cool Faith, keep your cool.

"This is awkward," I whisper to Paul on the phone, "He's just helping me with a ride."

"A ride to an abandoned house, he may be thinking this ride comes with a thank you benefit at the end," Paul says.

"He doesn't know about the house, not like that," I say to him.

"Just saying, you might want to be clear with your friend about this ride situation," Paul says.

"What's up with the house?" Tomas asks, shooting a glance in my direction, then looking back to the road, and then back at me and then continues, "And by the way, if you're going to talk about me—and yes it's that obvious—you might as well go to speaker phone," Tomas says.

I put up my index finger to Tomas, telling him to hold on a sec.

"Paul, my brother, is in trouble, like big trouble, and Tomas stepped up to help. That's it," I say.

"I'll meet you there," Paul says. I can hear him gathering keys.

"That's fine, but what's the address?" I push. Finally he gives me the address.

"How long before you're there?" Paul asks me.

I turn to Tomas, "Here's the address. How long before we're there?"

Tomas speaks the address into the GPS app on his phone.

"In one half mile, take the exit to the right," the GPS chirps.

"Thirty minutes," Tomas says, throwing the phone down to the center console.

"That's the guy, the one who just talked?" Paul asks.

"Yes," I say.

"You tell your friend that if he so much as gets a bad thought about you, I'll wipe him from this earth," Paul says.

"I'm not repeating that," I say.

"Give him the phone and I'll say it," Paul insists.

"No. I need help with my brother, not with this," I say.

"I'll meet you at the house," Paul says and hangs up the phone.

Well, my life just got more complicated.

CHAPTER SEVENTEEN

෨

GOING VIRAL

66 Well that was awkward, I'm sorry about that," I say turning to Tomas.

"For what, you didn't do anything. Your boyfriend seems like the jealous type though," he says.

"It's new, we're still sorting things out," I say. My cell rings. I glance at the screen, it's Kiara.

"Excuse me for a sec, it's my friend," I say to Tomas.

He mumbles under his breath, "*Boy*friend,"

"No, now hush," I say to Tomas.

He gives me a '*Are you telling me to shut-* look.

"Hey *KiKi*," I say into the phone, emphasizing Kiara's name for Tomas' benefit.

"You called? BTW I hear there's a reunion shaping up for the old house," Kiara says before even uttering a greeting.

"No, it's not a reunion, and how did you hear that?" I ask.

"Paul called me, said he was headed there," Kiara says.

"I just needed the address, Paul is making a big deal about it because I'm getting a ride there and it's not from him."

"Sounds complicated," Kiara says.

"It is. But listen, Eddie is in trouble..." I start to say.

"What kind of trouble? Is he alright?" Kiara asks.

"I don't know, what I do know is it has something to do with that house," I say to her.

"I don't understand," she says.

"Neither do I really, but it does, and I can't explain it, but I'm headed there."

"I'm in, just waiting on Michael," Kiara says.

"No, no you can't go, this guy is psycho. There was writing scrawled on the walls at home. I'm supposed to go alone," I say.

"What? You're not seriously considering doing that are you?" Kiara asks.

"Tomas is driving me, Paul says he's meeting us there," I say.

"Tomas? As in the dick from your school?" she asks me.

"Yeah, kind of, I mean I kind of misjudged. Listen, I'll loop you in later," I say glancing at Tomas.

"The dick that ruined your first day of that horrid school?" she asks.

"Yes, move on please. We have to focus on Eddie," I say.

"Well, I'm going. You alone is not safe," Kiara says.

"I won't be alone. Tomas is already going, Paul is going to show up...I just don't want to piss this guy off," I say.

"Then you're not going to like this—I thought it was a party and I posted a social media invite. I thought you wanted a big jacked up shindig," Kiara says.

"You did what?"

"Online invite—party this afternoon," Kiara says as if I'm thick-skulled.

"No, Kiara you can't, this is serious, this psycho *took* Eddie and if I don't do what he says then Eddie is in danger, and I think they're headed to *that* house," I say.

"Why that house, it's so random?" Kiara asks.

"Is that the part you're going to focus on, the house? Eddie, he took Eddie," I say pointedly.

"Damn," she says. Now she gets it.

"Yeah, damn, so no cops, no people...I have to sort this out one on one," I say.

"I think you should call the cops," Kiara says.

"No!" I scream

Tomas jumps in the driver's seat next to me.

"Sorry," I whisper to him.

He shakes his head, but the look on his face says he's doubting my sanity.

"Alright, alright, I hear you. I'll take down the invite. I can't have you doing this on your own. If he took Eddie, what could he do to you? I'm going, Michael too—he's added muscle if you think about it—we can stay covert. You need the guys there Faith," Kiara says.

"Fine. Just hang back until we assess the situation. I don't want to set this guy off. I don't know what he's capable of," I say.

Which is a lie, because if this is the *He* I think it is, he's not 'just a guy' he's something else. And I've seen what he will be capable of. I just don't know how long it will be before the vision moves to reality. I hope I get to Eddie in time. I'm not sure what I'm going to do after that. Maybe TheGirl can help, because I certainly can't do this on my own, and I don't think having my friends there is going to change things much, and hopefully it doesn't make things worse. I need the power the TheGirl has, but I can't even transform a simple acorn into an apple, and I don't dare reach out to her through the pendant while Tomas is sitting next to me in the car. If Enlitra is putting all their hope on me, the least they can do is help me understand—give me a fighting chance— or better yet, send TheGirl here. Why aren't they sending her? She knows how to use the power, why are they depending on me—someone who has absolutely no clue—*this* is what doesn't make sense.

Tomas pulls off the exit and I immediately recognize the area. We pass through Main Street with the barber shop pole twirling red and white, and then the town ends and we come to the fork in the road.

"I think it's left," I say to Tomas and GPS confirms my guess by telling us to make a left at the fork. Tomas eases the Civic from pavement to dirt road, following the sign to Kinderkamack Road.

"It's in the middle of nowhere," Tomas says.

"Yeah, that it is," I confirm.

"You guys were out here last night?" Tomas asks.

"How did you know that?" I ask.

"I overheard you on the phone," he says.

"It was two nights ago. I mean I was here last night too. Oh never mind. Here. I think it's here," I say pointing to a driveway that we pass on the left.

Tomas slows to a stop, and then backs up until he reaches the driveway. He turns in. Grass and weeds growing between the tire ruts brush the underside of the car.

"Yeah, this is it," I say as we approach the boulder that matches the car's girth.

"Stop here, don't pull up all the way," I say, "Let's keep the car hidden."

I open and close the door quietly, careful not to make a sound. Tomas slides out from his side...and slams his door. The sound echoes in the quiet.

"Tomas!"

"It's not like he didn't hear the sound of the car driving up, seriously, he'll know we're here," Tomas says.

I sigh.

There's goes the element of surprise.

We squeeze in between the car and the encroaching bushes, and peek around the boulder to survey the house overtaken by weeds, grass, and overgrown plants, with its wooden shutters askew and a holey roof.

"This is the place?" Tomas asks questioning.

"Yeah," I say.

"Doesn't look like anyone is here," Tomas says.

And he's right, the front of the house is empty—no cars—and the house stands silent and dark.

Maybe I made a mistake, maybe this isn't the place?

"Your pocket is glowing," Tomas says pointing to my pants.

The pendant again.

I pull at the chain in my pocket, and the minute the pendant hits the air the abandoned house explodes with a yellowish light—the same marigold light I saw on Enlitra when TheGirl showed me the En between the room and the landscape. Yellow flashes from the decrepit windows, around the branch still sticking out of the roof, and even through unseen cracks in the wood around the main structure of the house.

"What the…" Tomas exclaims beside me as he jumps back and turns his face from the bright light.

"We're in the right place," I say walking toward the house; I can't help it, I feel like a bug drawn to the light.

"You're just going to walk right up?" Tomas ask.

His question pulls me out of the trance.

"No, you're right," I tell him covering my eyes with my hand. Then I yell toward the house, "Hello! Are you in there? Eddie!"

It's then that I hear the clear sound of tires as they leave payment and move to dirt, the tread pulling up bits of ground into its grooves and depositing them back to the earth again.

I turn. There's a car moving down the road a ways, I can see it in between the trees. It's not a car I recognize and it's headed this way.

Please let it keep going.

It slows at the driveway. I move toward the boulder, and peer around it. The car turns into the entrance and eases its way in back of Tomas' Civic, and parks. There's only one occupant and he looks familiar, but it's not until he opens the door and steps out that I see he's a kid from my old high school—Raymond High—but I can't remember his name. He's dressed in jeans, a tee shirt and an open black zip up sweatshirt; his hair is gelled back and he's clean-shaven.

"Awesome light show! This has to be the party place, right," he exclaims.

I move toward him quickly, hoping to turn him around before he gets too invested in being here.

"The Party is canceled," I say quickly, dropping the pendant into my pocket.

"That looks like a party that is just about to start," he says pointing to the house.

"No, Kiara took down the invite, it was a mistake," I say fumbling over my words.

"Hey, Faith right? Remember me, Gerard, from Miss Blackwell's English a couple years back?"

Gerard, that's right, I do remember him, but if I admit I remember him then it will be harder to get him to leave.

"Sorry, a lot has happened, I don't recall," I say.

"Hi I'm Gerard," he says offering his hand to Tomas.

"Nice to meet you, man," Tomas says.

"So what can I do to help," Gerard asks Tomas.

"I don't think there's a party here, man, like she said," Tomas answers.

"What is it with you two, did I interrupt something, is that why you're trying to get rid of me. Oh I get it, a little somethin'- somethin' is going down before the party starts. I'm cool. I can wait here in the car until you're done. Is this a themed party, like a spooky, haunted house kind of thing," he says indicating the house with his thumb.

"There's no party," Tomas and I say in unison.

"Riiiiight. I'm not in costume, I got it. I can run to the store, just tell me the theme exactly," Gerard says.

I look at Tomas, he looks at me, and Gerard is looking at both of us.

It's at that moment that a voice echoes from the house, it's the same voice I heard over the phone when Eddie was taken.

"I said 'alone'," the voice echoes, and a black misty tendril plunges through the window next to the front door, shattering the glass, shooting forward into the air past Tomas and myself and hitting Gerard in the chest. Gerard goes stiff. The tendril pulls back bringing with it a twinkling dust as it slithers back to the house. Gerard falls to the ground. The light in the house flashes brighter and then the house goes dark.

Tomas reaches Gerard first, dropping down next to him.

"He's not moving," Tomas says. He bends down and places an ear to Gerard's chest.

"No heart beat," Tomas says.

"No, no, no, no, no," I say, shaking Gerard's lifeless body, "Wake up, wake up."

"He's gone, Faith. No heartbeat, no breathing," Tomas says.

"I knew him, I did...I just said I didn't so he'd go away. Oh god."

"What's in that house," Tomas blurts out.

"I...I..."

"This is some deep shit, you know that right?" Tomas says as he gets up, his hands behind his head, pacing.

Tomas grabs my arm.

"We have to get out of here," he says pulling me up and then toward the car.

"I'm not leaving," I say through gritted teeth, wrenching my arm away from Tomas.

"You're going to stay here, with that?" Tomas asks pointing toward the house.

"My brother is in that house," I say.

"How do you know? Have you seen your brother? Have you heard from him? There's no car, how would he get here?" Tomas asks.

"I don't know," I say

"Clearly something is happening here that is bigger than me, bigger than you, and I don't know..." Tomas trails off. He turns toward the road as the sound of another car approaches.

"Go! Stop whoever that is from coming down here!" I yell.

"Come with me," Tomas urges as he tries to grab my arm again.

"No, you go. I'll be o.k.," I say. I push him forward. "Go!"

Tomas squeezes around his own car, and Gerard's, and takes off in a sprint down the driveway toward the main road. I turn back toward the house.

"And now we are alone," the voice purrs while a soft light grows out of the dark interior of the house.

༄

CHAPTER EIGHTEEN

CONFRONTATION

"Where's Eddie!" I yell at the house.

"He is here," the voice answers quickly, the subdued yellow light pulsing with every word.

"I need to see him!" I yell, remembering what Tomas said, questioning if Eddie is even here.

I turn back toward the road, scanning for Tomas—he's running and flagging the car.

"Make your choice, your brother or the boy," the voice says. I turn back to the house.

"What?"

"You care too much about these people," the voice echoes.

"I care because that's what people do!" I yell.

"It makes you weak," the voice slithers back, dark and raspy.

I think of how my mom's death made me weak, destroyed me, and I wonder if there's truth to his words, but I will not give him an ounce of justification.

"It makes us stronger!" I yell.

"Are you sure?" the voice asks.

From behind me, the sound of fast & heavy footfalls echo. I turn to see Tomas and Paul both running down the driveway.

"Stay back!" I yell while they're still at a distance away, and then to the house, "Don't hurt them, or you'll never get what you want!"

"I wonder if you know what I want. Very well, go to them and send them away," the voice echoes.

Tomas is yelling as he runs, half out of breath, "I couldn't keep him away Faith, I'm sorry. I tried. I don't think he trusts me,"

"I don't know you," Paul says, leading Tomas by a couple feet.

"Make them go away," the voice taunts, "or your brother will go away."

The house goes dark again; I turn from it and run to meet the boys.

"You have to go. Please. You heard him," I say.

"What the hell is going on? Who is in that house?" Paul asks squeezing past Gerard's vehicle and meeting me in between the two cars.

"More like 'what' is in that house," Tomas says.

Paul gives Tomas a look of warning over his shoulder.

Tomas puts his hands in the air, and doesn't move past Gerard's car.

Paul and I duck down for cover at the back of Tomas' Civic, and Paul grabs me in his arms.

"Are you o.k.?" Paul asks, pulling me in close.

"I'm o.k., I don't know, I-I-I-I," I can't get past stuttering.

"Give her some space, man," Tomas says.

"Don't tell me what to do," Paul says to him.

"Is it true what he told me, or did he make it up so I wouldn't punch him?" Paul asks me.

I shake my head. "Gerard is up there, in front of Tomas' car." I point to the body still crumpled on the ground, the body of Gerard who was breathing and alive only minutes ago. I feel the weight of his death on my conscious.

"You guys have to go, both of you. Gerard's death is because I didn't follow instructions. I can't have anything happen to you, to him, to Eddie, or to anyone else. Please," I plead.

"I'm not going. As long as you're here, I'm here," Paul says.

"Pleeeeease," I plead.

"I can move back, if you're worried that this guy will freak out, but you have to take precautions; keep your phone in hand—yell to me, or speed dial me on the phone if you get into trouble and I'll come running—and no going in there alone. It's a compromise yeah?" Paul says

I shake my head.

I smile at Paul and pull the phone from my pocket, and show it to him.

"I'll call you if I get into trouble," I say.

"Don't go inside," Paul warns.

"I won't. Just talking," I say. He releases me.

"We have to get the body, man, we can't leave him there like that," Tomas says to Paul nodding his head toward Gerard's body.

"Fine," Paul says.

"Hurry up," I say, turning my head toward the house, checking to make sure it's still dark.

Paul & Tomas dart to Gerard's lifeless form. Paul grabs Gerard's shoulders while Tomas grabs his feet. They carry him toward Tomas' car, moving him into the back seat.

"Take both cars. I don't want people thinking there *is* a party here," I say.

"We'll be at the end of the driveway. We're not going far," Paul says. He slides into Gerard's car, the keys still in the ignition, and with his head out the window he blows me a kiss.

I kiss my palm and blow a kiss back to him, and wonder if this is our last kiss.

The boys have retreated, and I'm alone. The house is still dark, Eddie is nowhere, and *He* is here. Now is when I need help the most. I plunge my hand into my jean's pocket, pulling out the pendant by its chain. The center stone is dull white and seemingly lifeless. I touch the center. It does not respond, so I cradle the pendant with both hands and drop to my knees.

With eyes closed, I plead, "Please, if you can hear me, I need your help," and with that the pendant lights up, the oval center flashing with large flecks of red and blue, green and orange.

"I can-not bring you," TheGirl says through the stone.

"I need help," I say.

"He is near, I can-not open the way when he is so close," TheGirl says.

"That's why I need your help," I say, "I can't make the energy work here. I tried."

"You have on-ly tried a little. The fate of worlds rest on what you do, and you have cho-sen to spend your time fo-cused on other things. Did I not show you what is at stake?"

"You did, and I'm trying, but why is it me? I don't understand. Why can't *you* come here—you know how to use the power, I don't," I say.

"I can-not come there, that is why *He* has cho-sen to go there. We can-not use the con-nection, it is for-bid-den and we would not sur-vive the trip, so we de-pend on you," TheGirl says.

"*He* can come here and you can't?"

"Yes," TheGirl says.

"I can't do it. I tried," I say.

"You can, you have not tried e-nough," TheGirl says.

"Help me!" I scream.

"Remember the les-son I told you that you will not for-get?" she asks.

"I remember, I remember everything you told me, and I tried to do what you told me, but I can't translate energy here. I could barely do it there; re-member, you helped me? Can you send help through the pendant?" I plead.

"Ex-treme emo-tion will give you a boost, and a sharp-ness to push your tran-slation for-ward," TheGirl says, "what you fo-cus on is what will be trans-lated. So, think about what you want."

"I want Eddie safe," I say.

"Start with some-thing tan-gible," TheGirl says.

I open my eyes and scan the ground, picking up a twig beside my knee.

"What about this?" I say holding the twig in front of the pendant.

"That is some-thing not liv-ing, so it has less en-ergy—you need liv-ing En to boost the pro-cess, you need to bor-row from some-thing liv-ing," TheGirl says.

"You didn't tell me about that before," I say.

"There is a lot we did not get to, I was hop-ing we would have more time to pre-pare," TheGirl says.

"So how do I do it?" I ask.

"Look at a liv-ing thing, study it's ev-ery de-tail and you will start to see its en-ergy. There's a tree be-hind you, start with that, see its bark, the pat-terns on its bran-ches, the way it's roots dive into the dirt, study every part of it..."

"I'm looking at the tree—it's a Maple tree, its leaves are moving...like that?" I ask.

"See it as if you need to mem-or-ize it, as if you need to re-create it—top to bot-tom, leaf to trunk, every de-tail," TheGirl says.

I study the tree, analyzing all of its parts, pin-pointing details—the rough striated texture of the bark and the moss in between, the serrated leaves with deep green pigment, the way the sunlight re-veals tiny veins stretching like fingers, and the scent of the tree as the breeze moves its branches—earthy, green and somehow honeyed & sour at the same time. I breath it in, smell it—robust and intense—and the more I breath it in the stronger I feel; the effect is both energizing and calming.

"Now re-build the tree in your mind detail by detail, see the en-ergy part-icles that come to-gether to make up the tree, see the tree glow. That is its En. Once you see the En, you can pull from it and grab it. Now de-con-struct the tree, wipe a-way the En that makes it a tree, or re-arrange it so it changes into some-thing else, but re-mem-ber that "some-thing else" has to be clear in your mind, just as de-tailed as the tree was. Start with some-thing simple & small, some-thing that is not living and it will be less com-plicated to create," TheGirl says.

I picture an apple—since that's what I tried to change the acorn into back behind the—and I move the branches of the glowing tree to resemble the shape of the apple, condensing the branches into a small circle that will fit in the palm of my hand, melding the branches together, smoothing the rough bark, and changing its color, all by picturing the de-tails of the apple's design.

"I'm doing it!" I exclaim.

"Keep go-ing," TheGirl encourages.

The stem and the calyx of the apple are the last details, both fashioned from opposite ends of a small blooming branch.

"Hold out your hand," TheGirl says.

I do.

"Now drop the apple into your hand and open your eyes," TheGirl says.

Again, I do, and there in my hand is an apple, just as I had imagined it. I look up to where the tree stood moments ago, and the tree is gone—the space once occupied by the tree is occupied now filled with tiny rose-colored particles that float and bounce in its place.

"Those are the leftovers, the En you did not use. They will be ab-sorbed and trans-lated into some-thing else," TheGirl says.

"Did I just do that on my own?" I ask.

"I only guid-ed you, the rest you did on your own," TheGirl says.

"What happened to the tree?" I ask.

"You took all of its En. The tree as you know it is no more," TheGirl says.

"So when *He* took the En from the people in my vision, did he not take it all? They were dead but their bodies were still there, they didn't disappear like the tree," I say.

"There is so much I don't have time to teach, but you are right, this *is* im-por-tant. At the core of human En it is pure, but once past that there's a less useable en-ergy that is hard-er to translate, hard-er to digest unless it is re-fined," TheGirl says.

"Like gas?" I ask.

"I do not know," TheGirl says.

"Diesel & gas – both from petroleum but only gas is widely used because it's refined," I say.

"Yes, I think it is true," TheGirl says, and then continues, "Try one more, but this time take only a bit of en-ergy from sev-eral things and bring the En into you," TheGirl says.

"Why?"

"So you will not lose that which you take En from, you will not trans-late the whole thing but on-ly take a small amount of En from the thing, keeping it whole but still getting the En you need; you store that En in your body so you can use it when you need it," she says.

I move on to another tree and repeat the pro-cess following TheGirl's instructions, taking only a little of its En. I'm not deconstructing the tree but in-stead moving a few of its En particles toward me.

"Take a bit from many," TheGirl guides.
So I move on to another tree, and then other things around me like blades of grass, flowers, and tiny in-sects; each one with a distinct smell, and each giving bit after bit of energy. I dare not focus too long on any one thing, but instead bounce from one to the next. I don't want to destroy things, only borrow from them.

"Good, because a life can be siphoned dry of its energy and not reconstructed, as you saw with your friend and in the vision I showed you," TheGirl says.

I pause for a second.

"Does that mean I did to the tree what *He* did to Gerard?" I ask.

"Yes, in a sense," TheGirl says.

I stop completely.

"In what sense? You showed me how to take life?"

"You trans-lated the en-ergy into new life, *He* si-phoned the en-ergy and took it for himself. Un-der-stand?"

"Yes," I say.

"That is why I in-struct you now to take on-ly a lit-tle and move on," TheGirl says, "Do not be greedy, do not lin-ger no mat-ter how entic-ing the en-ergy is—it will some-times call to you in it's scent, taste, and tex-ture, much like food does—and if you in-dulge and take too much, you will strip life from life," TheGirl says.

I shake my head, but can't bring myself to voice my understanding.

What makes me any better than Him?

"I must go," TheGirl says quickly, "*He* is lis-tening. Go to your friends. You need to bor-row En from them. Hu-man en-ergy is the strong-est and you will need it against Him. Remember, take only a little. And one last thing, if you try to tran-slate some-thing dead from some-thing living, you can swap energies—the living can be-come dead and the dead alive—so be care-ful. Bring the En to you first. I must go. I will try to help if I can."

And then she's gone; the pendant loses its lus-ter and returns to a dull white.

The light in the house explodes to a brilliant yellow once again, brighter and thicker than before; it pulses now, I can feel the energy reaching out to me, calling to me.

"You have much to learn my child," the deep, raspy voice calls out.

"Where is my brother!" I yell getting up from my knees and facing the house.

"Your brother is here, but he cannot come out to play at the moment. He is not...ready."

"Ready for what?" I yell.

"I need but a short time longer. Then you and I *will* talk."

"Let's talk NOW!" I yell.

"You have something I want Faith. Very much. And I have something you want. An even trade, perhaps. But I make the rules. I make the terms. You are here now, and here you must remain until I call for you. Do not come in to find me, and do not send in your friends. If you do, their fate will be sealed as was the boy's. I will summon you when I am ready. I have business to attend to," the voice echoes.

And then the house goes dark again.

"Wait! Come back!" I shout standing frozen in place, staring at the darkness, on the cusp of running inside. Is he traveling back to Enlitra? Does the portal open every time the house flashes? Is it TheGirl he's going after; she did say he was listening. Or is He inside with Eddie, getting stronger, preparing to take me next? If I knew the answers to any of these questions, I'd know what to do next; I could make the right choice, but I don't know.

It's too much for one person.

But I'm not here alone. TheGirl told me what I have to do. I have to try. I have to get Eddie back. I have to stop Him before he does the things I saw in the vision. If it's me, then it's me, but I need a plan, I need practice, and I need En.

I get up and turn my back on the house, and I walk down the driveway toward Tomas and Paul. As I walk, I stuff the pendant in my pocket. Each step I take I feel my confidence bolstering. Eddie will owe me if I do this, all will be forgiven—all my bad luck and poor choices. We can go back to normal. I can have my brother back. And if what TheGirl says is true that the dead can become alive, maybe I can bring my mom back. It's a hope I can hang on to; it's a reason to stay alive.

❧

CHAPTER NINETEEN

THERE'S NO 'I' IN TEAM

Paul and Tomas are both outside Paul's truck; leaning against the side, arms folded, staring in opposite directions and neither talking to each other. They haven't noticed me yet, and I'm so busy watching them as I walk that I miss the tennis ball sized rock at my feet, the one I stumble on sending my upper body over my legs, my feet doing a funny twist and pirouette.

Both Paul and Tomas push off from the truck at the same time and head toward me.

"Nothing to see here. Stay there, I'm coming to you," I yell to them over the length of the driveway.

"What happened?" Paul asks, raising his voice loud enough for me to hear.

"Stupid rock jumped out in front of me," I say, almost to myself, probably not loud enough for Paul to hear.

"I mean, back at the house," Paul says taking a couple steps in my direction.

I guess he did hear me.

"I'm not sure," I say.

"But you're o.k.?" Tomas asks, inching ahead of Paul as if in an unspoken race to reach me first.

"Yeah," I answer.

"So..." Paul says with his hands emphasizing the one word.

"We wait," I say.

"Wait for what?" Paul asks, now moving ahead of Tomas and almost to me.

"We just wait," I say.

Behind Paul's truck, I notice, is another car; it's not Gerard's because his car is parked on the opposite side of the road, this is a blue Corolla, a car I don't recognize. A girl in a green Cheer uniform and a Raymond logo emblazoned across the front pops out from the other side of Paul's truck, and moves to catch up with the boys. As she gets closer, she targets me with an extended arm in my direction.

"Hi, I'm Melody," the girl says.

"I'm Faith," I say but I don't shake her hand. Instead I turn toward Paul and Tomas.

"Who's she?" I ask.

"I just said 'I'm Melody'," the girl quips.

"I know your name, but I don't know what you're doing here," I say to her.

"She got the invite from Kiara," Paul says.

"So why didn't you send her home?" I ask.

"She wanted to see the house," Tomas says.

"Why?" I ask.

"She didn't believe me when I told her what happened," Tomas says.

"O.k. and what did you tell her happened?" I ask.

Paul cuts in, mocking Tomas, "Oh you know, *he* told *her* about the 'light thing' and Gerard."

"Shut up, man, you weren't there," Tomas says.

"No, I wasn't but if I was maybe the dude wouldn't be dead," Paul says.

"Dead?" Melody asks like a frightened chipmunk.

"Yea, the guy's dead," Paul says to her.

"Someone's dead? You didn't say anything about someone being dead," Melody says turning to Tomas.

"Yep, and now you can't leave because you know too much," Tomas says with a deadpan face.

"Who are you to tell me I can't leave," Melody fires back at him.

"I can't win. I'm just kidding," Tomas says.

"How can you 'kid' at a time like this? Somebody is dead!" Melody yells.

"O.k., calm down. We know," Tomas says.

"You really are a poor judge of when to crack a joke," I say to Tomas, "and I can't believe you two couldn't handle this."

"Are you referring to me?" Melody asks.

Before I can answer, the sound of tires treading pavement echoes in the air. We all turn, looking in each direction, trying to pinpoint where it is; all three of us move our heads back and forth like tennismatch spectators as the sound echoes off the trees. We move toward the road en masse, as if drawn to the sound, but I'm not exactly sure why we'd want to be seen at this point. Then I recognize Kiara's blue Civic as it barrels down the road. She's coming fast. She doesn't even slow down until just before she reaches us, and then she slams on the breaks coming to a stop behind Melody's car only inches from the rear bumper. Michael lunges forward in the passenger seat nearly hitting his head on the front dash. I can't hear Michael, but I see his mouth moving and can guess the obscenities.

Kiara doesn't even wait to turn off the car. She jumps out with the keys in the ignition and the car still running, and runs to me, enveloping me in her arms.

"Oh thank god you're o.k," she says, "Where's Eddie?"

"I don't know yet," I say.

"Who is Eddie?" Melody asks.

"My brother," I say to her.

"Melody?" Kiara says looking at the girl in the Cheer uniform for the first time.

Melody looks at Kiara, and then the moment of recognition flashes in her eyes.

"Kiara!" she screams, and the two of them hug and bounce as if they haven't seen each other for years.

"What are you doing here, I canceled the party," Kiara says talking fast.

"I found *that* out after I was already here, and did you know somebody *died*? Is that why you canceled the party?" Melody asks.

Kiara turns to the three of us—me, Tomas, and Paul, "Somebody died?" she asks.

We all shake our heads.

"Who?" Kiara asks.

"Gerard," Paul says.

"Gerard!" Kiara screams, "Where is he?"

Paul points to the back of Tomas' car. Kiara and Melody tiptoe to the window and peer inside.

"Oh my god; there's a body in there?" Melody screams.

"Keep your voice down, you don't need to announce it!" Tomas yells.

"Who is going to hear her?" Paul asks motioning to the trees and the woods.

"You don't know if there's a house back there, or someone hiking, or walking their dog..." Tomas says.

"There's nobody," Paul counters.

"Fine. But we have to get rid of the body. It's in *my* car," Tomas says.

"We bring Gerard to the police after Faith is done here," Paul says.

"And say what?" Tomas asks.

"That he, I don't know, got hit by a falling tree, or something," Paul says.

"Do you honestly think the police will believe that? They'll believe foul play before a falling tree," Tomas says.

"I don't know, I've never been responsible for a body before," Paul says, stumbling over his words.

"None of us have," Tomas answers.

"We can't just leave the body in the back seat like that. What if someone drives up and sees it," Paul says.

"Exactly," Tomas agrees.

"How did this *really* happen?" Kiara asks. She's biting her lip now.

"For the record, I wasn't here. Ask these two," Paul says wagging his finger at Tomas and I.

The passenger door to Kiara's Civic opens, and Michael slides out, fist pumping the air.

"Yankees won. Wha—what! I had to catch the end of the game. So what did I miss?" Michael says sauntering up behind Kiara. He high fives Paul and ignores everyone else.

"Gerard is dead!" Kiara yells.

"What?" Michael asks.

"Look," Kiara says pointing to the back seat of Tomas' car.

"When I asked if I missed something, that's not what I was expecting," Michael says peering into the back seat, "He doesn't look dead, looks like he's sleeping,"

"He doesn't have a heartbeat," Paul says.

"You're going to, like, leave him there? Don't you think it might be better to move him to the trunk, instead of the back seat," Michael asks.

"We were just discussing that," Tomas says.

"Hey dude, I'm Michael," Michael says extending a fist to Tomas.

"Nice to meet you," Tomas says, fist pumping him in return.

"How can you guys be so cold? Gerard is dead, and you're fisting pumping each other! We have to figure out what we're going to do," Kiara says, near tears.

Michael turns to Kiara, putting his hand around her shoulder. "Babe, it'll be alright."

"Yeah, it'll be o.k.," Paul chimes in, "we just have to move the body for now, and we'll figure it out later."

"There's some super weird shit going on in that house—that's what killed Gerard, something in that house," Tomas says.

"He says the house is haunted," Melody chimes in.

And there's my alibi, what I need to explain to my friends what's going on. A haunted house is more believable than an evil tyrant from another world—of which I've visited. Yeah, that story would lose my newly minted boyfriend and label this already whacked out brain as certifiable. Haunted house works for me. Crazed maniac who kidnapped my brother hiding in said haunted house is even better.

"I can't even explain it," Tomas continues.

Kiara is staring at Tomas, giving him the stink eye.

"Why are you staring at me?" Tomas asks.

"So, you're Tomas? I heard about you, heard what you did to Faith on the first day of school. Low, really low buddy. She may have forgiven you, but I haven't," Kiara says.

"I don't even know you," Tomas says.

"Then let me introduce myself, I'm Kiara, Faith's *best* friend, and if you ever do something that cruel again, I will personally track you down and squish you like a bug. Splat!" Kiara says smacking her hands together.

Tomas backs away with his hands up in surrender.

"Lady, it was a joke, that's all it was. I explained that to Faith and she's cool, it's history. Right Faith? I think we might have bigger problems to deal with right now. Don't you think?" Tomas asks.

"I'm watching you," Kiara says.

"Yeah, me too," Paul says staring at Tomas.

"Speaking about 'watching', shouldn't someone be standing watch, making sure there's no cars coming before we move a *body*?" Michael asks, "I volunteer for that job. I didn't have anything to do with killing the dude and I'm not touching the body."

"You do that, let the *men* do the real work," Tomas fires back, opening the trunk and moving its contents to the sides.

"Hey jackwad, you want to take it outside?" Michael asks.

"We are outside, dipshit," Tomas responds moving from the trunk to the back door.

"Let's get this over with, are you ready?" Tomas asks Paul.

"Yeah," Paul answers.

"Clear Michael?" Paul asks.

"Crystal," Michael answers.

Tomas opens the rear door; Paul slides inside, grabs Gerard's ankles, and pulls the body toward him.

"Get his shoulders," Paul says

Tomas ducks inside the rear footwell sliding his hands under Gerard's shoulders, and lifts. The two boys carry Gerard's heavy, lifeless body from the backseat to the trunk, dropping him in one heave. The body lands with a thunk, and the car rocks on its axles.

"Did you have to *throw* him in there!" Kiara yells.

"He's dead. I don't think he cares if we throw him—not anymore," Tomas says.

"Shut up! It's called respect for the dead," Kiara yells, close to tears again.

Tomas rolls his eyes, slamming the trunk closed.

A wave of silence washes over the group; the body in the trunk is a heavy weight for everyone to shoulder, and I carry most of the burden. Gerard is dead because of me, and seeing Gerard's body tossed into the trunk is a stark reminder of what's at stake.

Gerard is the first death, and he may not be the last—life is what's at stake right now.

My life may not be important; hell I was ready to throw it away so many times since mom died—her death seems more distant with everything that's happened these last three days, but I can't forget, because her death is a prime example of how precious life is. Maybe I need to remember that to keep me focused. It's not just about me anymore, it's the lives of two worlds no matter how different they might be, even if I don't understand my role fully, I have instructions and that's where I have to start. *He* is real, and He has my brother (somewhere), Enlitra is in jeopardy, and I'm the only one it seems who can solve all those things. I don't know how yet, but I'll start with what TheGirl told me to do—gather En. Somehow I have to bridge the topic with the group, even if it is disguised as 'the lunatic kidnapper hiding in a haunted house', because how else do you transition from dead body to by the way I need to grab some of your energy so I can fight this bodyless entity who comes from another world.

"Guys," I say, feeding off of the courage from the pep talk to myself. Everyone turns toward me, silent and staring.

"Gerard is dead…" I start, but I can't get past the lump in my throat that emerges at the word dead. I can't continue, I'm stuck.

"I gotcha," Kiara says, "I think what Faith is trying to say is that maybe we should say a few words, for Gerard. Right Faith?"

Kiara, my hero. Except no one volunteers.

"Fine. I'll say something, because I knew him," Kiara starts, herding us into a circle and holding out her hands for others to grasp.

"We bow our heads, dear Lord," Kiara continues, then looks up at all of us staring at her—"Close your eyes, and bow your heads. Have none of you been to church?"

We do as we're told, and we wait for Kiara to continue, which she does; she continues with a prayer— "Oh God, by whose mercy the faithful departed find rest, send your holy Angel to watch over Gerard. Amen."

"Amen," we all repeat.

Then Kiara strings together a few words on what she knew about Gerard, his good deeds and how we should remember him. And as she finishes I find my chance, the lump in my throat gone.

"Guys," I say, "How about a couple minutes of silence? To remember Gerard."

"*Minutes* of silence?" Michael asks.

"A couple minutes," I say, "while we're still holding hands. For Gerard."

"Isn't it supposed to be a moment of silence, meaning a minute or less?" Michael quips.

"Please. Humor me," I say.

"Michael, if she needs a couple minutes, give her a couple minutes," Kiara says.

Did Kiara just side with me over Michael?

"I know a couple minutes seems long—*I work up some tears to sell the sizzle*—but after losing my mom, and now Gerard—*my voice cracks*—I know I didn't know him but, it's hard for me, I need a couple minutes," I say.

What I really need is to gather energy. I know that, you know that, but *they* don't that and I can't tell them that so please lord, let this work, let me find the connection. Two minutes is not a very long time. Everyone is talking at once now, mostly words of encouragement, although I hear a couple "Michael" jabs thrown in the middle.

"Let's settle down, I think 'silence' was the key word in Faith's request," Kiara says to the group, and miraculously everyone quiets, everyone except Michael who mumbles something under his breath and then sighs.

"Two minutes," I say, "close your eyes." I hope they listen to me like they listen to Kiara.

Two minutes. Go.

I take in a deep breath and turn toward Kiara—her hand clasped in mine—and study her; she'll be my first, and I have to be careful. I don't want what happened to Gerard to happen to her. And I only have two minutes.

I start with her hand, tracing her cocoa fingers with my eyes, the promise ring from Michael on one finger and a bracelet on her wrist, moving down her sweatshirt clad arms and shoulders, all the way down her torso over her jeans to her flip flop feet, then back up to the top of her thick black pixie cut. I close my eyes and recreate her body in my mind as if my brain is a 3-D printer, going over the details once, twice, three times until the 'her' in my brain matches the 'her' to my left.

Kiara's energy starts to form like a wisp of steam rising from her head, comprised of particles so numerous and compact I can see the wisp but not the individual particles.

Now to move it, toward me.

I think about TheGirl.

'Visualize something specific', isn't that what she said?

I picture my body like an intake vent—because it's the first thing that comes to mind and I don't have time to waver—my pores like openings in a grate and my body a mechanism to draw the energy forward. I pull at the air, breathing it in, coaxing Kiara's En forward, the wisp now a rose-colored dust. It obeys, and the En advances toward me. My body is ready to absorb it.

I continue to draw it forward, slow at first as my energy holds to the dust and prepares to absorb it at the same time. It's a lot to focus on, and I don't want to mess it up and have to start over. I only have two minutes.

Kiara's energy hovers over my skin. I picture my pores like tiny mouths inhaling, and will them to take a breath en masse, and it's then that the En assaults my senses with a sweet, fragrant scent that is everywhere, reminding me of lilacs at first bloom. The inundation of my senses is disorienting—my eyes tear up, my sinus' counter with congestion & a postnasal drip, and pressure builds around my face. It's like being assaulted by perfume walking through the fragrance department at Macy's. My head spins. I take in another breath, my intake mechanism on auto pilot, sucking at the energy like a baby to a bottle. My body goes numb, light and buzzing. There's a ringing in my ears. I gulp at the air because I like the way this feels, and I want to take in more, I want to taste it even though I've never wanted to taste lilac before; smelling is not enough because I *want* more. TheGirl's warning echoes inside my head, "...do not be greedy, do not lin-ger."

I search for a way, but my thoughts are clouded by the 'want' and the 'need' for more.

Pull away! A voice inside my head screams.

It's enough to jolt me from the 'want' for a second and in that second I feel the weight and presence of my body; it's enough clarity in the moment, enough knowing right from wrong that I cut the connection from Kiara, sending both sides, mine and hers, flailing like two whips recoiling. Kiara flinches beside me, the muscles in her hand tense in my palm and then release. I squeeze her hand. She squeezes back. She doesn't know I'm the one who caused her to feel whatever it is she's feeling, at least I hope not, but I know she's o.k. in our silent communication. Still her scent lingers in my nose and mouth.

I don't know how much time has elapsed, but finally the remnants of Kiara's energy twinkles and disappears in the sunlight.

Hands are still grasped in mine, and as I look over the faces in the circle around me, I see quiet contemplation, so I continue. They're still with me.

I'll try one more. Maybe two.

"A little longer, guys," I say out loud, hoping to curb any impatience.

Michael is across from me, Paul on my other side, Tomas and Melody fill in the gaps.

I wonder if it works the same from one person to the next, or if it changes based on the relationship, the history, the attraction. For the rest in the group, two are near strangers—Melody and Tomas—but

Paul and Michael, I'm curious how their energies differ, or if they'd be the same as Kiara's.

Michael, my gut is telling me. G*o with Michael next.*

Even though I'm curious to see what Paul's energy is, I don't trust myself, yet, I don't trust the attraction factor and I can't forget what happened in the parking lot when Paul and I kissed. I have to be careful.

I'll go with my gut.

I trace Michael's lean frame—skinny jeans and a burnt orange tee, his hair in stiff submission and his face in a perpetual look of smug confidence. I smell the stench of old smoke and greasy chips on his clothes. I follow the same pattern as I did with Kiara; I study him, then recreate every detail in my head and watch for his En as it forms around him. His energy is less wispy than Kiara's, more like a fast-moving cold front on a meteorological map. I pull it to me, engaging my pores to inhale again, and my question is answered...Michael's En is woodsy & pungent like the scent of a cedar chest, so very different than Kiara's lilac. It feels different in my body too, it doesn't elicit the feeling of 'want' like Kiara's did, instead it's as if Michael's energy is seeping into my blood, grabbing hold of my cells and shaking them awake. I like the feeling; I have more control with this one. There's no craving here. I can turn it off easily, so I release after only a few seconds.

Michael gulps, so loud I can hear it across the circle.

How does it feel to have energy taken from you, I wonder?

Melody is fidgeting across from me, shifting her weight back & forth from one leg to the next, while Kiara clucks her tongue to the roof of her mouth to some tune that sounds vaguely familiar, although I can't place it. Tomas has completely re-leased himself from the handholds, and is moving his hips as if dancing to a silent Salsa routine. I stop and watch for a couple seconds. He can move that's for sure.

I can't get distracted.

Everyone's eyes are still closed—even if they are getting impatient—and Kiara hasn't released her hand from mine, and neither has Paul, even if he does look bored to tears.

Do I dare try for one more—I don't even know what I'm going to do with this energy inside me? I may not get another chance before I face Him. If I face Him.

At the same time I'm curious. What is Paul's En like? I wonder.

I stare at Paul, and before I even realize I'm doing it, I'm studying him, tracing the lines of his chiseled features, his square jaw and chin, bright blue eyes, tapered dark brown hair. My eyes roll over his fitted flannel and jeans, to the bottom of his Timberlands. And then I rebuild him in my mind, and his energy appears different from both Kiara and Michael, still rose-colored but the particles are so tightly crowded that it looks like a bright rose-colored glow around his entire body.

I can already taste his energy in my nose and mouth, even before it reaches me, like tasting the air above the ocean. Instantly my lips dry. I pass my tongue over to moisten them. And then Paul's En smacks into me like a wave, nearly rocking me off balance—salty, briny, and powerful like an ocean current, so strong I *feel* the wave— cold & wet—engulf me.

I gasp for air swallowing water and nearly gag on the salty liquid that pours down my throat. I can't breathe. It's too real. A heavy wall presses against me, my throat blocked by water. My chest burns as my body tightens, desperate to hang on to air in my lungs. I cough the water from my mouth, gasping for air, and fall to the ground.

The connection to Paul's energy breaks.
Hands drop down to me—I can sense bodies, the circle closing in around me—and voices, but I can't tell who is who as the words muffle like I'm still under water.

"Are you alright?"

"What happened?"

"I think she's choking. Anyone know the Heimlich?"

"Give her space."

"Faith?" Kiara shakes my shoulders, turning me over and patting me on the back.

When she turns me over again, Paul's energy is gone; not even one rose-colored particle remains in the air.

Was that really his En or was it me translating it because I was thinking about the ocean?
I don't know.

"I'm o.k," I croak out, "my throat hurts."

There's a lot of noise around me, as if the volume on my hearing has been turned up, but it's more than that, it's as if my awareness is heightened. I hear footfalls moving away, quickly, a vehicle door—heavy and thick—opens then slams, and then footfalls again.

"Water?" Paul asks offering a bottle to me.

I hesitate; water from Paul is ironic. I grab it anyway and sip, not salty but sweet; the sound of my lips sucking at the bottle opening, magnified in my brain.

Someone is breathing heavy close by, short belabored breaths. I can't figure out who, the sound is getting drowned out by the acoustics of nature around me—animals and trees—normally relaxing, suddenly reminding me of a busy city street—the scurrying, digging, swaying, climbing, chirping, rustling, tweeting, and beating wings are loud acoustics volleying for my attention. And I can hear the three energies, plus my own, pulsing as I sit here on the ground; I feel them like shots of alcohol in my blood, nestling in between the ridges of my brain. My pores tingle; my fingertips, toes, top of my head, and tip of my nose burn and the hairs that cover my body pop to attention like tiny saluting soldiers.

And it's then that the light in the house returns, and His voice calls out.

"Faith. You are ready. Come to me."

⋔

WE'RE GOING TO DIE

E veryone is still, unmoving and staring through the trees in the direction of the house. The windows are full of pulsing marigold light; the same light streaming through the hole in the roof, around the limb, and around the cracks in the aging facade. Even in daytime the light glows as if through darkness.

"Help me up," I say to Paul.

He extends his arm, offers his hand and pulls me up.

"Time to kick this a-hole's ass," I say, looking down the long dirt road, trying to sound brave and confident, riding the wave of euphoria from the En inside me, while honestly I have no idea what I'm doing. But Eddie is down there, and He is down there, and so is my destiny.

"You were serious when you said there's some weird shit going on in that house," Paul says turning to Tomas.

"Told you," Tomas says.

"What *is* in that house?" Paul asks turning to me.

I don't speak for a few seconds, debating how to answer, to spill the truth or to bend it.

"I don't know," I say.

"And the plan?" Paul asks.

"I don't know yet, exactly, except you guys are going to stay here, and I'm going to go back down there," I say.

"That's not a plan," Kiara says next to me.

"It's the only one I've got," I say.

"I like the plan," Melody says. Everyone turns to look at her.

"I don't mind watching from afar. Besides, someone has to 'stand guard', right?" Melody says.

The air explodes with a flash of light, followed by His voice, "Fai-eeee-th."

"I have to go," I say turning toward my friends, "Stay here. Don't come down."

I turn back toward the house, and walk at a fast clip.

The sound of footsteps over gravel echoes behind me. I get to the large boulder on the right, stop, and turn, and there are Kiara, Tomas, and Michael, shadowing me. Melody remains behind with the vehicles, arms folded, and hips cocked to one side.

"Sounds like a death wish to me," Melody shouts, "but good luck!"

"Ignore her. You're not going down there by yourself," Kiara says sidling up, interlocking her arm with mine.

"Thought you wanted to *see* the house?" Tomas yells back to Melody.

"I can see it from here. I'm good," Melody answers.

"So you'll watch Gerard, then?" Tomas shouts back.

Melody looks at the trunk of Tomas' car. Her face loses its color.

"Maybe strength in numbers is a better philosophy," she says and jogs to catch up with the group.

"Kiki," I say looking at her directly, "please. I can't let you go down there."

"And why should I let *you* go down there. What makes me any more important than you," she says.

"He only wants me," I say.

"Why? Who is he?" Kiara asks.

"He's the one who has my brother," I say.

"Really? I don't see your brother. I don't hear your brother. What makes you think Eddie is in there?" Kiara asks.

She has a point, the same point Paul brought up earlier. I am relying on His word, but I still have no proof, but *that* gives me an idea.

"You're a genius," I say planting a kiss on Kiara's forehead, then pivoting back toward the house. I take one step only, and shout, "Hey!" You. In the house!"

"Yessssss," the voice echoes from inside.

"Show me Eddie," I say, strong & calm.

"You want to see your brother. And you want your friends by your side too? I can see your thoughts little one," the voice taunts.

"Yes," I say firmly.

"You don't follow instructions very well do you?" He says.

"If you want to get what you want, you're going to have to concede on this," I say.

"Very well. Your friends can come closer, but they cannot come inside," He says.

"And Eddie?"

"He will open the door for you. Then I advise you to follow instructions very closely. You'll *both* come inside," the voice says.

"That's not the deal!" I shout.

"Deal? There is no *deal*. I think I have conceded enough."

"You said we trade," I say.

"Yes. I *will* get what I want, but the 'deal' has changed. You for them. Your brother is already mine. And if you don't comply, they will be also."

"No!" I scream.

I hear Melody behind me, "I'm outta here," she says, her voice like a scared child in line for a haunted house who has chickened out.

"Do not move!" the voice from the house yells, simultaneously thrusting a glowing marigold filigree out from one of the windows.

Melody freezes in place.

"Don't let it hit you!" Tomas yells. "Something like that came out of the house and killed Gerard!" He dives for Melody, plowing her to the ground out of the filigree's path; the rest of us duck and watch the filigree as it circles around the perimeter, fencing us in.

"Do not cross the boundary, or you shall face the fate of the boy," the voice echoes.

Melody is shaking, her hands twitching like a dog with a scratch reflex.

Tomas helps her up, wiping dirt from the back of her shirt and placing his arm around her shoulder.

"It's o.k.," he says to her, but I can hear the doubt in his voice as he tries to mask it.

"I guess we're all in it now," Michael says smugly.

"I guess we are," Paul says.

The yellow inside the house flashes a hue brighter, and the front door opens as a husky shadow sweeps into the light—Eddie, standing in the doorway, hunched and silhouetted in a grayish shadow, five o'clock stubble over his cheeks and jaw. His face is gaunt, his eyes are set deep in their sockets and the whites have turned the color of charcoal. He's wearing a dark blue polo shirt, the shape of it no longer crisp or draping his body in clean angular lines, but instead wrinkled and frumpy. He opens his mouth to speak, and now I understand why *He* will not trade me Eddie—the body is Eddie's, but the voice is not. *He* speaks while Eddie's mouth moves, "You wanted your brother. Here he is."

"What have you done to him?" My voice is shaky and uncertain, the opposite of the impression I want to portray.

"It's time to get this over with, come inside," He says while Eddie's mouth moves.

"I want Eddie too," I say.

"Come inside, we have much to talk about," He says.

"I don't want to talk," I say, regaining some of my confidence.

"Should I make an example, to show how serious I am? Who should I start with? The best friend or the boyfriend?"

"No!" I shout. And I take a step forward, toward the house with Eddie standing in the doorway. Kiara reaches out to me, holding on to my arm.

"You can't go," she says.

"I have no choice," I say.

"Your *brother* is the maniac?" Paul asks.

"No!" I yell.

"But he's standing there, talking to us in that voice. He's the one making demands Faith. He's the lunatic," Paul says.

"No. It's not him," I plead.

"I say we tackle him, there's enough of us to take him down, six-on-one," Paul says to the group.

"What about that gold shit around the yard, how is he doing that?" Tomas interjects, "that's not normal."

"Maybe it's one of those paranormal things like you see on ghost hunting shows," Melody offers.

"I don't know. Some special effect," Paul says.

"It killed Gerard, dude, it's not just a special effect. No, this is some sci-fi, Chupacabra shit," Tomas says.

I don't know what Chupacabra is but I can't just explain this away anymore; Paul is ready to do something rash and Tomas is on the edge of figuring it out anyway. I can't afford either of these guys pissing Him off and probably getting everyone killed. I may already have a death wish, but the rest of the group doesn't have to, and as Michael says, 'we're all in it together now.'

I turn and sprint toward the house—toward Eddie—but Paul catches up to me in a few strides, grabbing my arm and pulling me back.

"You're not going in there alone," he says pulling at my arm.

"I have to talk to Eddie. Just let me talk to him," I say pushing toward the house, dragging Paul with me. I come to a stop at the steps. Paul doesn't let go of my arm, but instead moves his hand down to my hand and intertwines our fingers.

"Together," he says. I look at him and smile, then look up at Eddie, standing above me on the steps. His face is stoic and rigid and he's looking past me. I can't tell if he's spacing out or focused on my friends in the front yard.

"Eddie?" I ask in a whisper. I don't know if *He* is projecting through Eddie from the house, or inside Eddie, but maybe I can get through.

"It's me, Eddie, it's Faith. Can you hear me?" I ask, but he doesn't answer. He doesn't even acknowledge I'm here.

"Hey!" I yell, swiping my freehand in front of his face. He doesn't flinch, but his head does start to move in a slow robotic swivel, targeting me in his sites.

I stare into Eddie-not-Eddie's face, "I need to talk to Eddie," I say.

"How sweet you call to your brother. Is it disappointing when all you get is me?" He asks.

"If you won't let me talk to Eddie..." I pause... "...then I'm not coming in."

"Tsk, tsk, so many demands for someone so weak," He says.

I step up two steps—Paul is trying to pull me back but I still go forward—until I'm eye to eye with Eddie.

"If I'm so weak, why am I still here," I say working hard to keep my voice steady.

What I want to do is turn on my heels and run.

A smile cracks on Eddie-not-Eddie's face, not a smile I would expect to see from him, but a smirk that starts in one corner and spreads his entire mouth, his head tilts, and a low laugh like a slow, deep growl builds until it erupts in a full maniac howl with Eddie's body moving in a jerky fit.

This is not my brother.

"I told you he's a lunatic," Paul whispers in my ear.

"Shut up!" I say hitting him in the shoulder.

The laugh is unnerving me.

The full crooked smile remains on Eddie's face as the laugh subsides, and then He speaks.

"You're not taking me seriously Faith. Perhaps now you will. Say a farewell—eeny, meeny, miny, moe," He says, then a strand of filament breaks off from around the perimeter, whips past the group, and snatches Paul from my side, pulling his legs into the air. I desperately grab onto his shirt with my free hand and tighten my fingers around his.

"Help me!" I yell to the group. I can't tell if they are coming or not, I don't dare turn to see, I don't want to lose focus on Paul.

"Don't let go!" I yell at him.

His fingers slip.

I rush to grab his jeans, shoving my fingers into the belt loops but it's then that he is swept back with a powerful force, fingers leaving mine, and a scream follows him as he is swept into the house. Eddie is no longer on the steps. The door to the house closes. The house goes dark.

"Noooooooooooooooooo!" I scream.

I have lost them both.

"Bring them back!" I yell at the house.

"When I return, there will be no talking. I will not be gone long," He says.

All I can do is stare at the closed door and the dark decrepit house behind it, blurred by the watery film on my eyes and hot tears streaming down my face.

"Noooooo," I moan.

Melody is pacing behind me, kicking up dust and pebbles as she walks, mumbling, "I have to get out of here—I have to get out of here—I have to get out of here."

Tomas talks behind me. I don't see him, but I hear him, "You take care of Faith, I'll get Melody."

Why is it that bad things happen around me? People die; Gerard died, my mom died; I don't have anyone else besides my brother and he might be gone too, and Paul?

I AM bad luck.

"C'mon Faith, get up," Kiara is saying.

I've fallen to my knees on the front steps. Kiara moves to help me up and I drop my hand to my pocket and check for the knife.

I could end it all right now. End the bad luck. End people dying. End the chances that He gets what he needs to bring the end of the world.

Melody screams out, "I HAVE TO GET OUT OF HERE!"

"Get a hold of yourself, you have to calm down, freaking out is not going to solve anything," Tomas says.

I trace the outline of the knife through my jeans.

"Eddie, Paul—they'll be o.k.," Kiara is reassuring me, rubbing my shoulders and wiping tears from my face.

"You don't know that," I answer in a low, barely audible voice. I feel worn out & exhausted.

I don't have the courage to do what needs to be done, just thinking about opening the knife and making the first cut, I want to cringe. I am weak. He is right. How is it, a whole world puts their hopes on someone so weak?

"You are more im-por-tant, and much stronger than you know," TheGirl's voice whispers to me. I look up half expecting her to be standing beside me, but she's not. Instead, the pendant glows through the pocket of my jeans. I push my hand inside fumbling around blindly, plucking out the pendant by its chain. I let it fall into my palm, cupping it in my hand, wrapping my fingers around it. I close my eyes.

"I can-not bring you," TheGirl whispers, "Use the En instead, it can help you get clar-ity."

The pendant pulses in my hand drawing at the energies inside me—the En from Kiara, Michael, and Paul—stirring them to action inside my blood like a cup of coffee after a long night or a shot of adrenaline in the arm; my heart is beating stronger & faster, my brain alert, my nerves heightened.

I feel strong and confident. And ready.

How did you do that?—I think, hoping TheGirl can hear my thoughts as she has in the past.

"En streng-thened you, the pen-dant fun-neled it. It is a-nother way to use en-ergy," TheGirl says.

Kiara lays her head on my shoulder, "What's that?" she asks pointing to the pendant with its spar-kling flecks fully lit.

I look up at Kiara, "Um..." I start to say, my mouth and brain at odds with each other.

"Have cour-age. It is time for them to know," TheGirl whispers.

"Funny story..." I start, knowing Kiara will ap-preciate the facts wrapped in humor.

"All of them," TheGirl says.

I gulp. To expose this truth to all of these peo-ple—some of which are still strangers to me—is opening myself up for rejection, but TheGirl has not led me astray yet.

Time to let the crazy out and hope they'll stand by me.

"I want you guys to see something," I say loud enough for everyone to hear.

Kiara peers at the necklace over my shoulder.

"Can I hold it?" Kiara asks.

"Not now. I need everyone here," I say—maybe a little too direct—closing my fingers around the pendant.

"Fine," she says, annoyed.

I can't take the chance; I know Paul touched the pendant and nothing happened, but I can't take any chances right now.

"Michael! Tomas!" Kiara yells. Then she pats the ground between the two of us and motions to Melody, "sit here."

Melody obeys, lowering herself between Kiara and I, settling in sitting cross-legged with one knee touching me and the other touching Kiara. Meanwhile Michael slips in, hovering above the two of them.

"Sit," I say to Michael.

"Nah, I'm good up here," he says.

Tomas is the only one who isn't coming, he's in his own world walking the perimeter following the filigree that holds us penned in place, and he's mumbling to himself, "We can't leave, we can't get the vehicles, we can't go in—we can't, we can't, we can't—when do we get to 'we can'; we have to calm down and figure this out—I have to..."

"I'll get him," Kiara says pushing up from the ground and walking toward him. "Tomas, come," she says holding out her hand. He looks up, as if surprised to see her standing in front of him.

"Are you here to give me another lecture?" Tomas asks.

"Come, come join the group," Kiara says grabbing him by the arm.

"What's in that house?" Tomas asks.

"I don't know," Kiara says.

"Who knows what's in that house? Do you know?" Tomas asks pointing at Michael.

"I don't know dude," Michael responds.

"How about you, I bet you know," Tomas asks pointing at me.

"Yeah. I do know," I say.

Everyone stops looking at Tomas and turns to me.

"I know what's in that house," I say to everyone, "and what this pendant is for, and where that thing around us comes from, and all the weird crap that's happening to us. I know what it is. I just don't know if you're going to believe me when I tell you."

"At this point, not much *will* surprise us," Michael says.

"O.K.," I say taking in a giant breath. I pause, and then I start slow, "Inside that house...is something...from another world..."

There. I've said it. It's out.

I don't think it's enough, because everyone is staring at me, hanging on to what I'll say next, maybe waiting for me to say 'just kidding' or something.

I continue, "...inside that house is something from another world...a place called Enlitra." I stop talking, letting them take it in, giving them time to process the information.

Kiara looks at me sideways as if trying to figure out the meaning behind what I've said, and she's biting her lip. Beside Kiara, Melody stares at me, her eyebrows pushed up and her eyes like one of those squishy stress toys that you squeeze and their eyes pop out; Tomas has an "I told you so" look on his face and it's as if he's relieved to know that he's not losing his mind, and Michael—I can't read his face, it has lost the smug confidence he usually shows, and instead I see a vulnerability I've never seen before. On no one's face is the accusation of me being crazy, as I had feared. Maybe the timing, seeing everything they've seen makes it easier to believe what I've said.

I continue, "....inside that house is 'someone' for lack of a better word who wants *me* because I'm supposed to stop him, and he doesn't want to be stopped. You all being here puts you in the wrong place at the wrong time, because now you're a part of it too. I *have* to stop him or we're all dead, not just us, but everyone we know, everyone on Earth is at risk because I've seen what He wants to do, what he *will be* capable of doing if I don't stop him. A lot of people will die," I say.

I hold up my palm, open my fingers, and reveal the pendant to the group.

"This," I say, "got me to Enlitra. I've been there."

"What, the What—What?" Kiara says, "Hold the bus, you *went* there? When?"

"The other night, before we snuck out and came here," I start, "...and then again when I went to go pee after Michael pissed me off, when you guys couldn't find me, remember?"

"You lied?" Kiara asks.

"Now you sound like my brother, but yeah, I lied, I covered because I thought you guys would think I was crazy."

"I still think you're crazy," Michael says.

"I appreciate the vote of confidence," I say sarcastically.

"Not because of this though, just in general. This is actually pretty cool. What's it like, this Enlitra place?" Michael asks.

"Guys, seriously, nobody is freaked out about this? I am. Gerard is dead. Her brother and the other guy are inside with that *thing*. Who is next—you, me? This is way too much for me. I have got to get out of here," Melody says picking herself up from the ground and wiping dirt from her backside.

"Melody, please, you already know you can't leave," I plead with her.

"You're weird. All of you are crazy for listening to this crap. Seriously. Alternate worlds and crazy people. Who said we can't leave? Some maniac in a house that's falling apart. This is like an episode of Scare Tactics. Is there a hidden camera somewhere? A film crew hidden in the woods?" she asks. Melody heads away from us, walking fast.

"Melody!" I scream. I see what she's going to do.

"Oh shit!" Tomas says—he sees it too—sprinting to catch Melody before she crosses over; Michael and Kiara jump to join the pursuit, but they don't reach her on time, she crosses into the thin, tensile, marigold-colored filigree and it sparks like a high voltage electric fence as she touches it.

The light inside the house blazes on.

Melody shakes, her body tossing itself around in convulsions; the tensile filigree loosens and wraps itself around her, turning her like a spider wrapping its prey. En leaches out of her, rose-colored dust exiting her body while the filigree absorbs it, and then Melody's eyes roll back into her head. She stops moving; her limbs drop to her side, her head lolls back, and her mouth flops open. The filigree releases her, returning to its prior station—tense and taut—and Melody drops to the ground in a pile.

"Nooooo!" Kiara screams, her hands to each side of her face, and her eyes wide.

Tomas drops to the ground next to Melody, lifting her arm and checking for a pulse.

"She's gone," Tomas says, a look of fear on his face.

CHAPTER TWENTY-ONE

એ

DOWN TO ONE

I can't ask my friends to sacrifice any more. This fight is down to one on one. I will have to face Him alone; he calls my name, beckoning to me in his rough taunting voice, and I know he expects me to obey and I will. I have a plan—it wasn't until a second ago that the certainty of a plan, a partial one, started to form in my head—so I move slowly, purposefully, hoping He will take it as weakness or hesitancy. Instead, I am preparing.

The pendant in hand, I wrap my fingers around it in a death grip, taking in the life around me, grabbing bits of energy as best I can by picturing my breath pulling the En from the trees, the underbrush, and Kiara—since I drew from her before the connection comes fast and with very little work; I picture her, and the En begins to flow. I draw it forward, anticipating Kiara's lilac scent, promising myself I will only draw during the span of five steps as I walk slowly to Him; every time my foot hits the ground I will keep myself in check and when I step for the fifth time I will release. Step One—my head is dizzy as I'm inundated with lilac; Kiara's En more robust than the energy I pulled from the trees and the plants. Step Two—I'm breathing fast, pulling in En in big gulps. The pendant burns hot in my hand. I want more. Step Three and I'm inhaling faster than I can breathe, the breaths are too fast and too shallow, making my head spin and my vision blur. Step Four—I know I'm making a mess of it; there are bits of rosy energy leftovers everywhere, but I can't stop to collect those errant bits, I have to focus on the biggest flow. I should be moving on to Step Five, I know I should, but I also know I need as much En as I can get, and I feel the overpowering need for more.

Which decision is correct—it's hard to tell— do I stop or keep going? Do I take Step Five, or continue to strengthen myself?

I need more, I *know* I do, more is good, and it *feels* good, but then I hear a low moan from Kiara behind me and then she drops heavy to the ground— I can tell it's her because Michael is desperately calling out her name—and I have no choice but to move my foot to the ground for Step Five. I release Kiara, and before I can turn to check on her, *He* speaks to me in my ear—"Good girl. You are a fast learner. Just think, a little more and you would be no different than me. Now come."

And like an obedient subject, my sixth step is toward the house.

I don't look back to check on Kiara, I hear her talking, *and if she's talking she's o.k.*—I tell myself. Michael & Tomas will take care of her, and if I delay, I might not muster the courage again to go inside the house. I have to go *now*. I have to follow the plan.

I clutch the pendant in my hand and search for the newly acquired En in my body; I must keep it close and keep the connection to it fresh. I may not get the chance to reconnect once I'm inside. The door to the front of the house swings open, yellow light spilling out like a lighthouse beacon.

I climb the steps and stand on the threshold.

This is it.

I place my foot over the line—from this world to that—and I go inside.

It's hard to see. The light inside the abandoned house has now turned a brighter brassy-yellow and it's everywhere, and thick, and so very bright I have to shield my eyes now that I'm fully inside. I can barely make out the edge of the old couch with the faded red fabric just ahead of me; it's the only detail I can see, because everything else is hidden and indistinguishable behind the brightness that floods the room, and there's something else that floods the room too, a smell that reeks like rotten festering potatoes forgotten and liquefied into black juice. I cup my hand over my nose but it barely curbs my body's need to dry heave. I twist my head side to side like a bird of prey, scanning through light and dust for the source of the smell, for the source of the light, and for Him, but there's nothing.

The door creaks behind me.

I whip around expecting to see Him with his hand on the door in some form—as Eddie or Paul or maybe as something else—but instead there's only light and an empty space. The door slams shut on its own, and a dust cloud billows up, particles sparkling as the dust moves through the light. I squint, but I can't look away, if I look away I might miss something. I might miss Him.

I take in shallow breaths hoping my lungs can filter the air from the dust, but instead I cough as the dust clings to my throat, pushing into my lungs. The back of my neck prickles.

The floorboards creak.

I freeze; listening and training my ears to pinpoint the sound's direction but everything is distorted, sounds echoing around the space and light refracting in all directions rendering all things in the room invisible.

I freshen the connection to the En inside me, keeping myself prepared...and then His voice rings out like a bullhorn, and I jump.

"Did they tell you Faith who you really are?" He says, his voice ricocheting around the room. I can't pinpoint where he is.

"Who?" I say, trying to keep him talking so I can find him.

"You went to Enlitra Faith. You know who I'm talking about," He says.

"They say I'm their last hope."

"Yes. But did they tell you why?" He asks.

"No," I answer, looking around the room for a clue where he might be.

"Perhaps that is a question you should have asked," He says.

"Why don't you tell me if you know so much about it!" I yell.

"It's too bad they won't come to help you. Did they tell you they 'can't'? Such cowards. More like they 'won't'," He says.

"They can't come, they don't want you to get the portal," I yell.

"And why would I need the portal. I'm already here," he says.

I don't know the answer to that.

"Are we going to work together Faith?" He asks.

"Are you going to leave my friends alone?"

"Your friends are the least of my concerns," He says.

"Why won't you give me a straight answer, just tell me the truth," I say.

"The truth is much scarier than you think," He says calmly.

"Try me," I say through gritted teeth.

"The truest thing I know is before our time is over you'll be mine. Or dead," he says, his steely voice strong and unwavering as if delivering a proclamation.

"Don't be too sure of yourself!" I yell, and as the last word leaves my mouth, I push energy out from my body, with no form or direction, sending it out like a shock wave. The house shakes with a loud rumbling that crushes my ears. My first instinct is to flee—before the house collapses on top of me—now that I've pushed out the blast, so I search for a quick exit, but the door, like everything else, is again obscured by light. I drop to the floor. Here the light is lessening, burning off like a fog, and I can see something materialize beneath me; where the floor should be, wood changing into an uneven surface of pockmarked gray stone. I drop down and touch it with my hands looking for where the surface ends—hoping I can crawl out—but it doesn't end, instead it grows and continues even into the areas still obscured by light. The temperature of the room suddenly drops, the stone beneath my fingers turns cold, and all shaking ceases.

"Where did you go!" I yell, and my voice echoes back to me.

The stone grows from the floor to the walls, sealing out the light as it closes in around me in a space the size of a small living room, most of the light is gone, and all sounds inside and outside grow silent as if sealed from each other.

I look for Him, but he's not here in this small space. I look for a door, or some other way to escape, but there are no doors, or windows, or cracks to show light from the outside; there are no joints or places where the stone would fuse, the corners simply close into smooth rounded walls like an oversized 'rubber-room' made of stone.

He tricked me.

I was naive to think I could walk in here and have a chance at defeating Him. I lost before the battle even started.

"Hello!" I yell again. My voice echoes to the wall and then stops.

No one answers.

"I know you can hear me. Face me you cowardly piece of shit," I yell.

My own echoing words are the only sounds I hear. I am alone, in the dark, in this room.

And then I remember—*I have my phone*—my pocket bulges with it and I feel a jolt of hope as I pull it out. The light from the screen illuminates the air around me, but my hope quickly diminishes when I see there's no signal and I only have 6% charge. I draft a text to Kiara and hope it goes out—*Call the Police. 911. Hurry!*—but the text cannot be sent.

Using the light from the phone screen, I scan the space—it's empty except for me—and then turn off the phone to save charge.

I slide my back against the wall and stay alert, acquainting my eyes to the dark and searching for movement. I don't want to be caught unaware. The pendant and the knife are both in each respective pocket, I don't dare take them out and lose them in the dark—little good the pendant is though, it's as dark as the room—but the knife might come in handy although I don't know if it would be any good against Him.

I keep checking my phone. It's been three hours, and nothing. What is he waiting for?

My phone is dead. *I wonder if I will have the same fate too, soon.*

It feels like hours since I last checked the time, since my phone died. *I don't know what to do with myself. I'm going out of my mind.*

I get up and pace the room in the dark, taking one hesitant step after another, counting 29 steps, my hands and arms outstretched to ensure I don't smack into a wall, then 30 steps, then 35 steps. Is the room changing or am I not walking in a straight line? I sit back down, again with the wall to my back, but this is a different spot, the wall curves here, it isn't flat like the first spot I found. I wait, and it feels like more hours go by.

My stomach growls.

My lips are dry.

And I am so thirsty.

Is it day or night, the same day or another? There's no way to keep track.

I have to stay awake. I have to stay awake, but my eyes are droopy and my brain sluggish. I'm exhausted. My head dips toward my chest, and my eyes drop closed; I feel it and have enough sense to pull my head up, but I know it's a battle I won't win. The air is hot and stale around me. My head dips again.

Maybe I'll rest my eyes for just a minute. I'll need my strength.

A light wakes me up from my sleep.

I shoot up to a sitting position with my torso straight and the weight of my body on my legs and hips, sitting on the stone floor, and there in front me, several arms length away, sits Eddie in a wooden chair with a candle at his feet.

"Eddie!" I shout, getting up, pushing through stiff muscles that don't want to move. I run to him, but stop short when I hear His voice.

"Nice to see you too," *He* says in a deep raspy tone through my brother's lips.

"Is my brother in there, somewhere?" I ask, but all I get is a smile in response.

"Why did you leave me here!" I yell, so close to Him I shower Eddie's face with spit.

"Glad you found the accommodations pleasant enough to sleep," He says, "Now have a seat."

"No!" I yell.

"HAVE A SEAT!" A chair pushes into my legs from behind me, forcing me to sit. I try to get up but an invisible force keeps me in place.

"This will go much smoother if you follow directions," He says.

"Where's Paul?" I ask.

"The other boy? You should be more worried about yourself Faith," He says, "because this is when the real fun begins." He flashes a knowing smile at me, and that's when the stone walls begin to shift, contorting as if making room for something unseen.

"What are you doing?" I ask, watching the altering walls.

"Watch, and see," he says as tiny holes open in the walls—above, around, and under me—and out from each hole slides a crystal, sharp tips puncturing through stone and scraping the rock as they push through. The walls are filled with crystals, too numerous to count, growing longer and fatter until the tips are a foot from me in all directions. Only the space where Eddie-not-Eddie stands is free from the spires.

"What are these?" I ask with a quavering voice.

"I promised you fun, remember?" He says.

"My brother, please let me talk to him, before...please," I plead. *This may be the last time I speak to Eddie, or to anyone.*

"I take it this means you understand the gravity of your situation, yes?" He asks.

I don't answer, and an audible sigh escapes from Eddie-not-Eddie.

"I will give you a few seconds, but that is all," He says, and immediately a black mist begins to seep from Eddie's body, out from the top of his head— massive, filling the room in between the crystals with a haze—the candle flame flickers—followed by a rotten potato stench like the one from before. Black tendrils swirl and reach like fingers toward me, one touches my side—cold as darkness and death—I can't move away, and a pain fires in my stomach spider-webbing into my chest and through my limbs. I can't help but scream, and I do—long and loud; I hear myself screaming until my breath catches in my throat.

"Do not move," He whispers in my ear, removing the finger from my side.

"Faith?" Eddie says in his own voice, the whites of his eyes returned to normal.

"Eddie?" I say through tears, my chest convulsing with breaths as the pain ebbs away.

"What's going on Faith?" He asks.

"I love you Eddie and I'm sorry. I'm sorry for everything," I say.

"What are those things around you? Where are we?" Eddie asks.

"Don't move Eddie, please, just don't move. If you make it out, and I don't, please know that I love you and I am so very sorry," I cry.

Inky tendrils move back toward my brother, hovering around him.

"No, please," I plead, "just let him go."

"Who are you talking to?" Eddie asks.

"You are in no position to bargain," He says and with those words he engulfs Eddie in black mist once again, Eddie's eyes changing back to charcoal, absorbing the dark energy into his body.

You have to fight! I remind myself. I have *some* En left inside me, but not very much, because I used most of it for the blast in the house. I search the room for En. Everything feels dead around me.

"Let the fun begin," He says, taunting me. Tiny lights flick on inside each of the crystals. The room fills with an eerie green glow, and immediately I feel the presence of something crawling into my head and grabbing at the synapses of my brain, pulling at my blood and drawing from my energy, cutting off my ability to act—thinking and knowing what to do but unable to do it.

I have to block it. I have to maintain control.

In that instant, TheGirl's words come back to me, "En streng-thened you, the pen-dant funneled it."

The Pendant, maybe the pendant has some En inside it. I search for traces of the En inside me and move my hand to the outside of the pocket holding the pendant.

I have to bring the two together.

I imagine the En and the pendant united, the En moving in my body, down my arm, and to my hand to the exact point where my hand touches the pendant... now what?

I have to protect myself. A shield...

I envision a bubble around me, a translucent turquoise force field of a bubble, something that will block Him and his crystals. The En swirls in my blood, I surge it forward pushing Him out and pushing energy through my pores and into the air, pooling it around me, expanding it, bigger and bigger until I'm completely surrounded by it.

I stare back at my face reflecting off the shield. My eyes are red and droopy, my cheeks streaked with dirt, and my hair like a wild woman, but none of that matters if I'm dead. *Keep fighting*, I tell myself.

Eddie-not-Eddie flicks a hand toward the crystals—like a king to his subjects— and the crystals expand again in girth and length, the tips of them sharp, pushing in, threatening to burst my protection.

I should have made the shield hard.

The crystals inch inward. I push En out to strengthen the bubble, but there are too many crystals, and He's too strong. The shield bursts, bits of it exploding in all directions. The crystals ignite with a flash of green and pull at my blood, sucking life from it, my skin and bones feel as if they are being stretched, and every part of me burns as if on fire. My hands shake. The muscles in my legs and arms writhe, sending my body into convulsions. My head feels in a vise squeezing tighter around my brain. I see bits of my own rose-colored En exiting my body, moving toward Eddie-not-Eddie. Everything spins. Going dark.

"You must fight," He says.

Why does he want me to fight? Shouldn't he want me to give up?

I reach for any last remnants of En inside me, but it's hard to get past the pain and the cloudiness, but still I try.

I want to push Him out, I HAVE to get him out!

I imagine the fire burning in my body and re-member TheGirl's words—*Emo-tion will give you a boost*—so I focus on the En and the heat and the crys-tals and I meld them all together with anger—energy swells in me like an expanding tornado—and I push it; my blood burns and a wave of heat moves from the center of my body outward. My legs itch. My arms tingle. Heat explodes into my fingers. And I push it out.

My body obeys.

Green beams of light explode forward from my fingers and eyes. It pulls from my skin as it moves, and then it explodes, hot like a giant fireball, green and blue, hot enough to melt the crystals and the chair and the walls and everything around me.

I push some more.

One crystal bursts to my right, pieces of it shattering in the air, moving like projectiles, bits of it lodge in my arm and one in my face. I flinch, the pain adding to what already racks my body, but I don't stop. Crystal after crystal explodes and I try to direct the shards away from me to minimize the pieces that reach me, although a few more still do. I deal with them like I dealt with the first ones. And I don't stop until all the crystals are gone.

"I WANT OUT OF HERE!" I scream, and I continue to push the fire forward, melting the stone walls and the ceiling and the floor.

I have nothing left, the En is gone and I can barely keep my head up. Only the chair under me remains. The yellow-gray returns and I squint to see if I can make out my surroundings, but it's too bright and I'm too tired.

I don't know what happened to Him or to Eddie. I didn't see. I have to see, I have to know. I have to get up.

Slowly I push myself up from the chair, the room spinning, the yellow-gray around me swirling, and I force myself to stand. Strong. As best I can.

CHAPTER TWENTY-TWO

EVERYBODY DIES, NOT EVERYONE LIVES

The floorboards creak somewhere in front of me. I strain my eyes to pinpoint the exact location, but the yellow mist is too thick and bright to see anything. I push my hands into both pockets of my jeans, and grab the knife in one hand and the pendant in the other.

If I'm back in the house I can get outside, pull more energy, and stand my ground. First I have to find the door.

I turn, and search for a clue to orient me. There—several long steps ahead—is the faint outline of the door. I step forward.

"Going somewhere?" He says.

I whirl around in a ninety-degree pivot, and there standing in an area cleared of yellow mist is Eddie-not-Eddie, standing upright, gashes on his face, his dark polo shirt and jeans ripped and torn and covered in green dust.

I'm not ready.

I search for the tiniest particles of En—tidbits, morsels, anything leftover in my body.

"You have nothing left," He says.

"You don't know what you're talking about," I say too exhausted to yell or scream or shout, all that comes out is a tiny voice swallowed up by the mist.

"But I do. Everything I do has a purpose, and everything we have done together in this little reunion has led to this moment. Just as I had planned," He says.

I have nothing—nothing to say, nothing to do, not even the energy to continue to stand. I slump to the floor, still facing him, upright but sitting to conserve the little strength I have left.

"Very good. As I said, you're a fast learner," He says.

"Why do you keep saying that? I'm not learning anything from you," I say.

"But you are, you always have been," He says, "but don't worry, we'll be finished soon, very soon."

The brightness of the room dulls and the brassy-yellow mist thins in the space between us. The house's decaying living room begins to take shape once again—the old couch with the faded red fabric, the windows with white chipping paint around the frames, and the front door in full definition...and voices & shouts from the other side of the door, fists and palms pounding sending dust swirling.

I move to get up from the floor.

"Stay where you are," He says, "or you will miss the surprise I have for you."

I scour the room with my eyes—*there's got to be something here.*

The mist thins even more, clearing the space around the front windows and the bookshelf with its oddly preserved books. On the other side of the bookshelf, on the floor, are a pair of outstretched legs dressed in blue jeans and unlaced Timberlands.

"Paul!" I shout. He doesn't respond and his legs don't move.

Kiara, Tomas and Michael scream my name outside the house.

I turn my head toward the door.

"If given the choice, who would you choose?" He asks.

The door swings opens, and my friends pour into the doorway and stop, frozen in place.

A smile spreads on Eddie-not-Eddie's face.

"All of your friends are here, Faith, so what are you going to do? Are you going to run and leave them behind? Are you going to 'take a stand' against me to save them? Or you could just give up, and then all will be lost—you, them, the world. So which is, what do you choose?"

"I choose for you to go away, leave and never come back," I say looking to my friends, checking for signs of life; they are stopped mid-motion but still breathing.

"This is not Hollywood, Faith; this is not a movie where you simply wish something and it comes true. That's not how this works. You have to fight. *Show* me what you've got," He says.

"One minute you want me to give up and the next you want me to fight? Explain to me how this works?"

"You need to be controlled, and it's not what I 'want' from you Faith, it's what I 'need' from you, and unless you fight I cannot get it."

"So if I fight you, you get what you want..."

"Need. It's what I 'need' Faith, not what I want,' He reminds me.

"Fine, you get what you 'need', but then if I don't fight I lose what I 'need'," I say, "So it's a lose-lose for me."

"If we work together, you will not lose anything," He says.

"I will lose myself, and I will lose everything I care about," I say.

"You don't trust me?" He asks.

"No! Why should I?" I yell, "If I make a choice, you're going to take what you want anyway," I say.

"You must understand, I do not *want* to hurt you Faith," He says, "but sometimes hurt is the only language that resonates truth."

"Truth? What truth? I don't even know you."

"Ah, but there you are wrong. You do know me, and I have only always told you the truth. It is the others who have told you lies. I thought you would have seen that by now," he says.

"Then answer me this one question, and answer it honestly, how the hell can you say I know you. *That* is a lie," I say.

"You have forgotten so much since I last saw you," He says, "Perhaps this will help you remember."

Eddie-not-Eddie extends a hand and upturns his palm; from the center one single strand of black ink spirals into the air and makes its way toward me, the other end still connected to Him. I scoot backwards on the floor.

"Do not move," He says. I stop.

The inky strand moves toward me, and then hovers a foot in front of me.

"Extend your hand," He says.

"Is this some kind of trick?" I ask, keeping my hand on the floor.

"If it is, do you think I would tell you?" He says sarcastically, "Put out your hand or I'll pick off another one of your helpless friends."

I look to my friends just inside the front door, still frozen in place, and I drop the knife on the floor and put my hand in the air.

"Palm up," He says. I obey, and instantly the black strand drops its end to my palm and connects like an electric cord.

Voices sound in my head instantly—my own and my mom, and another I don't recognize, a man.

"Who is that?" I ask.

"Close your eyes, it will be better to see what you hear," He says.

"No." I say. I'm not leaving myself completely defenseless. I'm not *that* stupid.

"Very well," He says, and an image flashes in front of my eyes like a television screen. It's me as a child, maybe six or seven sitting with my mom on two giant brassy-colored pillows. The room we're in is sparse—only us and the pillows—windowless and door less, the walls and floor and ceiling looking like solidified butter. And there's a man, not really a man but a noncorporeal body, more like an outline of a body, standing at a distance, observing.

"What is this," I ask as the image fades and the inky strand retracts back to Eddie-not-Eddie.

"A memory," He says.

"A memory? It can't be a memory because I don't remember it," I say.

"You'll find you have many memories hidden inside you, this is but one of them," He says.

"Who is the man?" I ask.

There's a pause, and then He answers, "Me."

"You're tricking me. I have never met you before. It can't be a memory if I don't remember it," I say urgently.

"Did you never wonder why your mother never spoke of your father?"

"He was a loser, that's why," I answer.

"No. Because you don't have a father, Faith. You don't even really have a mother..."

"I have a mother!" I yell.

"Had," he counters.

"Shut up!" I yell, tears streaming down my cheek.

"She outlived her usefulness. I don't want the same fate for you Faith, but if you continue to disobey me, I will have no choice," He says.

"No. My mom died of cancer."

"Did she? Or is that what the doctors were lead to believe?" He says.

"I don't understand. Are you saying YOU killed her?"

"My one flaw with you is that I let you feel too connected to this world...but enough of this already, I lost you for too many years and now it's time to move on," He says, "It's time for one last game, Faith, and this one will give me what I've come for."

He waves a hand and continues, "By all means, friends of Faith, come in," he says, releasing Kiara, Tomas, & Michael from their suspended animation.

Kiara rushes forward, screaming my name.

"Stay back, Kiki! All of you!" I yell with my palm out, indicating for them to halt.

I get up from the floor, stand, and face Eddie-not-Eddie.

"What *is* it you have come for?" I ask.

"The power I hid inside you, it's time to bring it forward. It's time to use it," He says.

"So you can take over the world? If you ask me that sounds more Hollywood than anything else."

"No. This world is not my big life's plan. I would have thought you figured that out by now too. Earth is simply a stepping stone to bigger things. The universe is a big place Faith, and no one will miss this planet when it is gone. You think too much of this place. Next time, I will have to tweak that a bit," He says.

"There will be no next time!" I shout.

"Run!" I shout to my friends, but the front door slams shut blocking their exit. Tomas darts for the door, jiggling the doorknob, which falls apart in his hand.

"It won't open!" he yells.

Michael grabs Kiara's hand and pulls her to the hallway.

Tomas darts after them. "Come on Faith!" Tomas yells as he turns the corner.

I don't follow Tomas, or run; I stand tall & straight, and face Eddie-not-Eddie. I face *Him*.

"I'm not running," I say.

"I didn't expect you to. Had you run I would have been disappointed," He says.

Feet shuffle in the hallway, I turn my head and see Tomas peeking around the entryway, ducking behind the wall.

He whispers—"Come on!"—and extends his hand in my direction, which gives me an idea.

I need En.

"Take this," I whisper tossing him the jack-knife, and dividing my focus between the pendant in the other hand and Tomas, never letting my eyes leave Him for a second. I pull at Tomas' energy, bringing it toward me, my body feeding on it before it even reaches my pores—pine needles and sap—I feel a jolt in stamina and strength, and I pull some more until I hear Tomas yelp from around the other side of the wall, and I release.

"Now go!" I yell to Tomas.

En swirls below the surface of my skin; my fingers, hands, and arms tingle as I move En down into my hands, concentrating it so I can mold it into something usable—*fire, and this time it's not the crystals that are my target*—I focus all thoughts on hot flames in the palms of my hands...and there they are—green as the taffeta dress I wore to junior prom—flames licking the air like miniature camp-fires in my hands. I push the two fires together, pressing them into a sphere forcing the outermost flames to chase the flames in front until the sphere is fully formed—heads connecting to tails, caging the rest inside, the power of a roaring fire concentrated in a ball between my palms.

If I can scare Him out of Eddie's body, and then blast him while he's outside, maybe I have a chance at defeating him.

I pinpoint a spot to the left of Eddie-not-Eddie's right foot and send the fireball forward; it crackles as it soars, but just before it hits, He commands my brother's body to twist in a backwards bow—a move both athletic and unnatural—launching his body into the air and out of the vicinity of the blast.

The fireball hits the floor splintering the wood and sending fragments into the air like projectiles. I drop and duck into the crook of my arm; fragments pummel my arms and legs, ripping past my clothes and into my skin.

I scream out in pain.

Fragments continue to hit the ceiling and walls, then drop to the floor like wooden rain.

And then, quiet.

I unfold from my safe position, ready to target Him with another volley, but Eddie is gone, and *He* is gone. My stomach clenches.

Everything is eerily quiet.

There's a gaping hole in the floor, the wall is scarred with green soot & splintered wood, and the window closest to the damage is blown out with glass shards on the floor and some jagged pieces of glass still attached to the frame; pieces of wood and glass are strewn around the front yard on the gravel and lodged in the vegetation.

Brassy-yellow mist lingers in the air, now thinned enough to see most of the space in the room and Paul's legs motionless behind the bookshelf. I launch myself toward Paul; his head is lolled to the side, safely tucked behind the back of the bookshelf, which probably saved his life—several pieces of wooden shrapnel are lodged in the wall and scattered over the floor and over his body; a wooden stake is stuck through his thigh and another in his shoulder. I drop down to him.

"Paul!" I yell, shaking him by the one part of his body that seems safe—his right shoulder.

He doesn't react. I move two fingers to his neck and check for a pulse. He's alive.

Thank god for minor miracles.

I pull him by the arm, testing his body weight. I don't think I can carry him, but maybe I can drag him and get him outside, which seems like a safe precaution, but just as I pull hard enough to straighten his body, something moves at the edge of my peripheral vision. I scurry my legs to the side releasing Paul back to the wall, and turn just in time to see a hand flick the air as if guiding a wand to tap a magician's hat. Something fiery is flying from Eddie-not-Eddie toward me, gunmetal gray tinged with blue that ripples in the air like heat rising except its moving forward and not up, and it's FAST.

I am slow to move, too slow, and the gunmetal fire grips me like a hot hand. I push at it, trying to free myself. My efforts only constrict the energy leaving me less and less space until I am wrapped so tightly in its hold I'm unable to move...until He decides that I should, and He flings me up into the air.

My legs lift from the ground, my body pushes upwards until my head hits the ceiling. I flail, arms and legs desperate to gain leverage, until I'm squished to the ceiling like a specimen between microscope slides. All I can do is grope the ceiling blindly; the old wood disintegrates between my fingers. And then He releases me. I tumble forward mid-air. He grabs me again and holds me hanging upside down; blood rushes to my head, and dizziness follows. The upside down room spins. And He watches me through Eddie's body from below with a smile, then jerks me backwards, flinging me quickly through the air. My back hits the opposite wall, and then my head. Hot breath spills out of my mouth as my lungs compress on impact. Bits of decayed wood and dust shake from above, raining down around me.

He releases me. I drop, my elbow hits the floor first with a crack followed by the full weight of the rest of my body crumbling on top.

"You son of a bitch!" I scream in a thin voice, exhausting the last of my strength. Short, rapid gasps are all I can manage, and my elbow feels broken; when I move my arm, pain shoots out to my hand and up my shoulder. I roll onto my back.

I have to get up, but I can't.

"Faith! Over here!" Tomas yells, looking at me from around the corner.

"Get out of here Tomas," I barely croak out.

"Come on, we can get out the back window!" he yells.

The back window. They can get out.

"Go. You three get out!" I yell to him.

"C'mon!" Tomas yells again, his arm outstretched to me.

"Come, come, come out to play," Eddie-not-Eddie says in a deep sing-song taunting voice, grabbing Tomas and pushing him forward with an invisible force extending from his hands. Tomas skids across the main room.

"Leave him alone!" I yell through big breaths, still on my back on the floor.

I force myself up onto my stomach, and then up to my good arm inching my way up to my legs, shaky and weak.

Tomas flies into the air.

Desperate for leverage and a spike in energy, I try something I should have tried from the beginning. Why I didn't think of it until now I don't know. I search the room for the largest pocket of yellow—a place where the mist is still thick and the color bright—and I pull the air toward me the same way I pulled the En from my friends—imagining my pores like intake fans sucking it forward—and immediately I can tell my intuition is correct. The brassy mist is full of En.

The hairs on my body stand at attention as I draw the yellow to me; it's oily on my skin and smells like crushed nuts and coconut. This is not En from Enlitra—although it looks similar—it can't be, this has character and body while the En from Enlitra was bland, filtered, processed—as if not yet infused with any individualizing attributes. But if not from Enlitra, where did all this come from? Drawn from the trees and animals maybe...or people? What if Gerard and Melody's energies are mixed in here?

I could be drawing the energy of the dead into me. I shudder as I think about it.

But I have no choice.

Tomas is now pinned upside down to the wall above the broken window, shards of jagged glass protruding menacingly just below his head. If He releases Tomas, the glass will kill him.

I pull at the En quickly, half into my body and pooling the rest at my hands. There's no time to invest in 'trying' something new, I have to go with what I already know works.

"Tomas. Are you with me?" I ask, already feeling the strength of the En filtering into me.

"Yeah," he says feebly, his voice thin and squeaky.

"Promise me something; when I get you free, you'll run to the back and out the window, and make sure Kiara & Michael get out too," I say, dividing my attention between him and the energy I'm molding in my hands.

"They should already be out," Tomas says, his voice full of fear though he's trying to hold it together, "Michael was lifting Kiara to the window when I left them."

"Why didn't you go with them?"

"I had to tell you there was a way out," he says.

"Promise me you'll get to the back and out," I say again.

"What about you?" he asks, his eyes trained on the glass below him.

"Promise me!" I yell.

"I'll get to the back," he says.

"And..." I say.

"And, I'll get out the window," he says.

"Good. I'll give you a couple seconds warning but that's it," I say.

"Warning for what..." he starts, moving his head up to look at me.

"You'll see," I say.

"And you, you have to get you out too," Tomas says, "...promise *me*, that."

"I'm going to try," I say, priming the fireball in my hands, and then yelling to Tomas with his couple second warning—"Now!"

I push the ball of energy forward, targeting the wall below Tomas, leading the fireball toward the glass; I visualize the shards pulverized, fiery fingers of the fireball's perimeter scooping the glassy particles into the center of the circle...and it obeys, my fireball does as is commanded, clearing the glass from under Tomas' head and containing the debris.

I blindly send a second fireball, quickly made, in the other direction toward Eddie-not-Eddie. There's a whoosh of air and then Tomas plunges to the floor in front of me, curling to protect his head as he drops, falling on his shoulders with a thud.

"Go!" I yell to him.

He gets up and runs, just as he promised, but he stops in the hall at the doorway looking back at me.

"Go!" I yell again. He stares at me for a second, and then turns and runs, disappearing around the corner.

I scan for Eddie-not-Eddie and find him by the front door, as if blocking it; perhaps he thinks Tomas might make a dash for it, or he thinks I will.

"You told me I would either be yours, or dead. So which is it going to be?" I say to him calmly, hoping to focus his attention on me and away from Tomas.

"I'm not the one making that decision, it's you Faith; if you agree to work with me then it's the first choice, if you disobey me then it's the second," He says, "so far you're not being very obedient, and there are consequences for that."

"Are there consequences for being an asshole?"

"I see you haven't lost your humor. We'll see how long that lasts," he says.

"We'll see how long *you* last," I counter.

I don't know where I get off thinking I'll be the victor in this scenario, my track record so far puts me far from winning this battle, but I can't give up, there's too much at stake.

I squeeze my hands into fists, slowly pushing En into the center of each, imagining two fiery tennis balls with En building inside each one, ready to explode.

My blood pulses as the energy flows...

...heat in my palms...

...skin itching...

...hair at the nape of my neck standing stiff.

Glowing circles surround each hand. I open them, one by one, to allow the balls to grow.

Eddie-not-Eddie takes two steps forward. I focus all the energy to my palms, and in a fluid, quick movement, I shoot my hands toward Him. Two fireballs whiz through the air trailing long green tails and emerald flashes. The air in the room crackles and stirs with electricity. I hold my breath. Every second ticks like a minute.

He remains still, he doesn't charge Eddie's body to move as he had before, this time he doesn't react at all and yet I know he sees what is approaching. I watch his charcoal eyes track the fireballs as they move toward him—closer, and closer, and closer—he's still not moving. And then Eddie-not-Eddie's eyes change, the dark color replaced with normal pigment, the whites to white and the pupils to brown. He looks confused.

"Eddie?"

"What the hell is that?" he shouts with a perplexed expression that quickly turns to fear.

"Eddie! Move!" I yell.

He doesn't move. I don't know if he's frozen in fear or if he is unable to.

I search for the energy I've released, trying to connect to the fireballs that are on a collision course with Eddie, but I can't stop them, they are too far from me and going too fast. I swipe my hand trying to move them off course but they don't budge.

"Move Eddie, move! Move!" I shout.

A burst of green explodes in the air. There's a smell of sulfur and burning flesh. The house shakes and debris slams the wall. I lose Eddie behind the flash but hear his body hit the floor followed by an agonizing scream. I run to the sound, covering my head with my hand to protect against falling debris, and ducking around pieces that have already fallen.

Eddie is writhing on the floor; his clothes, skin, and hair are charred and his polo shirt and jeans ripped into shreds. He's holding a hand over a fleshy wound between his hip and ribs with blood running down his side and onto the old wood under him. He's screaming, and twisting as if to escape the pain, but there's no escape, his flesh is burning and his movements are exacerbating the agony. His screams are relentless.

"It hurts!" he yells in between howls.

I drop down next to him. He's sobbing now.

I feel helpless and responsible.

I *am* the one who did this to him.

I pull pieces of his shirt from his lacerated flesh in between his writhing twists. He's losing blood, and I have to stop the bleeding. I strip down to my bra and press my sweatshirt hard to the wound, which sends him into another fit, his body moving to escape the pressure, his screams reaching a crescendo until he just stops...screaming and moving. I look up as his head lolls backwards and his body relaxes against the wall. I grab his wrist and check for a pulse—he has one—then I put my hand in front of his mouth to make sure he's breathing, which he is.

I have to get him out of here and to a hospital. Surveying the room, I look from Eddie to Paul—still prone on the floor beside the bookcase—and realize

I now have two bodies to drag out of here, and Him to contend with.

Where is He anyway?

He's not inside Eddie; maybe he's in the air in that inky black form, but I don't see him; maybe he moved to another room.

Boys out to safety, then I'll find Him and kick His ass.

I drop down to Eddie and loop my arms under his armpits, and pull him up from the wall, but he's too heavy for me to carry. I drop him back down to the floor where he slumps like dead weight.

Is he still breathing?

I place my hand in front of his mouth, and hot breath hits my palm.

I can't lose him.

I kiss his cheek and turn, kicking debris and pieces of glass out of the way. I can drag him—in fact I'll probably have to drag them both—I don't want to leave either one alone for too long, so one to the door then I'll get the other one; then one *through* the door and then the other...and then I'll burn the house down—*I'll burn Him down.*

Still no sign of Him anywhere in the room.

Kneeling next to Eddie's limp body, I wrap the sweatshirt around his torso and tie it tight to further stanch the bleeding and protect the wound. I grab the opposite arm and pull. He's heavy but moving, and no matter how tired I am, I'm getting him out. I heave, and pull, and slip a couple times on the fine dust that coats the floor, but finally I get him to the front door, and I prop him up against the wall.

Now to get Paul. I turn, and that's when I see Tomas outside the front window—the one with the glass blasted out. Tomas is ducked down, with only the top of his head and his eyes showing inside the glassless window frame.

"Psst," Tomas sounds, trying to get my attention.

"What are you doing?" I whisper.

"I can help, with Paul and Eddie." I see his eyes rest on bra adorned chest, and then quickly move back to my face.

My first reaction is to tell him to just get out of here, to run, but then I think about the plan. Tomas could get Eddie and Paul away from the house. He could get them both to the hospital. I head to the window.

"O.k. But you're not coming in," I whisper, "Eddie is at the front door. I'll open the door and you drag him out".

"You sure that *thing* is not inside him?" Tomas asks, fear oozing from his voice.

I shake my head.

"I'll get Paul. Same deal. Got it? Then you have to get them away. Get them to the cars, get them to the hospital. What about Kiara & Michael, they got out?" I whisper.

"I haven't seen them. I assume they got out," Tomas says.

"You saw them going out the window, right?" I ask.

"Yeah," Tomas says.

"Alright. Let's do this fast, meet you by the door," I whisper and head in that direction.

The second my fingers slide in the hole where the doorknob once was, the air inside the house reverberates with His voice.

"You are NOT leaving," He bellows.

I ignore him, and pull the door open.

"Tomas, grab him!" I yell pulling Eddie's arm and extending it to Tomas through the door. Tomas grabs Eddie, and pulls him over the threshold onto the steps. The second Eddie's legs cross the opening of the door, the door slams shut.

"Tomas, go!" I yell through the door, and I turn toward the center of the house.

Two feet in front of me stands Paul, but like Eddie before him, I can tell he's not my Paul, not 100%—his eyes are charcoal and his face is emotionless.

"Get out of him!" I yell running toward Paul, and when I'm close enough to touch him I pound on his chest.

"If we are to work together Faith, then you will have to leave these petty relationships behind. You are too attached. I left you alone too long in this world without guidance, and now you think you are just like them, but you're not," He says.

"I'm not like you!" I yell.

"But you are, my pet. Do you think just anyone can pull energy from the living like you can do? No. It takes someone with a very special gift to do it, and where do you think that gift came from? Oh...but let us not dwell on the wheres and the whys—instead let's *explore*, shall we.

I don't have a Plan B—what do I do?

Convince him you are with him. Buy time.

"O.k." I say.

"O.k. as in you are ready to accept your destiny?" He asks.

I shake my head yes.

"Verrrrrry good. Are you ready to say goodbye to these meaningless shells you call your friends?" He asks.

"Yes. But one last request, please, let me say a proper goodbye. You gave me that with Eddie, give it to me with Paul. Please."

"It shouldn't be necessary," He says angrily.

"It's what *I* need. Do you want me to be obedient?" I ask.

"Very well," He says.

"So give me back Paul, but give him back to me whole and conscious," I say quickly.

"You will need to get past this attachment, Faith, but very well, say your goodbyes—it *is* the last time you will see any of them," He says seeping out of Paul like an inky ocean mist. He doesn't go far, He hovers just over Paul's head, as if waiting.

"Some privacy, please," I say to his inky form in the air.

He slithers around quickly in the air as if annoyed or impatient, then moves away from Paul but not before rushing around my head, amorphous and inky and sounding like a current through an electrified fence, hissing and buzzing. The sound of him fills the room. It's a warning.

My head spins like a Tilt O' Whirl. I feel every ache, every battered and bruised part of my body, every gash in my skin, and the pain pounding in my elbow, and still there's hope, *this* is my chance.

Paul stares at me, his face wan and confused. I move my face close to his.

"This is for you Paul, this is goodbye and I love you," I say, the words spilling from my mouth. I trace the lines of his mouth with soft kisses, and then press my mouth full to his. I press my lips and give him a goodbye kiss, a kiss charged with emotion—fueled by longing, anger, sadness, guilt, and every other emotion that has bubbled inside me over the last few months, all there in one kiss.

And that is part of the plan.

My whole body ignites with warmth. Paul comes alive, his mouth begins to move—working his lips over mine—until he takes the lead playfully grabbing at my lips with his teeth and tongue, the intensity of his kiss growing, his hands pressing against my back and then slipping down to grab my ass. I let him take the lead; as we kiss, I search Paul for En and draw it forward.

The tingle starts first in my lips, then spider webs over my jaw and cheeks. My face burns. As the En flows to me through our kiss, I taste him—salty and wet—his energy just as strong as last time, it floods me with a hunger for more, and the more I get, the more I want.

My whole body vibrates. The tingle radiates down my arms, spreads to my fingers, my legs, and into my toes. The room grows noisy with the sounds of breathing—rising and falling, heavy and fast, mine and his.

Paul's energy engulfs me completely, his salty lips turn even more brackish. Cold. Wet. Like the sea. The waves of his En threaten to take me completely; I hear their roar in my ears, feel their surge on my skin. His energy presses up against me like a heavy wall, my chest burns, and my body tightens. This time I don't panic, because if I panic everything will go to Him. I steady my breathing and open my body to receive the full power of Paul's En. I push my lips more vigorously into his. His En wraps around mine, and like flint on dry, brittle firewood, it ignites in my veins.

The walls of the house shake, dust and sediment fly in the air, and the floors shift on the foundation. A flash of heat explodes over me. My body tingles everywhere now, each and every cell ready to burst out of my body. My lips are the only thing grounded, grounded to Paul as the rest of me floats, light and pulsing with energy.

I keep myself locked to Paul even though the alarms are ringing in my head—*Don't pull too much from him*—even he must sense it as his lips try to pull away, but I don't allow it. I need more En.

The inky cloud is back, gathering itself above me, buzzing in my ear, tendrils like black fingers reach out to my skin as if searching for a way in. I nudge Paul forward as we continue to kiss, guiding him slowly toward the closed front door.

"Let me in," *He* says in a booming voice.

I call En forward in my body, holding it just under my skin and at the ready.

Paul wobbles on his knees and his lips quiver. I look to his skin—so close in front of me—and can see his color has dropped a shade, looking ashen and weak. I bite down on my lip to distract myself from the allure of his En, and blood fills my mouth. It's enough. I wrench my lips free and cut the connection to him while surging the En forward pushing Paul to the still closed door, pushing him with enough force that he breaks through the door, crashing outside.

"Tomas! Get Paul!" I scream and turn to face what waits for me in the center of the room.

"Never," I say steady and loud to the black cloud hovering around my head, answering his demand to 'Let me in'.

His inky cloud bulks itself up, growing bigger and thicker in the space of the room around me, and then He advances, darting forward with half a dozen tendrils aimed like spears in my direction. I duck to avoid them, but they follow me like heat seeking missiles, so I sweep my hands upward, pushing En into the air, imagining a wall of flames lighting the room; flames of green and blue, thick and wild burst from my hands and flash like a flame thrower at the inky spears and the dark cloud closing in around me. He is barely phased by it, his inky form simply dissolves in the spots where the flames hit, regrouping in a corner on the ceiling, dark and ominous like an impending storm cloud.

It's all or nothing. You have to go big.

I feed the flames, stoking them vigorously with En, and will the fire to grow higher and wider.

I want it to consume the house, consume everything in it, and consume Him.

The ceiling sparks, the old wood an easy tinder, and flames soon swell the entire roof—bright orange, yellow, and blue.

Smoke is in my eyes and in every breath I breath, but I can't leave until I know the job is done.

"You must protect yourself. Finish the job from up high. Remember our lesson."—It's TheGirl, she's back and speaking to me in a whisper in my ear.

She's right. If I stay here, I will get caught in the house as it crumbles, or my lungs with seize from the smoke, and I could die before the job is done.

He is still in the corner.

I gather En in my fist and push it forward, as hard as I can, aiming for the ceiling just above Him. The wood splinters and buckles, the wall groans, and then a section of wood blasts outward, and He scrambles, stretching his inky cloud to avoid fire, blast, and debris.

I translate my own En into the look and feel of an eagle, hoping the memory of it will still be in my body. I stretch my arms into wings, wiggle my feet imagining them as claws, twist my head as if scanning for prey, imagine my mouth elongating and hardening into a beak and my body covered in feathers. Three fourths of me forms into an eagle as I watch it happen, but I lose a bit of concentration as the smoke thickens in the room—my eyes burn, a tickle worms through my lungs, and a cough threatens to erupt in my throat.

Only half my body has developed feathers, the other half is down to naked flesh, and my clothes have disappeared. I jump up hoping my wings can catch enough air even in this semi-finished state, but I barely get off the ground when a ribbon of fire zips over and past my face—a part that still has no feathers and is still not fully formed into an eagle. My cheek burns as heat scorches my skin. My eyes fill with white dots of light. Barreling down after the fire is Him, his inky mass descending on me, coming in fast as if he means to propel into me.

I duck my eagle head down and to the left like a boxer avoiding a jab and He skims my ear, sending a blast against the side of my head; pain shoots through my temple as if my head is in a lemon squeezer, and I scream but it comes out as a screech. Bits of the flaming ceiling fall around me. The crackle of burning wood is deafening. Debris, smoke, and flames make it hard to see where He is. I think past the pain, completing my picture of the eagle, pushing

En to those parts that need finishing elements, and then I jump in the air again, and I catch some air beneath my wings, and it's then that I see Him again, his dark energy a silhouette against the conflagration that looms above, and next to him is a hole in the ceiling big enough for me to fly through.

I'm getting out of here, AND I'm going to burn him alive.

༆

CHAPTER TWENTY-THREE

KEEP FRIENDS CLOSE AND ENEMIES CLOSER

I lower myself onto thick, muscled, feather covered legs—extending my wings to the side and up—and propel myself into the air with a push and pump; my body lifts, my wings catch air beneath them, and I'm airborne, but I'm not in open space like I was on Enlitra, this space is confined and like an obstacle course as I swerve to avoid fire and debris, nearly hitting the wall, and then there's also Him to contend with.

I target the hole in the roof and pump my wings to move me there, but an inky tendril shoots up to my leg just above the claw and yanks me down and around, swinging me like a lasso. My head spins.

He forces me forward toward the flames. I beat my wings to try to escape but his grasp is too tight.

"I did warn you," He says, "either we work together, or *you* don't work at all."

The flames are hot on my face. I twist my head away from the heat, but my skin bristles as flames lick my neck and chest, the smoke and smell from burning feathers works its way to my beak.

I screech and struggle to break free, but my free claw only slices through air. I pump my wings hoping to power out of His grip, but he only pushes me further into the flames; feathers completely burn from my body, my skin bubbles as the fire eats away at it.

"Last chance," He hisses in my ear.

My 'never' comes out as a high pitched screech again, but He must understand because he pushes me into the flames even deeper. My skin continues to burn on my neck, but this time I wrap energy around the closest flames and whip them head to toe toward Him instead.

He releases my claw. I drop for a couple seconds before finding my wings again and pumping them, bringing me back on track for the hole in the roof. I pump and fly putting all my efforts into moving forward, and finally the hole, which has gotten bigger as fire disintegrates the old wood, is just above me. A chunk of fiery ceiling drops and I swerve to avoid it. I pump my wings three times fast and then tuck them to my side as I slide out of the hole and into open air. The sky directly above the house is full of smoke and ash, so I aim higher, pumping my wings fast, all the while dividing my attention between my target and the house below me. For my plan to work, He cannot escape the structure.

Cool, clean air slides into my mouth and down my throat. I swallow and push the air down into my lungs, clearing them of smoke and ash. My body bolster with En from the air—organically, with little conscious effort—as I pump and soar, pump and soar, and circle the house from high above. I swoop down close to the house, searching for Him, without flying through the main plume of dark smoke billowing up into the air.

The fire needs to burn hot and fast and I have to keep him inside.

I divert En to the house, targeting the flames, bolstering the fire's temperature, tending the flames from the air and imagining them hotter than any fire has ever been, pulling at the blaze with invisible hands of head to tail energy on one side, siphoning energy from another side and using it to strengthen the heart of the blaze. The fire whirls in a tornado of flame—crackling and swirling—pushing fast over the wooden structure; smoke billows thick into the air.

Looking down through the skeleton of the roof, past the flames, I see the effects of the fire—curling wallpaper falling & incinerating, the books & bookshelf like tinder fueling the flames along the wall, the red fabric of the couch engulfed, and even the old kitchen is now enflamed with remnants of gas sparking the old rusted stove and wooden cabinets igniting in a fast swoosh.

As the heat increases, so does the smoke, making it harder to breath. The air is dry and thin and full of ash. I stand my ground, exhaustion settling in; everything aches, the burn on my neck and chest sears with heat and every touch of wind reignites the pain, and the wing connected to my injured elbow flaps weaker than the other side. It's taking more effort to stay on track; diverting the energy to the flames is weakening me in the air. I miss a pump of my wings and my body drops into a lower current, slipping closer to the house, and it's then that I see a ripple across the roof—gunmetal gray tinged with blue—rippling like a patch of intense heat boiling the air but instead of the heat moving up it's moving horizontal along a section of roof clear of flames. I push energy from adjacent flames toward that patch of roof, trying to catch Him before he escapes, but He scoops up the flames, churning them inside an invisible container, pressurizing them, and then he releases the fire—a blast rocks the house; windows shatter, sides rip from the foundation and collapse on the ground, remnants of the roof blast outward, strips of wood and debris propel in all directions, and glass shards spew into the air. In the middle of the blast, a dark inky hand reaches for me—*His* hand— so fast it reaches me before I can react. I screech as his fingers wrap around my throat, electricity surging from his fingers to my skin, constricting my ability to breath. I feel myself dropping in the air, no longer pumping my wings to stay in flight. His thumb digs into my collar bone, his fingers round my windpipe. My head spins, and with the last remnants of energy, the bits that are keeping me in air and keeping me in this form, I pinpoint as many energy sources as I can and I pull and meld them together, fusing them with the power of the blast below me and His inky form. A high pitched wail explodes from the black tendril that grasps my throat, as it softens into a thick goo suspended in the air. He releases my throat, his form moving slowly, not dead but dormant; parts of the black twitch and writhe in the air. He seems impossible to kill, but maybe that's the point, maybe I'm not meant to kill him, but to imprison him. I can cage him like he did with me in the cave, into something small, manageable, without a means to escape and I can give him to TheGirl, and then Enlitra can deal with him.

One more push, *fast before He has time to awaken*, I form a box with the last remnants of En and the last of my strength, and encase Him in it. The box I make is a box with no escape. I meld the corners together around him, from material hard as steel, formed from one continuous sheet so there are no seams that can be broken, a box made from materials without organic compounds—nothing to draw energy from—*a box of my imagination, a box only I can open*. This, I think, as I push the last of my energy into sealing Him inside.

I grasp the box in my claw. I'll hold it as long as I can, but I've pulled from all my resources and my eagle is falling apart, with bits of me as eagle and bits changing back to human. One claw has already disappeared; feathers, beak, and eyes follow—one by one I return to a human, naked and dropping to the ground fast, but still I cling to the box with one last eagle part, one last claw...and then all my energy is gone. I don't have the strength or clarity to pull more En from around me. I am exhausted and spent and I have no more to give. My body is done.

I can only hope that the impact will kill me instantly as I continue to drop. I did what I had to do, my friends are safe and two worlds will continue. My life is a simple sacrifice for what I have accomplished. I close my eyes and wait for the impact.

Images flash in those seconds, they flash on the inside of my eyelids, images projected like a moving scrapbook. Memories.

Mom, binoculars dangling on her chest, a straw hat with a big yellow daisy perched atop her head

– flash –

A car, my first, a red junker with nearly bald tires, a relic in the yard of my old house, hood open, the smell of grease and oil

-flash-

A young boy, ten, lanky in brown corduroys, perches over me with a band-aid in hand; he snatches me in his arms and squeezes me – "You'll be o.k. sis, everything's ok after a boo-boo hug," he says.

-flash-

My old room, teen mag pictures pinned to the walls, the smell of boiled tomatoes and browned meat wafts in from the kitchen

-flash-

Mom in a casket, thin, skin painted to her bones, her hair like strands of frayed twine

-flash-

White sand, thatched huts at the edge of a beach, dark fog perimeter. Enlitra.

My brain stops on that, like a record player that skips from a scratch, the image of Enlitra plays and then skips back and plays again. Enlitra. The pendant. I open my eyes and look to the jeans that are no longer there because I didn't translate them back. I'm naked, which means I don't have a pendant in my pocket. I call to TheGirl but have no idea if she can hear me without the pendant.

"Help," I say in a tiny voice.

The ground is close, the length of two telephone poles end to end.

"I did what you asked me to do," I say, and I close my eyes.

When I hit, it isn't as hard as I think it will be, mainly because I don't hit the ground directly. First there's a tree, with branches full of leaves that seem to reach out to me like arms passing me along, cushioning the velocity of my fall. The branches seem endless until there are no more branches and I'm dumped to the ground where I lay now, unmoving and numb. I've broken some bones, I felt them crack and bend at odd angles when I hit, but I'm numb and unable to tell which bones they are, and for that I am thankful.

My breath is slow and ragged in my chest, a mix of too many smoky breaths, His strangle hold on my throat, and the impact of my fall. My throat burns as I breathe.

The house is down to its skeletal frame – I can see it from where I lay—barely standing, its wooden framework continuing to burn and smoke.

Something shiny glints in the sunlight an arm's length away—a box—and I know I mustn't let it go, so I reach my right hand toward it, with pain shooting in all directions as I move, and I pull the box close.

We keep our friends close and our enemies closer.

There are sirens in the distance and footsteps running, getting closer, pounding the ground hard; the house is getting fuzzy, my head is spinning.

I want to get up but I can't remember how to do it.

I'm so tired. So tired. Tired.

CHAPTER TWENTY-FOUR

I WILL NOT DIE AN UNLIVED LIFE

I think I blacked out 'cause there's a break in my memory and I can't place the snapshots that flash in my head...a gasp and hands moving my arms and legs out of knots...a rough material dropping on my skin, water on my lips, and a voice.

"Faith," the boy calls to me, *he knows my name*, "Can you hear me Faith?"

He's kneeling beside me. I think his name is T, or starts with a T, I can't remember. I can hear him but I don't know how to respond, I can't find the energy to move my mouth or to form the words. My brain can barely function to process the question.

"Help is coming," the boy says. He slips his hand in mine and squeezes, gently as if he's afraid of breaking me. It's hard to break what's already broken.

I think I smile, but it could be my memory is distorted.

I move to look for the boy, to see his face, but I can't. I can't move.

Tomas. That's his name.

I fade out.

The cackle of a police radio wakes me, more voices close by. I don't recognize these. Hands grab me and lift, pain explodes through my body. I want to scream but I can't find the way, my body won't obey; I'm screaming inside my head, it's hard to breath, I gasp, and black out.

When I wake, there's a loud siren blaring above me and plastic ripping next to my ear, a pinch on the skin on my arm, and the smell of antiseptic. I wrinkle my nose.

"She moved," a woman reports to someone close by. The woman bends down to me, I can smell faint traces of her perfume; she places a hand on my upper arm and calmly asks, "Faith, are you with us?" I think I'm Faith. I did move my nose. I shake my head yes.

"Good," she says. I smile. I've done something good.

I black out again.

I was asleep, but now I'm awake, and my first thought is—honest to god—*why do pajamas have to twist and wedge up the crack of your ass while you sleep?*

I must be feeling better.

My brain is still a bit foggy; my eyelids heavy and hard to open, and my brain is unfocused and strangely empty. I rarely wake up with an empty brain. The bed feels foreign, harder than I'm used to, and I don't think I slept so good because my body is tight and achy, and there's a pain that comes and goes.

Someone left the lights on, I can see the light through the slits of my eyes. My head feels like it's sitting on one of those Guess-Your-Strength carnival attractions where the giant hammer slams down, the weight racing up the back is like the pain shooting up the back of my head. Foggy brain turns to dizzy brain. I grit my teeth and clench the sheet that covers me until the shooting pain passes, and even after the pain has gone the muscles around my head clutch my brain as if in expectation of the next spike. I move a hand to massage my temples, and that sends a different pain up my side. I try to move to find comfort but my arm is in a cast and my chest tightly wrapped so I breathe through the pain until it passes.

I open my eyes all the way, hoping the brightness of the room won't send my head into a spasm. So far so good. I study the room. White sheets are pulled up around me. I must be in the hospital; there's an IV taped to my forearm and the room smells of antiseptic. There's a rhythmic recurring beep somewhere close to my head. I turn to find my vitals dinging and flashing on the machine next to me.

I move to sit up, but my torso is stiff and wrapped tight—a testament to the extent of my injuries; the second I sit up, pain spider webs over my ribcage sending flashes of white into my head. My stomach turns nauseous and my head spins. I hear a moan and realize it's me, moaning in between each breath. I close my eyes—I might topple over if I don't steady myself—and lay back down, slowly, careful not to put too much weight on my ribs.

How was I sleeping just a few minutes ago?

I blindly search the sheets around me for a button to call the nurse.

I know there has to be a button, somewhere— sheets, blanket, more sheets, dizziness…got —I push it and try to breath, but my breath is too thin and shallow to fill my lungs.

Footsteps and wheels down the hall, turning the corner, and coming closer.

"Nice to see you awake," the female nurse says as she pushes a mobile workstation toward me, then moves to check the connections on my IV and pulls my arm from under the sheet to check my pulse. She types notes onto the computer.

"I can't breath," I say.

"Alright, let's get you some oxygen then," she says matter of factly as if this happens all the time, which it probably does, but it's the first time for me and I'm desperate.

"Let's put this on," she says grabbing a mask attached to a tube that disappears behind me, pulling it over my head.

"Breath in and breath out, like you normally would," she says, and then after thirty seconds or so, she asks "better?"

I shake my head yes.

"I'm going to send the doctor in, he's got some questions for you, so hang tight," she says pushing the workstation and disappearing around a curtain that closes in a semicircle around me. I listen for her footsteps, and the cart, until they get lost down the hall.

I wait for the doctor, which feels like an eternity. I have nothing else to do but lay here. There's a bedside table to my right and a pitcher of water with condensation forming on the outside, and a stack of plastic see through cups beside it.

My lips are dry and chapped.

I really want that water.

I look beyond the table to the curtain which keeps me from seeing the rest of the room. I don't know if I have a roommate, or if I'm alone.

I am soooooo thirsty.

I move the sheet from the top of me, very carefully. What I thought was a pair of pajamas is instead a hospital gown, bunched up and twisted and barely covering anything. My legs are completely exposed, pale, and full of gashes and blisters—*No swimsuits for a while*—and very stiff, as if they haven't moved from this spot for days. I have to shimmy them off the bed while being mindful of the IV and oxygen I'm connected to, but as I start—even though I'm careful to move slowly—the pain spikes up my side. I take in air in a huge gasp through the mask on my face and hold it, hoping it will help me over the top of the pain. Then I move again, and the pain spikes worse. It's then I hear footsteps approaching, down the hall and in through the doorway. I pull the sheet over my legs, but don't have time to shimmy them back into bed or even lie down.

The curtain pulls open and a doctor who looks old enough to be my father stands in a white coat, khaki pants, and a button up shirt and tie.

"What are you doing out of bed?" He asks, not harshly but concerned.

"I need water," I say in a gravelly voice.

"You can't have water yet," he says, lifting my legs and placing them back into bed. I wince at the pain.

"That hurts?" he asks.

I shake my head.

"You're lucky you can even move them," he says now helping me scoot back into the bed, propping a pillow behind the back of my head.

"I'm really thirsty," I say; my voice sounds foreign—deeper and older than normal.

"O.K. we'll take care of that in a minute. This is the first time you've been awake in three days, so it makes sense that you're thirsty. A couple questions, then we'll get you something for that thirst," he says.

"Three days?"

"You are one lucky girl," he says.

"I don't feel so lucky. I'm in a lot of pain, every time I move," I say.

"That will get better. We can up the pain meds for now," he says as he watches the machine pinging and beeping beside me.

He proceeds to ask me questions about my medical history, specifics about what happened to me and how I got my injuries—I keep most of those details to myself, and cover my story by saying I don't remember much about what happened. I know better than to say I was a bird, flying in the air, battling something from another world. Yeah, I watch enough television to know that kind of answer would buy me a one-way trip to the Psych Ward, so I say as little as possible.

"I'll have the nurse get you some ice chips. You can only have a few at a time and if you can hold that down, we'll start you on some liquids. And we'll up your pain medication. Your body needs rest. Oh and one more thing, you have some friends waiting to see you. They've been in and out the last few days, and they're here again like clockwork, but I told the nurse to have them wait until we had the chance to chat. Are you feeling up for visitors?"

I shake my head yes.

"I'll check in on you before my shift ends," the doctor says. And then he leaves.

Not long after, there's a commotion outside the door, whispers and shuffling feet, and then I see them—Kiara & Michael filing into the room. Kiara has a bouquet of flowers and Michael is carrying a stuffed elephant – gray, fuzzy, and holding a sign that reads 'Get well soon'.

I want to cry at the sight of them.

Kiara bends in to me; she pushes her face into my shoulder and hugs, and I tense as the pain spikes.

"I'm sorry," she says loosening her embrace, backing away from me, and wiping tears from her eyes.

I shake my head, wincing as the pain crests.

"You look like shit," Michael says.

"I feel like shit," I say, "but I'm so glad to see you both."

Kiara slowly eases herself onto the end of my bed and Michael settles into the boxy armchair by the window.

"I thought they had you on pain medicine?" Kiara asks.

"They do. It's when I move too much. But the doctor said he'd up it, thank god."

"That's good," Kiara says sounding hesitant and reserved.

"Right here is a good spot, if I don't move I'll be good," I say.

"Can I get you anything?" Kiara asks.

"Water," I say.

Kiara gets up and pours water from the pitcher into one of the see through cups and hands it to me.

"Oh my god, water never tasted so good," I say sipping it slowly, mindful that the doctor told me not to have it.

"Thank you," I tell Kiara, and she lights up, and then I ask her, "Are you OK, both of you? Paul? Tomas? Eddie?"

Kiara and Michael glance at each other, as if they're balancing the weight of a secret between them.

"What?" I ask.

"Nothing," they both say in unison.

I turn to Kiara and stare at her.

"I know you too well Kiara Leigh Jackson— spill."

Kiara starts in with what I think is a Greek accent but it comes out more like a bad Godfather impression—"No one loves the messenger who brings bad news," she says obviously trying to lighten the mood.

"It's Antigone with a horrid Greek accent, now stop trying to change the subject," I say.

"There's good news and bad news..." she starts tentatively.

"Isn't there always," I say interrupting her.

"...which do you want first?" she asks.

"Give me the bad news," I say.

"You sure?" she asks.

Michael steps in. I guess he knows it's going to take Kiara a long time to spit it out—"Nutshell, Eddie's in intensive care, Paul is two floors down but he'll be o.k. He's got amnesia."

"Intensive care..." I start, and my voice cracks.

"Yeah, he'll pull through," Kiara says reassuringly.

"Honestly, the doctors won't give us much since we're not family and we're minors, but Kiara's mom was able to get a little info," Michael says.

"Did you go see him?" I ask.

"No. They won't let us see him," Michael says.

Poor Eddie. I have to get out of this bed and go visit him—I am the only family he's got—he needs to know I'm here for him.

"I've got to go see him," I say.

"You've got to work on *you* first. They won't let you go see him yet," Kiara says.

"We asked," Michael says, "because Kiara knew you would ask."

"Ask your mom to keep checking on him, please," I say.

"Yeah, I will," Kiara says.

"Paul's o.k. you said?" I ask.

"Yeah, I think he's going to be released this afternoon. He was up here yesterday when we got here, checking on you," Kiara says.

I smile. "He was?"

Kiara shakes her head.

The nurse walks in. We all turn quiet.

"Are you in pain?" the nurse asks, walking to my IV.

"Yeah, off and on," I say

"We're upping the pain medication, the doctor told you?" she asks.

I shake my head yes.

"You'll probably get drowsy once it hits. Let her sleep," she says looking at my friends, "Oh and this is for you," she says handing me a child's size cup, half full of ice chips.

I half smile. I won't tell her I had the water.

"Can I have more than that?" I ask.

"Take it slow, and not all at once. If you keep it down, I'll bring you more in a half hour, keep that down and we'll start you on liquids," she says with a straight face.

As the nurse leaves, I watch her stride out of the room, and a feeling of Thankfulness washes over me. I'm thankful for her being here, to take care of me even if it is just her job. I'm thankful to have Kiara and Michael here, thankful that Paul is o.k and ready to be released, thankful that Eddie survived and is getting the care he needs.

I hope he'll be o.k.

I move the tiny cup to my lips. The ice is like a small bit of heaven.

I'm lucky to be alive. Lucky to have survived the fight, and thankful to be in one piece.

I'm feeling a bit loopy now, and tired. My eyes are heavy. But I'm happy, and I can't say I've been happy in a long time. Not since before Mom passed. But I am, happy, and the proof is in the huge grin widening on my face. I let my head fall back to the pillow, soft and fluffy behind me. It feels nice.

"Getting tired?" Kiara asks, obviously seeing my head fall back to the pillow and my eyes flutter.

"I'm trying—stay awake," I say skipping a couple words as another round of pain medicine hits me in a warm wave of tingling numbness.

"Tomas you didn't mention?" I say, my words slurring together as if I'm drunk.

"Get some rest, we'll talk later. We'll be here when you wake up," Kiara says patting my un-casted arm.

And I do, I drift with the sound of Kiara's voice fading, the beeping of the machine fading, and the room fading. I'm fading, fast asleep, wondering what's up with Tomas, drifting deeper, deeper, until I start to dream...about Him, and in my head one sentence haunts me in the deep dark sleep—

Where is the box?

ACKNOWLEDGMENTS

Writing this book took fifteen years, and in that time there are a lot of people who have influenced this story, and I'd like to take the time to say thank you. Thanks to...

My husband who is always supportive and my most honest first reader. Without you, this story would not have been told. Thank you to my son, who has seen me at soccer practices and events typing from the sidelines or from the front seat of our vehicle. Thank you for inspiring me to keep going. Thank you to my mom and dad, my brother George, and all my amazing family. You are the core of who I am, who I started out to be, and who I will continue to be.

Thank you to the amazing writing friends I have made. The ever supportive groups at Writers Studio and #wschat, #PitMad, #PitchWars, #SonOfAPitch, #AuthorMentorMatch, and #OnThePorch. Thank you to the incredible staff at Highlights Foundation, where I did some of my best writing & editing in their cozy cabins; the feedback and inspiration I received helped shape this book.

Thank you to National Novel Writing Month (aka NaNoWriMo) for forcing me to write without editing, and then edit without overthinking. Your events and camps have been the backbone of many drafts.

Thank you to the beta readers who have given feedback and helped to make this story better than it started fifteen years ago.

Most of all, I want to thank YOU. The person holding this book. The reader. You bring the story life by reading it. Thank you.

Write a Review

Won't you consider posting a review?

Help other readers discover the magic of *En*. A review can be as short as a few words, or as long as you want, posted to your favorite review site like Goodreads, Amazon, your personal blog, or on social media. Tag your review with the #ENtheBOOK hashtag.

THANK YOU!

ALSO AVAILABLE FROM
Michelle Reynoso

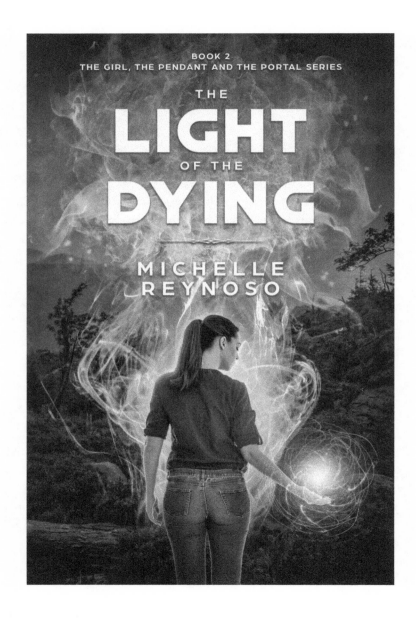

Michelle Reynoso—poet, technical writer, and novelist—is also an avid photographer and nature lover. Her work has been published in magazines & literary journals, and her debut book *Do You?* was a finalist in both the Writers' Digest International Self-Published Book Awards and the New York Book Festival.

Visit Michelle online at:

Website: www.MichelleReynoso.com
Twitter: http://www.twitter.com/MichelleReynoso
Instagram: https://instagram.com/mtrwriter
Facebook: MichelleReynoso-Author

CPSIA information can be obtained
at www.ICGtesting.com
Printed in the USA
BVHW030856021019
560005BV00007B/39/P